More Than One Way to Kill a Cat

BY THE SAME AUTHOR

Novels/short stories

Simon Says

Goeie dood wat saggies byt

Tafel vir twee

Poetry

Watervlerk

Fluisterklip

Die dood is 'n mooi blou blom

Waar die oog van stil word

More Than One Way to Kill a Cat

Ilse van Staden

Colour and Quill

2019

First Printing: 2019

ISBN 978-0-9943405-5-9

Colour and Quill

New South Wales, Australia

www.colourandquill.com

No animals were harmed in the making of this book

Killing snails

Harry Green is a gardener. And a murderer.

Or so he is told by his five-year-old daughter Martha. She watched as he caught snails, probing into the cosy hidey-holes among leaf litter and mulch in their front garden. Her blond eyebrows went up in concentration, her mouth pursed. She held onto the edge of the scuffed black bucket while he dropped the snails in one by one. Even at the tail-end of the afternoon, it was hot, and where the scattered sunlight fell on the bucket, it was warm to the touch.

The snails landed with a dull thud on the bottom, nearly weightless in their calcium carbonate shells. After a moment of concussion-induced immobility, they started to unfurl their squashy feet and tried out the plastic sides of the bucket for grip, which, despite the sprinkling of salt, they found for a moment.

Then Harry reached for the saltshaker and dashed off a few more shakes of pure Australian sea salt onto the unsuspecting molluscs.

"Murderer," Martha whispered.

"They aren't humans, Martha. They are pests."

"But you kill them, Daddy! That's murder."

"It's pesticide."

She considered the word in silence, giving Harry time to focus on his snail hunt. He moved to the next patch of garden and felt among the plant debris with gloved hands.

"Can I keep one?"

"What? A snail?"

"As a pet, Daddy, before you pet... petti... murder it."

Harry paused with a snail between his fingers. He looked from snail to Martha and back again. The snail tentatively poked out its head (or foot) in the limbo of its existence. Harry dropped it into the bucket, where after a short lag period it started to foam in salty death throes.

"No," he said.

Martha, never one to sulk for long, sat back on her haunches. She watched her father intensely, then promptly fell over onto the soft lawn.

With impulsive playfulness she hugged her knees to her breast and rolled over. And over. And over, tumbling down the gentle slope till with a final bump she came to a stop against the low edging of a flower bed. She lay immobile in unconscious imitation of a concussed snail, her green T-shirt riding up to reveal a streak of skin. She squinted at Harry.

"Daddy," she called. "Can I have a dog?"

Harry plucked another couple of snails from the false security of a philodendron's axilla and pretended not to have heard. A pair of rainbow lorikeets landed in the palm tree above him and started screeching at each other or maybe at the world in general.

"Daddy!" Martha had scrambled upright again and ran back to him. She bumped into his side, upsetting his balance, and they both landed in a tumble on the lawn. The lorikeets flew off, raucously scolding. A snail dropped out of his hand. A most ungraceful child, he thought, to go bumping into everything. She giggled, her breath warm and ticklish against his arm.

"Careful, Martha," he said, sitting up.

"Can I have a bird, Daddy? Please?"

"No, Martha. Now, I think that is enough snail hunting for today. You take the salt in to Mommy and I'll meet you inside for a cup of coffee."

When she had dashed off, Harry pushed himself up off the lawn. The lost snail died in a slimy crunch under the heel of his hand.

Beaches and bicycles

Although he knew it was only a matter of time before the question of a pet would resurface, Harry had counted on it being at least a few months. That would have given him enough time to work on his arguments against the acquisition of what he regarded as a time-consuming, money-guzzling, logistical nightmare of a hobby, not to mention the emotional cobweb of attachments that went with pet ownership.

As a child, when Harry had been not much older than Martha was now, he had secretly yearned for a pet. It was not something that he would have dared mention to his father, a loving and tolerant man in general, but intolerant of any mess. As a chemistry lecturer at the university, Dr Green's life centred around formulaic and controllable events like an electron around its proton. At home as at work, his was a constant and vigilant battle against entropy. Children were tolerated. They seemed to be one of life's necessities, and as a chemist he had a secret interest in genetics and how this would manifest in his progeny. But pets were total anathema.

At the first sign of a rat infestation in their house, he had handed Harry a stack of rat traps and told him to get rid of the pests. His wife had pleaded for a more natural approach, a cat for example, but he would have none of it. His son would solve the problem and normality would return. He did not want to see or hear any more of it.

Harry, still dreaming about a pet—a cat, if he couldn't have a dog—and hoping his mother would win out, had nevertheless dutifully set out the traps. Within days he had caught four rats. The dead rats with their lolling heads were ugly but also strangely fascinating. But then one morning there had been something else in the trap—the tiny body of a hamster. The trap had slammed down over its chest and nearly cut the animal in half. The ghastly sight had set Harry gagging. His career as a rat trapper ended there.

Fortunately, it seemed to be the end of the rat plague. He never found out whose hamster it had been, and it was an uneasy memory that he preferred to steer clear of. He never got a dog or a cat, although his father did eventually relent and bought him two goldfish for his fourteenth birthday. They at least would be clean and contained, although Harry never saw the attraction as pets. He could not even remember what happened to them, only that they seemed to disappear from his life, or he from theirs, at the end of his school career.

If Harry thought he would have enough time to get his arguments in line, he was seriously underestimating his daughter's mind, which had latched onto the idea of a pet like a burr in a poodle's fur.

The next morning being a Sunday, Harry set out early for a bike ride with a friend. He wasn't a passionate rider, but he enjoyed sitting down for his exercise. He usually cycled at a leisurely pace, mesmerised by the rhythm of the pedals going round and round and round.

"We'll get a brekky somewhere," he said, giving his wife a quick hug. His cycling helmet bumped awkwardly against Nancy's head.

"At Jenny's?"

"Perhaps. You want to meet us there? No? Just for a cuppa?"

"We'll see. I might go to the beach with Martha. It's a beautiful morning."

"It is. Well, see how you go. See you later, then."

"Bye. Enjoy the ride."

Long before Nancy was ready to go, Martha was waiting outside the front door, her own bicycle at the ready. With its training wheels, it was a less elegant version of her father's and had a small wire rack in front on which she had placed her favourite doll—Priscilla the pink elephant.

"Put that away, Martha," Nancy said. "We're going with the car."

The esplanade and beach weren't all that far from their house, enough to make a good outing on the bikes, if that was your main purpose. But today Nancy just wanted to enjoy the sunshine and the beach, without putting too much effort into it.

"But I want to bicycle, Mommy."

"It's too far, possum; it will take too long. And you'll tire."

Martha contemplated this. "I won't, Mommy. I never tyre my bicycle. And when Daddy tyres his bicycle, he fixes it again. With glue."

"He sure does," Nancy chuckled. "Well, put it away, then. Here, come in, we'll just leave it in here for now."

Martha held onto one handle of her bicycle as Nancy wrangled it through the door, making sure that her doll was sitting snuggly.

"Priscilla can stay here, Mommy."

"That's a good plan, yes."

"She can ride all everywhere, because she won't tyre, will she?"

Instead of going to the esplanade with its long beachfront and pretty gazebos, they headed for Canoe Point, a park near the river mouth. It was elevated, with a view over the sea and barbeque facilities under the large trees. A staircase led down to the beach.

It was a popular place, and on such a fine morning there were already a few cars in the parking area. A man was loading a big black dog onto the back of his ute. It had clearly had a swim and gave its whole body a shake as Nancy and Martha walked past, sending water droplets flying.

"Eow!" Martha giggled, running ahead.

"Sorry about that," the man said, waving to Nancy.

"That's alright," she said and trotted after Martha.

They passed another man with a dog—a fat, panting Labrador—coming up the stairs. Several people were making the most of the early morning to enjoy the beach with their pets or family. The mud flats near the river mouth extended more than a hundred metres from the shore and were exposed at low tide, so one could walk far out. The shallow pools in between were ideal swimming spots for children.

Martha had picked up a piece of driftwood and was trailing it behind her in the sand, looking back every so often at its squiggles. As they walked on the sand, strewn with pebbles and shells, Nancy marvelled at the ever-changing nature of the shore. It never stayed the same for long. A tide or two could change the shoreline. If you stayed away for a week or two, it would be different when you visited again. A rock would become exposed or covered by sand, a small lagoon would form, or a new sandbank. After heavy rains or a storm at sea, there were always new flotsam on the beach—driftwood or shells or plastic rubbish. Even large tree stumps became embedded in the sand, part of the landscape against which dogs cocked their legs and waves broke and where birds alighted momentarily. Once a whole beach umbrella had been buried and then slowly exposed again by wind and waves.

Nancy and Martha ambled along the shore for nearly an hour, picking up shells and discarding them again, hunching down to watch small crabs scurrying into their holes, and splashing through the shallow waves. A terrier dashing after a ball hurtled past, throwing up sand. A wayward breeze swept a woman's hat off and she ran after it. Martha stomped in the wet sand, making deep tracks, then turned around and waited for Nancy to catch up.

"Mommy," she said, slipping a hand into Nancy's. "Can we have a dog?"

"Uh, I don't know, Martha," Nancy stalled. "A dog? Probably not. We'll have to ask Daddy first."

Martha did not pursue the issue. They walked back to the park, Martha racing up the stairs with seemingly endless energy and waiting for Nancy at the top. A dog might be just what she needed, thought Nancy, a playmate to spend all that energy on.

They watched as a fluffy white poodle strained against its lead, barking at something in the garden shrubs. Its owner, a middle-aged woman with blue streaks in her hair, bent down, trying to calm the small dog. The poodle twisted, slipped free of its collar and went bounding into the bushes. Its bark turned into a high-pitched yelp as a tabby cat suddenly flew out of the shrubs and streaked away across the lawns, the dog in pursuit. The blue-haired woman let out a yelp of her own. She trotted after the dog, calling its name in frustration.

"Poor cat," Nancy murmured to herself, as they walked on to the car park.

"Mommy," said Martha, "can we have a cat?"

Martha wants a cat

When, after their Sunday afternoon coffee, Martha's energy had been diverted—the empty cardboard box from Harry's new hedge trimmer was just big enough for her to fit into and she was fantasising her way through the ocean in an ark—Nancy returned to the lounge with a smile and a small shake of her head. Harry glanced at her, lifting his eyes from the newspaper without moving his head. She answered the question of his glance with a widening of her smile.

"She wants a cat."

"A cat now, is it?"

"She started out with a dog but seemed to have a change of heart. We saw a stray cat at Canoe Point this morning."

"No, no. She started out with a snail."

"A snail?!" Nancy grimaced.

"She was trying to save one from the jaws of death yesterday." He let the newspaper drop onto his lap. A new survey showed that fifteen percent of Queenslanders fished regularly. There had been a spate of petty crime at a shopping centre over the last month. And the price of coal was climbing again, despite predictions by environmentalists. He wondered if there was a hidden message in all that.

"So what did you tell her? About the cat."

"I said that we would think about it."

"Aw, Nance! Really?"

"She's lonely, Harry. She can only spend so many hours at kindy; for the rest she's at home. She doesn't have many close friends."

Nancy flopped down next to him on the couch and nuzzled his neck. She smelled of vanilla and roses. He put a hand on her thigh and let her tangle his fingers with hers.

"Hmm. She's never alone, though."

"It's not the same and you know it."

"Yes. I do. So, a cat."

"A cat."

"A cat that leaves its hair on the furniture and dead mice on the doorstep."

"A cat that's cute and funny and beautiful."

"A cat that needs to be boarded when we go away."

"A cat that purrs when you cuddle it."

"A cat that gets pregnant or run-over or cat flu or..." He swept a hand over his face, as if to wipe away the rest of the visions of catastrophe.

Nancy disentangled her fingers from his and crossed her arms across her chest. She pouted, an older version of Martha.

"A cat or a sibling."

"When pigs can fly," he grunted. Nancy's eyes turned shiny with tears. "O darling, I'm sorry. I didn't mean it that way. Oh, come on, Nance. I was joking. We've been through this a dozen times. I thought we were on the same page by now."

She shrugged, unable to speak. A single sob escaped, like an air bubble breaking the surface of a deep pond.

"Really, love, owning a pet is a big responsibility."

"Have you ever owned one?" she asked.

Harry thought of his goldfish. "No, not exactly. But I know."

"Sure."

"It's worse than having children. It ties you down. And it's hard work."

"Children are also hard work. And marriage and... and nearly everything worthwhile."

Harry folded his newspaper and put it away on the coffee table. He turned towards Nancy and looked her straight in the eye. She didn't waver.

"Okay," he sighed. "A cat? You're sure?"

"Yes."

"Sure-sure? With all the complications?"

Nancy stiffened. Stubbornness was winning out over sadness; Harry could see this turning nasty. As Nancy took a deep breath to reply, he stalled her.

"Okay, damn it, okay. She can have her cat, okay? Nancy?"

She relaxed again, trying a smile. "Thank you, Harry," she said and kissed his nose.

A woman who purrs when you cuddle it, he thought longingly.

How to get a cat

Despite the go-ahead of both parents, Martha had not necessarily set her sights on a cat. It was essential to push the boundaries. For the next couple of weeks, she explored the various options regarding possible pets. Cats and dogs and birds did make her list, but only as the more familiar possibilities. She had a transient love affair with green frogs after discovering one in an abandoned plant pot behind the shed. Butterflies and cows and bearded dragons also came under her scrutiny. Harry had by now made peace with the idea of a cat and would not budge on the question of species.

"A cat?" Martha screwed up her face, contemplating the matter. "Are we getting a cat?"

"Well," Nancy explained. "It will probably start out as a fluffy little kitten. But yes, we shall get a cat and it will be your very special friend."

"Will it be a boy cat or a girl cat? Because I want a... hmm... So, it will be my cat friend?"

"It will be your cat friend, yes. But we shall have to see whether it is a boy or a girl. I do not know that yet."

"And will it be my baby cat friend?"

"Yes, love."

"My baby girl cat friend or my baby boy cat friend. Mommy," she suddenly realised the possibilities. "Can I have a baby girl cat friend *and* a baby boy cat friend?"

"No, Martha. Only one cat."

Even one cat, Nancy thought, when in conjunction with a girl like Martha, would be quite enough.

When their friends and neighbours heard that the Greens were in the market for a cat, it did not take long for the felines to line up at their door, so to speak. Tracy from down the road was the first to let it be known that her niece's sister-in-law had two kittens for sale from a rare litter of Devon Rexes. Discounted, mind you, on account of their being three months old already, but with all the vaccinations and vet treatments up to date.

"Discounted?" Harry was unconvinced. "At eight hundred dollars? You could buy a racehorse for that price!"

"O come, Harry, don't be ridiculous."

"Can I have a horse, Daddy? I can call him Cat."

"Look, all I'm saying is, that is way too much for a cat. What are our other options? What about the RSPCA—aren't they always looking for homes for unwanted pets?"

"I was getting to that. Tracy was the first on the list, that's all."

"You have a list?"

"I have a list." Nancy waved a slip of paper in the air like the Queen's hanky. Harry rolled his eyes but kept his mouth shut.

"So, the next one is Mary. Her neighbour has a litter of three. Mary isn't sure of their age or gender. All she knows is that they're all black."

"Mary's neighbour has a litter? All black and of an unknown gender. Interesting."

"That's not even funny, Harry. The neighbour's *cat*."

Martha was down on all fours at their feet, bucking and whinnying like a rodeo horse. "Look, Daddy! I'm a horse. A black racehorse, a black rex horse. Eehihi! What is a devil rex, Mommy?"

"Shush, Martha. Now, the next one..." Nancy had to wait for Harry to retrieve his arm and his attention from Martha's pawing equine impersonations. "The next one is a bit weird. My uncle Bruce who lives in Toowoomba..."

"In Toowoomba? Holy cow, have you advertised to the whole state that we're looking for a cat?"

"A devil rex and a holy cow. Can I have a cow? Cow-cow?"

"Martha, just stop it, will you? And stop clawing at my feet."

Martha rolled over like a submissive dog, aimed a last pawing at Harry's foot and then lay still, meowing softly. Harry ignored her, pulling his leg away.

"My uncle in Toowoomba," Nancy continued, "has a mentally handicapped stepson. A lovely boy, must be about sixteen now, but mentally probably Martha's age, if that. He's had I don't know how many pets, but they're always dying or running off or getting lost, I don't know what."

"You see?" Harry cringed at the horrors of a pet-owning future. "See what I mean?"

Nancy's haughty look stopped him in his tracks. His mumbled comments faded into Martha's meows.

"The last cat has been with them for about six months, and now it has suddenly taken to peeing on the son's bed. They do not want to put the cat down. The vet says the cat is stressed. Uncle Bruce was thinking maybe a change of scenery..." She glanced at Harry. "On second thoughts, scrap that one."

"Where do other people get their pets from? What happened to good old-fashioned pet shops, like they had in the old days?" Harry lamented.

"Pet shops don't really sell pets anymore, except maybe goldfish. Not around here, anyway."

Harry was briefly reminded of the so-called coffee shops in Amsterdam. They did not sell coffee, either. He wondered what pet shops did sell, being after all called pet shops. He had an inkling that he would find out soon enough. It was not a thought that gave him much comfort.

"So," Nancy said. "That leaves two on the list."

"I'm all ears."

"The notice board outside Woolworths had an ad for kittens." She read from her list. "Two males, two females, various colours, eight weeks old, wormed but not vaccinated. Fifty dollars each."

"Yes?"

"And then obviously there's the RSPCA. They have a pet adoption day next Saturday."

Harry nodded, contemplating the options. Choose your poison.

"What time? I'm cycling on Saturday."

"Nine to noon. We can go by ourselves, though, Martha and I. No need..."

"No need, indeed. Except that I don't quite trust the objectivity of your decisions when it comes to things like fluffy baby cats. As for this little piglet," he nudged Martha with his foot, "she would come home with a litter of tiger cubs, if you let her."

"I would, Daddy, I would!" she giggled, sitting up, and hugged his leg.

"Anyway, I should be home by ten and we can set out *en masse* to see what's on offer at the RSPCA. Okay with you? Now, let go, Martha. I'm starving. What's for dinner?"

A kitten delivered

The Universe, however, was not to be cheated out of its own matchmaking plans, plans that would surely go awry if a five-year-old is let loose in a veritable paddock full of felines. So it pulled a few strings in the fabric of time, causing only the mildest snitch elsewhere (a small herding boy in Zimbabwe came home with an extra calf that had appeared out of nowhere and joined his herd of Nguni cattle), and nudged fate in the desired direction.

Harry was not home when fate knocked on the door. And because Nancy was busy placing an expensive sheet of paper ever so precisely over her latest inked wood print block, it was their offspring who answered the door.

"Tell them I'm coming, Martha," Nancy said. "I won't be a minute. I just... have... to..." she continued as she found the mark and let the paper drop down, "...make this one print."

The teenage boy with chemically transformed hair and a stretched T-shirt dedicated to a generic demon or dragon (because that was whom fate chose to do its bidding) was mildly surprised when Martha opened the door. A motorcycle helmet dangled from one long-fingered hand. His other hand enfolded a tiny kitten. He ventured a quick glance over Martha's head into the interior of the house. He could hear a woman's voice from somewhere inside. Then he thrust the kitten into Martha's arms.

"I nearly hit your cat with my bike. You should keep it inside until it's bigger. It's the law, I think. Okay? See ye." And off he went.

"Who is it, Martha?" Nancy called. "I'm nearly done. Be there in a tick."

"It was the postie, Mommy," Martha answered, needing no great leap of imagination to pretend that the postman had changed overnight from an overweight greying man in yellow high-viz uniform to a gangly teenager with a twisted sense of fashion.

She hugged the fluffy parcel against her chest, where it uttered a feline version of "what the *%#*!" or some such profanity. Martha got the message and loosened her grip.

"He brought my kitten. See, Mommy? O Mommy, he's hungry!"

Nancy, whose attention was now drifting back to the real world after printing her woodcut and then scrutinising it with a critical eye, turned toward Martha with a few innocent presumptions—that someone was either waiting at the door or had been let in, failing which the someone had left either a message or indeed a parcel (did Martha say it was the postman?) and that someone was hungry. An agitated and ruffled baby of the feline persuasion was not on her list of expectations.

"Martha? Is that a kitten?"

Martha sensed that all might not be as straightforward as she had thought. She huddled defensively over the kitten, who gave an indignant squeak.

"It's my kitten, Mommy. The postie brought me a kitten. It's mine."

Nancy was about to protest. That it couldn't possibly have been the postman, that there had been some mistake, that someone else must be missing a kitten. That Daddy would, well, be ever so slightly upset. But then, after all, there was more than one way to acquire a cat. She smiled complicitly. The deed was done. Time enough to deal with Harry when he got home from work.

"The postie? Now isn't that nice of him!"

Stones move, trees speak

She was one of Harry's oldest clients, in more than one sense of the word. While other clients had come and gone, she had somehow stuck around for a good six or more years and at seventy-nine Cecily Stone was dead set on sticking around for quite a while longer. Her garden, and Harry's fortnightly visits to tend it, was one reason she was not planning on dying just yet.

Mrs. Stone had invested time, money, effort and a considerable amount of dreams in her garden, the way some people would invest in their careers, their pets or their children. She had not had a career since giving up nursing for the sake of matrimonial bliss in her early thirties and the only children Harry knew of was a daughter she had mentioned once or twice, with enough reluctance to discourage Harry from further inquiries. She had never shown any interest in animals other than the birds that frequented her garden, which had become her sole monument to life.

She always referred to her late husband with great widowly respect and a lingering sadness, yet it was not beyond her to flirt lightly with her gardener. Harry at forty-two was still a good-looking specimen, tanned and muscled from his daily work, with eyes the colour of shaded leaves and inky hair just touched by grey. He was hard-working and polite and knew when not to voice his opinions even when it must have been obvious that he did not agree with her.

Cecily never answered the door when he knocked, and he had learned not to bother. If he just got on with the job, she would soon appear, wearing a smile and a dash of gardenia. He would be bending over a weedy garden bed or snipping away at the lawn edges when he would get a whiff of her perfume and there she'd be, waving at him from a few paces away. The same applied to the end of his shift—sometimes she would be there to see him off, but just as often she would either be gone, away on an errand or visit in town, or just not bothered to say goodbye.

It was a beautiful morning, shimmering with filtered sunlight and busy insects. In a couple of hours, he knew, it would be as hot as a stew in a crock pot. Better to get going while there was still some respite.

He knew what needed to be done and how—which parts of the garden needed watering or weeding, which pot plants got a specific fertiliser and how often, which paths he had to sweep clean and which ones to leave to become springy and soft underfoot. There was also the new garden bed to plant, but Cecily Stone was particular about that and he would wait to hear her thoughts.

This morning he did not have long to wait. He had just fetched some tools from his vehicle, when he saw her at the front door. She gave a little wave, and he walked up the driveway to meet her.

"Lovely morning, isn't it?"

"Morning, Cecily. Indeed, it is. For now."

She gave a tight little laugh. There was a small white flower in her hair and Harry wondered whether it was real. While she talked, her hand kept reaching for the pearly necklace at her throat and he noticed a band-aid around the base of her thumb.

The blue colour of her blouse, made from a soft and shimmery fabric that Harry thought was called chiffon, reflected in her eyes. She must be going into town today. Or was it today her visitor was due?

She sometimes met with friends for morning tea or volunteered at the art museum, but this morning she looked somehow more breakable. He supposed at nearly eighty fragility was par for the course.

"You're right. Another hot day for you, for sure. I'm sorry."

"Not at all. It's what I do."

"I got the plants. Shall we have a look?"

He followed her along the steppingstones to the back of the house, a spade in the one hand and a garden fork in the other, like the weapons of some medieval garden knight. They were even marked with what he jokingly referred to as his coat of arms, a logo Nancy had designed and spray-painted onto the handles—Green Gardens, the green lettering entangled in curling black leafy tendrils.

He was interested in seeing which plants Cecily had selected for the new garden bed. About six weeks ago, when summer had arrived overnight, knocking spring off its precarious and ephemeral perch, she had unexpectedly proposed digging up a large bed of herbs and flowering shrubs next to the patio to make way for some new plantings. While the lavender and rosemary were indeed in need of replacement, having grown woody and untidy, it had surprised Harry to hear that she wanted the whole bed dug up. The azaleas had always flowered profusely, the hibiscuses carried masses of flowers of a most unusual peach colour, and the single camellia was again flourishing after a strange infection of scald a year ago and gave no cause for such drastic purging.

Despite Harry's diplomatic protestations, Cecily had been adamant that she wanted the plants removed. Dug up roots and all, she had said, no stone unturned, giving the vague excuse of wanting something new. She had not decided what that something new would be and had seemed uninterested in any suggestions Harry had made, as if she could not for the time being focus on anything beyond the clearing of the space. Harry had relented and spent a good few hours digging up the plants during his last visit a fortnight ago.

Cecily had been strangely tense during the whole episode. It reminded Harry of the time, just before Martha's birth, when Nancy had had her long hair chopped off, hair that she had been nursing and nurturing for years, that had been her pride and joy and the envy of friends and enemies alike. She had been on edge for days beforehand yet could not be persuaded to change her mind. Once the deed was done, she had relaxed, a weight literally taken off her shoulders.

Cecily had hung around while Harry dug up the plants, coming out frequently to check on his progress, before disappearing again with a nervous smile. But the cleared garden bed had been an anticlimax, no weight taken off anyone's shoulders, unless you counted the breather that he could take to rest his own arms and shoulders.

"It looks empty," Cecily had commented ruefully.

"It *is* empty," Harry couldn't help answering. Bits and pieces of plants were stacked high on the back of his ute like brown skeletons, roots still clinging to the dried soil. He had tried to save a few flowers for Nancy, but they were already wilting in the heat. "You don't regret it, do you?"

Cecily had been silent for a moment. Then she had sighed and smiled. "No. No, I don't regret it. You will still dig it over, though, won't you, Harry? Dig it over nice and deep. And put some compost in?"

"Of course. I'll do that when I do the planting. Now, about the new plants..."

They had spent another half an hour in discussion about the replacement plants, but when Harry had left, Cecily had still been undecided. The choice of plants would be hers and hers alone.

As much as she trusted him with decisions on the general maintenance and occasional upgrading of her garden, Cecily was very particular with the plants themselves. She liked to make an outing out of buying plants, organising half a day of browsing all the local nurseries, catching up with friends over tea and cakes on the way, around the more practical task of restocking her garden. That Harry could have collected and delivered the same plants with half the effort was beside the point. A visit to the nursery was a social event, not something she delegated to her gardener.

As he now followed her around to the back garden, Harry felt the happy anticipation of a child unwrapping a birthday present. In front of the empty new garden bed, she had placed a collection of shrubs still in their nursery pots.

They inspected the new plants. There were three small grevilleas, their intricately curled flower clusters a beautiful dusky pink. The full green foliage of lily pillies would form a backdrop, and to complete the picture there was a bunch of both green and variegated liriopes and low growing jasmine groundcovers.

Excellent choice, he had to admit. He had suggested crotons and heliconias, but Cecily had outdone him. She had also decided exactly where she wanted each plant. All he had to do was put them in the ground.

"Look, I know it's going to be a hot one and there's a lot to do. Maybe you can start with the planting and we'll leave the mowing until next time. Or maybe if you have an opening later in the week? You know you can come even if I'm not here."

"No, no. I'll get them in today, no worries. But I'll do the maintenance first."

"Oh. Okay. Well, they are such lovely plants." She seemed suddenly unsure again, a hand at her throat. "See how you go, then. I'll leave you to it. I'm just... Yes, just see how you go."

By the time Harry had mowed and trimmed the lawn, cleaned up the fallen palm fronds and done the weeding, his shirt was soaked with sweat. He took a breather in the shade of the large mango tree in the corner of the garden, sipping water, pushing back his hat to wipe the sweat from his brow. It was barely ten. This summer was going to be another scorcher.

Sometimes he wished he could just retire and take it easy, hang a notice on his door—'Gone fishing'. Not that he had any liking for fishing, but it seemed like a message people were prepared to accept. You wouldn't put up a notice saying 'Gone hiking' or 'Taking a nap' or 'Gone reading', but fishing seemed to be an accepted pastime, for even more than fifteen percent of the population. Maybe it had a ring of activity to it— providing for your family, putting food on the table and so on.

But even if he'd had the financial means—playing at gardening and collecting rent did not a rich man make—Harry knew he could never just let the days slip away. He had to *make* something of them. He had to shape them into a life, his own life, no matter how insignificant it seemed to others.

A grasshopper whirred past and landed among the leaves of a bushy native ginger. Harry made a mental note to keep an eye out for more of them. Cecily did not like grasshoppers; she would insist on poisoning them. Harry detested poisons. Since he was a gardener in her employ, this was a dilemma he tried to steer clear of. It was in the interest of his cognitive survival to prevent a grasshopper population explosion. Nip them in the bud before it was too late.

Harry moved over to the new plants and started to place them in the garden bed according to Cecily's instructions, moving a plant a little this way or that way, fitting in another one, standing back to contemplate the placement. You had to get the spacing right. Too far apart and it would look mangy. Too near and you would end up with an overcrowded garden that needed clearing and cutting in a few years' time.

Satisfied with the arrangement, he filled a wheelbarrow with compost from the compost heap and lugged it to his workplace. The shrubs he had removed the previous time had left the soil superficially crumbly, but there was more digging and soil turning to be done before he could stick the new plants in any decent hole.

At this time of the morning there was no shade in this spot. He took another long swig of water, rolled his shoulders, and picked up his spade. There was another old spade stuck into the soil at the back of the garden bed and he pulled it out and put it aside. He wondered whether old Cecily had had a go at digging herself. That would explain the band-aid. Maybe the barrenness of the new bed had been more of a shock to her system than he had thought. Poor dear woman. He would get all the plants in today and give her nerves a rest.

Thanks to the automated irrigation system, the soil was pleasantly moist. The spade sliced into it like a knife through cheddar. Years and years of composting, fertilising and cultivating by various gardeners, presumably also by Cecily herself in the mouldy past, had turned the native mixture of clay and rock into lovely sandy loam.

Apart from the occasional small stone that jarred his shoulders as the spade struck against it, Harry's digging proceeded without incident. Cecily had appeared a couple of times during the first hour of planting, but she had said little, just nodded her head approvingly and smiled. Now she seemed to have relaxed and left it to him to finish. He would knock on her door before he left to show her the final product.

He was busy with the last of the bigger holes, for the grevilleas and lily pillies, leveraging the spade against the side of the hole to get at the loose soil, when the blade scraped against something hard. Harry poked at it. It was metal, that much he could tell from the sound it made as he pulled the spade across its surface again.

He scooped out the loose soil, poked again at the hard edge. A clod of soil fell away. It was a small metal box, like those cookie tins you saw in the shops around Christmas, but much smaller.

Harry got down on one knee to have a closer look. He used the broken end of a planting stick to scrape away the dirt around the edges. Wedging it in along one side, he pushed, lifting the small tin out.

He could now see that it was a sweet tin, or had been in a previous life. Now, after perhaps decades underground, it was rusted, the paint flaked and fading, but he could still make out the remains of words—'toffees' and 'flavour' and 'limited edition'. It was highly unlikely that anyone would bury a tin full of lollies in the garden, so this had to contain another kind of treasure.

Harry wasn't given to flights of fancy or dreams of winning the lotto. He knew that the likelihood of the tin containing great treasure or valuable jewels was tiny. Life might be stranger than fiction at times, but it generally wasn't as romantic. The prince bypassed the real princess for a rich coquette, the bottle with the letter got smashed on a rocky uninhabited shore, the X on the treasure map led to the grave of a forgotten family pet. Yet life had a way of dishing up small, quirky surprises that nevertheless delighted, notwithstanding their apparent worthlessness.

The tin wasn't empty; he could tell that much by giving it a gentle shake. It was too light to contain any gold coins and too noisy for a stack of love letters. He wiped a gloved hand over the lid and pried it off. Then he sat back on his haunches with a wistful smile, before returning the lid and carefully putting aside the tin.

It took another hour to get all the plants in and spread mulch around them. Surprisingly, Cecily had not appeared again to inspect his progress. Before packing up, Harry walked around to knock on the front door and noticed that her car was gone. He had not heard her leaving. He knocked anyway.

"Cecily? Are you there?"

As expected, she did not appear, and Harry was left standing with his precious find clutched in one dirty gloved hand. He just had to show this to someone. He could not leave it. Decisions, decisions. He collected his tools and drove away.

Almost a daughter

Suddenly the old sorrow was back, pervading like a bad day of arthritis in winter, when the pain seemed everywhere and yet she could not put a finger on it. The planning of the past few months had dulled that ache, as she pushed it down into a dark corner of her mind, knowing full well that it would not disappear and she would soon have to face it again. But for now, she had to focus, had to believe that this was the right thing to do, that after all these years they would be able to lay some demons to rest. God knows, it would be her last chance; she wasn't getting any younger.

She steered the Corolla into a parking spot and killed the engine. She was way too early; the plane wasn't due for another half an hour. Cecily leant back in her seat. Soon it would get too hot in the car and she would get out to wait in the air-conditioned arrivals hall, but in the meantime, she would just sit back and breathe.

The photo was on her mobile phone. Michelle had sent it to her a week ago. "So you'll recognise me at the airport," she had said on the phone. "Thirty years is a long time."

Thirty years? It had astounded Cecily, and she was sure that Michelle had gotten it wrong, but when she had calculated the time later on, it had added up. Twenty-eight years, to be exact, but thirty was near enough.

She fished the phone out of her handbag. It was a very basic phone that she had bought only three months ago, and she still felt immeasurably proud of every call made or message sent. She had even taken a few photos of her garden—the hibiscus and the azaleas and even an amazing white orchid that had bloomed early this year—and of some friends at a recent birthday celebration. You could zoom in on the photos, a boon for older eyes, which is what she now did.

Michelle had been right—Cecily would not have recognised the woman that she had become—grown-up, attractive, darker blond now (surely dyed), the shorter hair and clever make-up setting off her delicate features. And yet, strange as it had always been, she had kept that amazing resemblance to Anne.

Cecily sighed as she slipped the phone back into her bag and got out of the car. She walked across the bitumen and through the sliding doors into the cool interior of the terminal building. Ten minutes to touchdown. She sat down on a bench, clutching her bag on her lap, her throat dry, her heart fluttering. Her bladder was filling up, pure nerves, but she could not go to the bathroom now, fearing the plane would arrive while she was gone.

There was no huge crowd gathered to welcome the travellers. A mid-week mid-term flight would be mostly made up of industry workers, flying in for another shift on the mines or construction sites, their cars conveniently waiting in the long-term parking lot, no need for someone to pick them up. A woman in a green sundress sat down next to Cecily, a toddler in tow. She whispered to the bouncy boy to be quiet. He danced around her on unsteady legs, little feet stomping in their sneakers. His bottom was thickly padded with a nappy under his pants. Tantrum coming or another full bladder, wondered Cecily.

She did not see the plane land, nor could she decipher the announcement over the public address system, but soon enough passengers started entering through the sliding doors. It was a small domestic airport, with minimal bureaucracy to slow things down. Some commuters with only shoulder bags or briefcases walked straight through to the parking lot, looks of tired resignation on their faces, their confident strides reflecting the familiarity of this routine—coming and going on a weekly or fortnightly basis, no more excitement or novelty than if it had been a car ride to the office.

The rest of the passengers headed for the luggage carousel or quickened their stride to meet whoever was waiting for them. The young woman had stood up, hitching her son onto one hip while they waited. Cecily stood up as well, her eyes scanning the crowd for Michelle. She took out her phone and searched for the photo. When she looked up again, the woman from the photo was coming straight towards her, a smile spreading from her eyes to her mouth.

"Cecily."

"Michelle?" Cecily managed, already enfolded in the younger woman's arms. She smelled of sandalwood and old books and a little of travel sweat. Her body was soft and welcoming. When she released her, Cecily had tears in her eyes.

"You're so... you look..."

"Thirty years older?" Michelle chuckled, the skin around her eyes and mouth crinkling into well-worn laughter lines. She had on the barest of lipstick and only a hint of dark blue eyeliner accented her paler blue eyes. A necklace of wooden and amber beads lay close around her neck. She was the woman in the photo, yes, but she was also different—she was real.

"No, no," Cecily said. "Not that, not just that. Oh! Michelle, you're so grown-up!"

"That I am," she said. Her accent sounded weaker now than it had over the phone, as if the memories of an Australian childhood were diluting it. "It is so good to see you, Cecily. You look wonderful."

"I have grown old," she said, shaking her head. She ran a hand over the thin skin of her cheek and down her wrinkled neck. Suddenly her bladder was full to bursting.

"You still look wonderful."

"So."

"So. Shall I get my luggage, then?"

"Sure, sure. I'll just..." she waved toward the ladies' room. "I'll meet you here."

Washing her hands in the bathroom, Cecily stared at herself in the mirror and sighed. The physical relief she felt was not only from an emptied bladder. She had met Michelle again. So far, so good. She took her phone out to take another look at the photo, then slipped it back into her bag's outer pocket.

When she came out again, Michelle had collected her luggage—a turquoise hard-shell case on wheels and a smaller backpack—and was waiting for her. She smiled, a bit uneasily this time, the excitement of their initial meeting subsiding into awkwardness over the circumstances.

"So," Michelle said.

"You must be tired after the flight."

"It is a long haul, yes."

"My car is outside. Did you want to... Have you decided what you want to do?"

"I think I have."

"We can go home, get you freshened up. I've prepared your room. You can even have a nap if you want to." Cecily smiled sheepishly. "I always do. That's why it's called a nanna-nap, isn't it? Not that I'm a nanna or ever will be, bless my dear girl's soul, but maybe, you know—you're sort of my daughter, aren't you? And forty isn't that old yet. These days many women have children in their forties. Even... I'm sorry."

Michelle grinned. "I'm not quite forty, but I will be. Next month."

"Yes, I know. No partner? No?"

"No. But listen, Cecily," she said. "Uh... I'm not sure I'm quite up to this yet."

"No?"

"No, but look, how shall I put it?" Michelle smiled reassuringly, then looked away, as if she could find the right words in the advertising banners plastered on the airport's walls—Your gateway to the Reef. Visit Heron Island. Here for the community, here for you. If only words were easier, if you didn't have to search for the right ones like a copywriter dreaming up a slogan. Words were like puzzle pieces.

Sometimes you could persuade yourself into believing that you had the right fit, even if it was obvious that you were squeezing the wrong word into the available space. The picture wasn't perfect and it would have repercussions down the line, but for now a less-than-perfect fit would have to fill the gap.

"It's not the house, really," she finally said, looking back at Cecily. "Or the garden even. I think."

"It's the memories."

"It is. Which, I know, you've been living with for years. But if we could just do this one step at a time. So, would you mind if we just went for a coffee first? Talk about things?"

"Of course!" Cecily let out the breath she had been holding. She looked at her wristwatch. Ten to four. The afternoon was still young.

Snails and dolls

If Harry thought he would surprise his wife and daughter with his strange find, he was not only disappointed but also mildly aghast at the surprise they in turn had in store. Martha met him at the front door. It took him a moment to realise that what she was clutching was not one of her soft toys, but a living creature, and while he had reconciled himself to the acquisition of a cat, its sudden appearance right under his nose was unsettling.

"Her name is Snail, Daddy." She held the unprotesting kitten towards him for inspection.

"What? How? Nancy? Nancy! Where did this cat come from? I thought..."

Nancy appeared from the kitchen, brows lifted enquiringly. "Yes, Harry? Hello, Harry."

"What is this? I... Oh, hello dear." He yielded to her greeting kiss without taking his eyes off the cat. "The cat?"

"You agreed that we could get the kid a cat, Harry."

"Yes, but... what about Saturday and the RSPCA and... There's no way this cat..."

"Her name is Snail, Daddy," Martha repeated. She had returned the kitten to the relative comfort of her embrace, where it huddled, eyeing the humans.

"No, no, no, no! *Not* Snail. You can *not* name that cat Snail."

"But Daddy..."

"Relax, Harry. It's the sixth name she's had in so many hours. We'll settle on something better in the end."

"Damn it all! A cat." He dropped into a chair at the dining table, shaking his head. "And how exactly did... this cat make its entrance into our house?"

To which neither Nancy nor indeed Martha had any clear answer. All they could say for sure was that someone had knocked and left the kitten behind.

"I have asked up and down the street, in case it was someone's stray kitten, but no luck. The guy at number fifteen thought he had seen a kitten in the road when he drove past this morning, but where it really came from seems to be a mystery."

"A mystery."

"Yes."

"And we are to keep it?"

"Of course, Harry. How not? I can't exactly throw it out of the house. So, unless someone turns up to claim her, she'll stay. It is a she, by the way. Yes, I'm sure."

"You can take it, her, to the RSPCA."

"Yes, I can," she agreed, her voice honeyed with sarcasm. "And pick her up again on Saturday, after paying an adoption fee. Good thinking, Harry."

She gently took the kitten from Martha and, joining Harry at the table, held the tiny creature on her lap. It gave a little shake and started to groom the ruffled down that was its coat. Patches of brown, black and orange seemed to crowd onto its body like the work of an overenthusiastic but sloppy painter. A touch of white relieved the jumble of colours under the chin, a bigger patch on the belly and four daintily socked white paws.

"She *is* beautiful, isn't she?" Nancy purred.

Despite his misgivings Harry had to admit that, yes, she was beautiful. He gave his wife a barely perceptible nod and the wisp of a smile. Martha, sensing a relaxation of the tension, came to stand next to him. He patted her arm.

"So, Missy Martha, you have a new plaything, yes?"

Martha nodded. She reached out a hand to stroke the kitten. It gave her a few licks. Martha squirmed and giggled, then leaned into Harry for a cuddle.

"Now," he said with a gentle smile. "To return to more serious matters. Three guesses what I dug up at Cecily Stone's today."

"A dinosaur?" Nancy tried.

"Not quite as old."

"A treasure?"

"Near hit, maybe, but no, you have to be more specific. One more try."

"A tree!" Martha cried and shrieked when he aimed a tickling hand at her waist.

"Nope, not a tree."

"But you do dig up trees, don't you, Daddy?"

"Quite right, although I prefer to plant them. By the way," he said to Nancy, "talking of trees, remind me about Fred Holmes, will you? I need to order his plants. Now, no more guesses?"

He left the room and came back with the rusty tin from Cecily's garden in his hands. He laid it on the table.

They leaned forward to have a better look. Nancy reached out a hand, wiping the surface with her finger, and then turned it over. The kitten on her lap let out a disturbed meow and jumped off to sit at her feet.

"What is it?"

"Go on. Open it." Clichés still came in handy. Harry felt like the hero of a romantic story urging his beloved to open the jeweller's box inside which he has hidden an engagement ring.

"Aw! Wow! Where did you find it, Harry?"

"I told you. In Cecily Stone's garden bed."

"What is it, Mommy? Is it for me?"

"No, wait, Martha. Just a moment, love." Nancy picked up the small object inside the tin. It was an old Kewpie doll made of hard plastic and barely five centimetres high. Its pinkish brown body was still smooth, though scuffed in places and with a patch of paint scratched off over one eye, which made it look like a baby pirate.

"Oh, it's beautiful, Harry."

"It's just an old doll." Harry had found many strange objects in many gardens over the years—rusty screws, a golf ball, bones of various shapes and sizes, even an old flashlight with the batteries still inside, all leaked out and corroded, and once a full set of dentures. This was something stranger, if no more valuable. The main value he saw in the doll was as a trinket to please Martha, even if he intended taking it back.

"Oh, but don't you think it's beautiful?"

"Sure. It's kind of pretty."

"What did Cecily say? Didn't she want to keep it? Gently, Martha, don't break it. See, it's a little doll. It's very old." She looked up at Harry again. "Do you think it's actually worth anything? You did show it to her? To Cecily?"

"I'm not a thief, Nancy. But no, when I left, she wasn't there. Her car was gone, so she must have gone out."

"And so?"

He shrugged. "I'll see her again in a fortnight. Don't worry; I'll give it back to her, of course. I couldn't very well put it back in the ground."

"You'll have to ring her, then. I'm sure it will have some sentimental value for her. It would if it were mine."

"Sure. Don't panic. I'll call her."

Martha was cradling the doll in her small palm and stroking it with one finger. She sank down on her haunches and tried to attract the kitten's interest. "Come, Blossom, see the little dolly."

"I wonder whose doll it could have been, though," Nancy said. "She doesn't have any children, does she?"

"Oh, she does. She has a daughter, I think, somewhere up north. Or was it in Perth? Anyway, she's never said much about her and the daughter's never been down here. She's getting a visitor this week, someone she calls her spare daughter, but I don't think she's actual family. Cecily mentioned she would be away for a few days. Next week? Yes, and it was north, I think Mackay or Ayr. Maybe they're going to visit the daughter."

"That's a long way to go just for a few days. They must be pretty close."

"She could be staying longer, I'm not sure. Although I got the impression that they're not that close, really. It's as if she doesn't want to talk about her. Not the way some of my other clients go on about their children and grandchildren. Not like Mary Atkinson, for sure."

"Men! How would you know?" Nancy was close to her own mother and would defend her sometimes erratic behaviour with the ferocity of a she-wolf. She became agitated at any mention of troubled mother-daughter relationships. Harry sometimes thought she did protest too much. Not that he would have blamed anyone for having a troubled relationship with his mother-in-law.

"I'm not a total fool. I can read people as well, you know."

"Gmf. Men are just so... Never mind." Nancy picked up the empty cookie tin and turned it over in her hands. "But what a strange thing to do, to actually bury a doll. Children playing? Or do you think someone just lost it?"

"In a tin? No-one loses a doll in a tin."

"No, I suppose not."

"I can't see that it's of much importance really," Harry said. "I just thought it was a quirky thing to find."

"I don't know. Another mystery. I'd love to hear what she has to say. You could have left it there, of course," she mused.

"In the garden?"

"No. On her veranda or at her front door or somewhere."

"Like a..." He glanced at the kitten in Martha's lap.

"Don't say it!"

"Like a stray kitten." He watched her, grinning. Waited.

"Touché."

"Thank you, thank you. Now," he said, bending over to watch the threesome on the floor, "what did you say her name was again?"

"Blossom! Her name is Blossom, Daddy."

But in that, everyone was mistaken. The cat, pretty and delightful as a flower though she was, was only Blossom for one night.

A storm forms

While the afternoon was still blazing on Central Queensland's coast, further east over the Pacific Ocean, the day was losing its grip on the sun. Nevertheless, in the Coral Sea between Australia and Vanuatu the ocean waters had been warm enough for long enough. Hot, moist air had drifted upwards, leaving an area of low pressure below it. Cooler air moved in, swirling upwards as it too became warmer, curling into thunderclouds. Already a tropical storm had formed, driven by the spinning earth, and it was moving south and east. It would be a day or more before it strengthened into a cyclone, but its path had been projected and weather warnings were popping up on websites. The Bureau of Meteorology already had a name ready.

Memories

Morning couldn't break soon enough. For the first time since her daughter had moved out twenty-four years ago, Cecily had wished for another living soul in the house. Even a pet would have been welcome, a cat to snuggle up to or one of those small dogs that some of her friends kept for company, with fluffy hair that needed to be groomed every few months and smelly breath and small mounds of pooh to clean from the lawn every day. Just another breath, God knows, even a wet breath from a goldfish would have sufficed. It had been a night for talking and the walls weren't such good listeners, after all.

After picking Michelle up from the airport, they had gone to the nearby Coffee Club for what Michelle had called an interlude. As if they were part of a play or an opera.

"I never realised how emotional this would be," she had confessed, stirring her cup of black, unsweetened coffee as if trying to dissolve something. "Coming back. I thought I was prepared for it. Do you mind if we just stay in the present for now?"

They had talked about the flight from London and the time zone and seasonal difference. She had told Cecily about her job as occupational therapist and the unit she shared with a Burmese cat called Mittens. She was a keen horse rider, a passion she had discovered in her late-twenties, unlike so many horse-mad teenage girls Cecily knew of. And unlike Anne. The only thing she had been passionate about riding had been a surfboard. Cecily pushed it from her mind.

It was history, a past they had put aside for the time being. Cecily had imagined Michelle on horseback, with her hair tied back in a ponytail, clear blue eyes under the riding helmet and a gentle hand on the horse's neck. Elegant, she would imagine. As she had always imagined Anne might look.

In turn, Cecily had told Michelle about her circle of friends in town, the occasional volunteering she still did at Rotary Club or the art gallery, the craft mornings twice a month, the

Bingo nights, and of course her garden. She had shown Michelle the photos of her flowers and explained about Harry and the new plants.

"He should be done by now," she enthused, glancing at her watch. "I can show it to you. It's the garden bed... you know... Perhaps... perhaps he'll have found it after all."

Which had plunged them back into that tricky subject again. They had spoken at the same time.

"You're not coming to the house tonight, then?"

"You'll have to get going, I think."

There had been a moment of uncomfortable silence, just the span of a breath, before Michelle spoke again.

"I can't," she said, looking down at her hand tracing the rim of her empty coffee cup. "Not tonight."

"But where will you stay? I've prepared a room for you and there's dinner. I thought... How will we..."

Michelle had reached out a hand to still Cecily's agitated gesturing. Her touch had been warm and firm, her voice reassuring.

"We'll have dinner together; I'll shout you. Then I'll book into a motel and tomorrow we'll go on as planned. Just not tonight, please, Cecily. I couldn't stand it, not just yet. Maybe it's the jet lag; I still feel a bit... fragile. Give me time."

And that was that, really. They had gone for dinner at a local Thai restaurant whose food Cecily normally enjoyed. Despite the delicious food, it had not been successful. Not even a glass or two of cabernet could relax the stilted conversation, which had now depleted current events, and danced around the past like a terrier around a snake – waiting for an opening, yet too afraid to strike.

They had finished while dusk was still lingering outside. Cecily had dropped Michelle off at a nearby motel and promised to pick her up at nine the next morning, giving her enough time to sleep off some jet lag.

So here she was again, after a night of tossing and turning and dreams full of memories, waiting for the time to pass until she could leave, listening for a phone call from Michelle to say they could leave earlier. Her suitcase was packed and ready at the door.

As soon as she had had a cup of tea, she had put on a light cardigan over her pyjamas and gone out to look at the new garden. Harry had once again done a good job. He was perhaps not the most green-fingered gardener she had ever had, but he was diligent and caring and creative. She liked Harry and she trusted him. It had pained her that she hadn't been exactly honest about her reasons for replacing what they had both known to be perfectly good plants. And it had been all for nothing, anyway.

No matter how wonderful the new arrangement looked—the lily pillies all expectant in their greenery, the tricolour jasmine just waiting to push forth new leaves, the delicate spidery flowers of the grevilleas already attracting insects—it would always be a reminder of her sentimental folly. What an appropriate name—Cecily's Folly. All it needed was a curly pergola and a cast-iron bench.

She had thought of taking a picture of the new garden—maybe the grevilleas would make a good photo—to show Michelle, to entice her to come back to view the real thing. Surely there would be enough time for a quick look before they left. She had even gone back into the house for her phone but could not find it. It was not in her handbag, where she last remembered putting it. She had searched her car, thinking it may have fallen out there, bending down on her old knees to squint beneath the seats, but it wasn't there. Neither was it in any of the spots in her house where things got deposited in passing—the corner of the kitchen bench-top, the coffee table in the lounge, the top of the bookcase in her bedroom.

There was still her old digital camera, but the disappearance of her mobile phone had so unsettled her that she had lost any inclination to take photos. Besides, she did not want to leave the house again, for fear that the phone might be somewhere where she would hear it ring, in case Michelle called her.

Now dressed in a comfortable pair of pants and a lilac cotton top, she stood in her lounge looking down at another photo. There was still half an hour to go before she would leave. Her hands trembled as she peered at the scuffed image of two girls in blond ponytails. They could have been twins, how often had she not thought that. Everyone had thought it. Newcomers were amazed at the strange resemblance between the two girls, and it had been their particular joy to play up to expectations. Whenever they had a chance, they pretended to be twin sisters, even wearing the same clothes. Seen from a distance, she was sure they could have fooled even their own parents at times.

The photo had the hazy, washed-out look of certain poor-quality colour prints of the time, as if it had spent some days yellowing in a blazing sun. The girls must have been about ten at the time. It was one of the last photos of them together, standing on either side of their favourite teacher. Cecily could not place the garden they were in, but it wasn't hers.

They had the same beach-blond hair, straight, and shoulder-length when not tied back. The arches of their brows followed the same curve, and they both had fine noses and narrow lips. The blues of their eyes differed only in hue, which often varied in a different light, anyway. When you looked closely, though, you could see a difference in their bone structure, Anne having the sturdier cheekbones and chin, Michelle's finer, yet only the variation one could expect between natural siblings.

Cecily fingered the photo again, before putting it back on the shelf, on top of some library books she had been meaning to return. It would have to wait until she got back. She picked up a bundle of mail and junk mail from yesterday that she had not bothered to go through. There were two bills, a thank-you letter from a charity she supported, a letter addressed to The Home Owner, and a roll of colourful store catalogues. She browsed through them, the specials and half-price offers from supermarkets and department stores, before dumping them in the kitchen recycling bin.

She had packed the provisions for the day's trip north—mini quiches and sausage rolls, cherry tomatoes, carrot sticks, fruit, a thermos with tea, and two packets of Anzac biscuits. It would be a long journey, but they were hoping to make it to Bowen before dark. She picked up the cooler.

She carried the food to her car and returned to get her suitcase. Then she pulled the door closed behind her. Time to go.

Perhaps it was better after all that she did not have a dog or a goldfish that needed looking after. She could leave knowing Harry would care for her garden, and the cleaner had a key of her own and would only need to come in once while she was away.

As she settled into the driver's seat, Cecily felt a buzz of excitement. She smiled, took a deep breath and turned the key in the ignition.

Click, went the car.

She tried again. Click, click.

And all the apprehension and tension and excitement burst in her like a dam wall and flooded out through her eyes. Her sobs were not just because of their trip being delayed—she knew after all that problems, even motor car problems, could usually be solved and that, even though they had already booked accommodation for tonight, it could be changed. She cried with all the truth and passion of years of sadness which she had thought dealt with and buried, but which Michelle's arrival had scratched open. She heaved with sobs, making soft mewling sounds like a baby animal, and wiping at her eyes and cheeks with bare hands.

When she had recovered somewhat, Cecily went back inside the house. It already felt deserted and cold, as if she had been gone for days instead of mere minutes. She found some tissues to blow her nose, then picked up the phone to call

Michelle but realised she didn't know the number. It was an Australian mobile number from a prepaid SIM card, and it had been on her own smartphone. Fortunately, she had copied it into her address book, which was in her handbag in the car. She went back to the car, found the book, returned to the house and dialled Michelle's number.

"Morning, Cecily."

"Morning, Michelle."

"All set? Did you have a good night?"

"Michelle," Cecily said and heard the tears leaking into her words. "My car, it won't start. I'm so sorry, I don't know what to do."

"Oh no! Could it be the battery? Did you perhaps leave the lights on last night?"

"I... I don't think so."

"Let me think. Are any of the dashboard lights coming on?" Michelle asked.

"I don't know. Hang on."

Cecily lay the phone down and went outside again to check. All the little red and yellow lights came on. She turned the key again, hoping against hope. Click, went the car. She returned to the phone.

"Are you there, Michelle? Yes, the lights come on."

"Perhaps it's not the battery, then. Could you ask a neighbour to have a look, do you think? Perhaps they can try to jumpstart you."

"Oh, I don't know, Michelle. I think everyone will have gone to work by now. Connie is my one neighbour, but she's as hopeless as I am." She gave a hopeless chuckle. "There's Megan across the road, but she's eight months pregnant. I don't want to bother her. And Gareth, well, we call him Grumpy Gareth. I could try him, I suppose."

"Could you? Call me back if you don't manage, will you?"

"Of course. I'm so sorry, Michelle. I don't know why it had to happen today."

"Don't stress, Cecily. We'll work something out. If the neighbours can't help, we'll find a mechanic, okay? I'll wait for your call."

Cecily's neighbour was a pharmacist who had moved into the house next door with his wife about ten years ago. Cecily had barely known her, since she had had a stroke within a few months of moving in and had subsequently been moved to a care facility. The husband had worked long hours at a local hospital and on the rare occasion when any of the neighbours had seen him, he seemed taciturn and unwilling to partake in any casual small talk or socialising. They had only learnt about his wife's eventual death through the grapevine some months after the event.

Now retired, Gareth kept to himself, with only the company of an elderly Kelpie that he took for regular walks. The dog was as unsocialised as his owner and quick to bark at anything and everything. Cecily was wary of its shiny teeth. As she knocked on Gareth's front door, the dog immediately started barking somewhere inside and she stood well away from the door while she waited.

There was a shout, but the barking continued, until a second louder shout brought it to a stop. Cecily heard approaching footsteps and then the door opened. Her neighbour stared at her from under a frowning brow. He did not immediately speak.

"Good morning, Gareth," she said, smiling meekly. "I'm sorry to bother you."

"Yes?" he said.

"Uh... my car... my car won't start. You won't be able to jumpstart me, perhaps?"

Gareth didn't respond immediately, just kept staring at her, his grey eyebrows twitching. His mouth contorted, as if fishing bits of food from his teeth with his tongue. Cecily wouldn't have been surprised if he had spat something into the bed of agapanthus beside the door. She was about to thank him and leave, when he gave a grunt and a curt nod. He closed the door behind him.

"Well?" he said gruffly and indicated for her to show the way. He smelled of linseed oil or old timber furniture.

"Oh, thank you so much, Gareth. It just won't start. It was perfectly fine last night. We think it may be the battery."

"You didn't leave the lights on." It was a statement, not a question, and Cecily wondered how he could be so sure.

"I don't think so," she said.

"You didn't."

"Well, if it's not the battery…"

They were at the car now and Gareth inelegantly plopped into the driver's seat and turned the key. Again, there were only the dashboard lights and the click. He didn't even bother to try again.

"It's not the battery," he said, getting out of the car.

"What is it, then?" Cecily asked.

He shrugged. "Spark plugs, filter, starter motor? I'm not a mechanic."

No, she wanted to say, but you're a man. And men are supposed to know about cars, aren't they? She was sure her Jack would have known. Instead, she just nodded in silence.

"Thank you, Gareth."

"Hmm." And off he stomped, back to his own house.

Michelle answered on the second ring.

"Cecily. Any luck?"

"It's not the battery," said Cecily.

"Not? What could it be then? There didn't seem to be anything wrong yesterday."

"No, there wasn't."

"Could you get a mechanic out to have a look, maybe?"

"I'll try," Cecily said with a sigh. It was already past nine. They should have been on the road by now.

She searched her address book for the number of her regular mechanic, a man she trusted, where she had been taking her car for servicing for years. It was his apprentice who answered the phone. Yes, his boss was there, but they were very busy today and would not be able to do a house call until the afternoon. No, he couldn't tell her what was wrong but besides a dead battery, there were several other possible causes and no quick fix. He could give her the number of another mechanic who might be able to help.

Half an hour and two more phone calls later, Cecily again called Michelle.

"Cecily! I was worried. I've been trying to call you, but it keeps ringing engaged," Michelle said. "And your mobile just goes to voicemail."

"Oh, yes, I'm sorry. I seem to have lost my phone. I've been calling from the landline."

"Could you find someone?"

"No. I don't know what to do. It's already so late; we'll never make it to Bowen tonight."

"Yes. I've been thinking. Why don't we fly? Wouldn't that be quicker and easier? We can rent a car when we get there."

"No," said Cecily miserably. "There's no direct flight."

"What?"

"Yes. You have to fly south to Brisbane first and then north again."

"Isn't that crazy! Well, we'll rent a car here, then."

"But..."

"No buts. I'll rent a car and I'll come and pick you up, okay? Just stay put. We'll sort out your car when we get back. Now have a cup of tea and relax and I'll be there as soon as I can."

Relaxing was easier said than done, but Cecily made herself a cup of tea and sat drinking it in her favourite chair on the veranda, enjoying her garden. With the little sleep she had had the night before, she nodded off after a while.

She dreamt of Anne. In the dream Anne was a little girl again, except that she looked older, the same age as Michelle. She was sitting in a chair opposite Cecily, covered in soil and leaves, drinking water from a paper cup through a green plastic straw and making those gurgling, slurping noises you got when trying to suck up the last bit of liquid. Cecily had reprimanded her, but Anne had only smiled and said she was still thirsty. She had then jumped up when she heard the ice-cream van tinkling away in the street. In the dream, Cecily had been struggling to get up to follow her, when she had woken with a start to hear the doorbell ring.

It was nearly twelve o'clock when they left. Only when they were a few kilometres away, Michelle still finding her feet in the rental car, had Cecily realised she could have shown her the garden before they left. She was about to mention it, but there was something else nagging at her, pulling her thoughts away. It was the vague sense of something forgotten, something important that had slipped her mind, and she could not pin it down.

Properties properly

Thursday mornings always felt somewhat decadent to Harry. It was his nominal day off, in the sense that he did the garden maintenance of his own properties. Besides the house they lived in, there were three properties—two residential and one business—that he had inherited from his parents and continued to rent out. They still brought in a dependable flow of income. Sometimes the tenants wanted to do their own garden work, but he kept an eye on those. All too often, a garden would become neglected once the troubles of daily life nibbled away at people's time and interest. All his current tenants were happy to have garden services included in the deal.

This meant he had one day on which he had no-one to answer to except himself, although admittedly he could not let down his tenants. But at least no-one would await his arrival and he had greater freedom in shuffling his priorities.

That said, with the summer being what it was, it paid to get in quickly and get it done with or else wait for the small temperature benefit of late afternoon. This left a midday gap of several hours, which in some faraway southern European country would have served as siesta time. Harry, haunted by childhood memories of darkened rooms and forced afternoon naps when he would much rather have been outside climbing a tree, did not take kindly to nanna-naps of any kind. He had a pile of admin to attend to—invoices, bills, quotes—but today he was using the bonus hours to attend to business.

You could still call it climbing a tree, in a metaphorical sense. There were branches, for one, and things you could reach for and footholds and balancing and views. And if you were lucky, there was a real tree or two.

The street parking outside the local Real Property branch was two spaces short of non-existent, so Harry never even tried to park there. Besides, halfway down the block was an open lot with tall gum trees reaching out over the street. At this time of day Harry could almost always get a spot in the shade, a pleasure for which he gladly walked the couple of hundred metres back to the estate agent.

Inside the air-conditioned office, Harry was on familiar ground. After nearly a decade of being a multi-property owner with the same agency in the same building, he knew the outlay of the office, the scuff marks on the wall and the way the entrance door closed slowly on its springs before slamming shut the last few centimetres. The carpet which had been replaced only two years ago was already showing signs of wear in a strip in the middle and the perspex pamphlet holders had unexplained scratch marks obliterating parts of the lettering behind them, so that from a certain angle you could read "Qui t location, lock gar ge, mode bathroo, swim in poo..."

Although there was a quick turnover of staff, Harry knew most of them by name. The previous rental agent had seemed a solid and immovable part of the agency, dull but dependable. Helen, bless her Irish soul, may have looked like your least favourite primary school teacher or the Sunday cashier at the local newsagent, but she was as tenacious as a bulldog with problem-solving a property issue. Both tenants and owners could rely on her courtesy and logical reasoning, but Harry had often wished (and fished) for a hint of humour to soften her efficiency.

Now Helen had left, gone who knew where to share her retirement with a widowed sister and an aging Chihuahua, and into the vacancy had stepped Tanika, a curvy brunette with skin that whispered of Pacific island breezes and a laugh that promised the realisation of impossible dreams. Harry hadn't quite made up his mind about her, but he was open to suggestions.

No-one, man or woman, could deny her sensuality. Even the regulation red work shirt, with the Real Property logo embroidered on its chest pocket, seemed unable to contain Tanika's presence. In other words, he admitted to himself, the view was good. But Tanika still had to prove her mettle in the market.

She spotted him as soon as he approached the reception desk. "Harry!" she mouthed and nodded to him through the open doorway of her office. She had a phone clutched between ear and shoulder while her fingers darted across the computer keyboard. A lock of thick black hair had strayed from the intricate to-do on top of her head and she kept blowing it from her forehead during pauses in the conversation. She wore a shade of lipstick that reminded Harry of a camellia in bloom and lips to match her figure.

"Until the end of the six-month period, yes. So, you're looking at about February."

Tanika's hand steered the mouse with one confident tilt of her wrist. A glint of light on two filigreed silver bracelets. The curser scrolled down on dates. Click, scroll, click.

"That's right, Colin. We can always reassess... Of course. I will get that ready for you."

A quick sideways glance as her mobile phone beeped on the desk beside her. Then back to typing and clicking and scrolling. In the middle of this busy-ness, she still somehow conveyed a message to Kristy at reception. So not only a looker, but clearly a multi-tasker to be reckoned with. Whatever was she doing in real estate? Harry wondered.

Kristy produced a file that she handed to Harry. He opened it, scanning through the property jargon to pick up the relevant facts. The lease renewal on one property was due in two months, but he knew the tenants were quite happy to stay on, so that was mainly a case of paperwork and signatures. At the business property, a neighbour had complained about noises at night. Why would there even be anyone around at night to hear noises? It could be rats, he supposed. He'd have to look into it. And then, of course there was Flinders Street. Because Harry had heard a rumour that Tanika had bought a house halfway down the block in the same street.

"Not at all. I see," Tanika was saying into the phone. She rolled her eyes under thickly mascaraed lashes and smiled at Harry. "No worries. I'll make a note and get one of the ladies onto it ASAP. Of course... Thank you, Colin, and the same to you. Goodbye."

As she hung up, letting out a relieved sigh, her mobile beeped again. She glanced at it, gave a small irritated shake of her head.

"Harry, good to see you. I just need to get this," she said as she picked up the phone, a blush threatening to colour her cheeks. "I won't be a second."

Harry waited while Tanika tapped away at a message on her mobile. There was a returning beep, then tap-tap-tap, another beep. At last, with an apologetic smile, she pushed the phone away and stood up to greet him. A hint of spicy perfume came with her.

"Sorry about that. Please come in; have a seat. How have you been?"

"Hi, Tanika," he said, sitting down opposite her. "Not as busy as you, I see. Property market booming?"

She shrugged. Again that momentary blush, a flicker of light at the wrist as she brushed her hair back behind an ear.

"Up and down, up and down, you know how it is. I mean..." Her eyes darted away, then back. They were enthusiastic and shiny as a child's.

"I do. It comes and goes. People come and go. Buyers, I mean, or tenants. I wasn't referring to you. You just have to hope there's more coming than, uh, going going on. If you know what I mean." Harry was inexplicably getting tangled in the words, as if pulling on one loose end of a string just caused a tangle somewhere else.

"Of course. Yours have been stable enough, your tenants." She gestured at the file in his hands. "Have you had a look? See the one about Hanson Road, the noises?"

"The Salvos, is it? Yes. I'm doing the gardens at Hanson this afternoon, so I'll have a look around, see if there's anything strange going on."

Tanika looked up as Kristy peeked in through the door. "Sorry, Tanika, will you remember...?"

"Flinders. Yes. Thanks, Kristy." She turned back to Harry. "Something that's not in there, which I need to mention."

"Yes?" I already know, thought Harry. You're just down the road from me. Well, not me exactly, my house, my property. Oh God, he could get tangled in these bloody words.

"Flinders Road. The tenants phoned this morning." So, it was something else. Harry felt unreasonably deflated. "The main bedroom—they say the blind cords are broken and there's something up with the ceiling fan."

"In the bedroom?"

"I know."

"What do they get up to in there?"

"Exactly. I'll get a handyman over to look, shall I?"

They discussed the various issues about Harry's properties, their conversation interrupted three times by a demanding beep from Tanika's mobile. Each time she cast it a furtive glance, but did not respond, though Harry could feel her attention wandering. Messages from an irate customer? Or an arduous admirer? he wondered. She must have plenty of those.

He kept his eyes on the documents, signing in the designated spaces. He wouldn't bicker about increasing rental fees, not today. Christmas was coming. Next year would be soon enough.

"Well, thanks for coming in, Harry," Tanika said, standing up. "You let me know about the noises and I'll let you know about the bedroom."

"Sure." He hesitated. "I hear you're in Flinders Road now?"

"I am." She smiled. "I might see you around."

"Your place or mine?" It made her laugh, but not before a quick blush had lit up her face again.

They were still saying goodbye, idly commenting on the hot weather and the lack of rain, when Tanika's mobile phone rang shrilly. Some insistent customer, for sure. She picked it up but did not answer immediately, fitting in a few final words to Harry. Then she turned her back to him as he walked out of her office and he heard the annoyance in her voice as she answered softly.

"Fred. What is it?"

Rats alive

The property in Hanson Road had been in Harry's family for nearly three decades and had housed an array of different businesses. In his parents' time there had been a supplier and installer of window blinds, an auto electric workshop and an accounting firm. At the time he had inherited it, a landscaping business had occupied it.

But, as he had told Tanika, people come and go. When the owner of CQ Landscaping had been paralysed in a motorcycle accident, the business had fallen apart, as if its own backbone had been severed. Harry had been tempted to take over the dregs and rebuild the business, but he knew his own limitations. After nearly a year of standing empty, with the heaps of sand and soil in the yard getting incrementally smaller, carted away in trailer loads or washed into the ground, the buildings had been occupied again, this time by a furniture warehouse.

The gardens of the property were necessarily minimal and low maintenance. There were certain council standards and regulations to be complied with, but not even Harry would expand beyond the mandated requirements.

At the front, there was the obligatory strip of lawn, barely worth the effort of unloading the mower. Behind a row of edging bricks two garden beds framed the concrete driveway entrance. On one side, the garden made a curved left turn to continue along the front of the four-space parking lot. The original shrubs—a few weary ixoras and three gardenias that hadn't produced a decent bloom in years—had recently succumbed to Harry's excavations. In their place he had planted a group of palms, under-planted with philodendrons, no-fuss flax grass and creeping irises. A thick layer of mulch kept most of the weeds away.

Harry parked in the street outside the shop, slapped on his hat—the palms still provided minimal shade at this time of day and he was beginning to think an actual tree might have been a better choice—and started unloading his tools. His head was bent over the edge trimmer, intent on refilling the line, when someone spoke close behind him.

"Hello there. Excuse me? Good day to you."

The voice had a grating politeness like crystallised honey. The man inclined his head and smiled at Harry, his fingers entwined and fidgeting like a zealous salesman. His face bloomed like the moon above a dark blue shirt with the Salvation Army logo across the chest.

"Morning."

"Yes, morning, morning. How are you? Harry, yes?" The man held out an eager hand.

"I'm Harry, yes. And you are...?"

He beamed and pointed at the paper label stuck onto his shirt. It had "Lennie" scribbled on it in lopsided letters and its stickiness was already coming undone at the edges.

"That's me. I'm Lennie."

"Nice to meet you, Lennie. And you are from... here?" Harry pointed his edge trimmer in the direction of the Salvation Army op-shop next to Homespun Furniture.

"I am, yeah. I am." Lennie nodded emphatically and with a laugh he pointed again at his shirt and the obvious logo, just in case anyone still had doubts about his identity and current employment status.

"I see." Harry looked thoughtfully at a spot somewhere between the two properties, seeing nothing. "They tell me you've been hearing noises."

"Oh yeah, yeah. Noises at night they've been, yeah."

"What kind of noises? Who heard them?"

"I did. I heard them myself, Harry," Lennie said, eyes like an owl's in his moony face. "Just noises. Like something was there."

"Footsteps?"

"Not footsteps, no, just..." His hands wrestled each other as he searched for a word to convey the exact sounds. "...noises?"

"Like something was in the building, you mean? Say, scuffling or rattling? No? Scurrying? Scratching? Banging? Were they scary noises, then?"

Lennie gave up. His hands abandoned their shared pursuit of linguistic clarity. He waved them in the air and shrugged his shoulders. A cloud drifted across his face.

"Just like something was there," he repeated lamely. "I didn't see anything much. It was dark; I'd only switched on the one light. It was only me, Harry. Leonore couldn't come and no-one else had a key."

"No matter," said Harry. "But what exactly were you doing here at night?"

A smile replaced the anxiety on Lennie's face. He was back on familiar ground, dealing with basic facts that needed no interpretation.

"Someone dropped a heap of stuff at the door, after we had closed. Just left it there. You're not supposed to do that," he admonished, gathering pace. "So JB called Leonore because he was only going to come the next Friday and Leonore couldn't come on account of her son, but I had a key. My next shift was only on Monday, that's a couple of days, but they said as I could maybe come and just put the stuff inside. Which I did and then I heard them, the noises."

"Thank you, Lennie," Harry said, breathless for the sake of the other man and feeling cross-eyed from trying to keep track of everyone's whereabouts. He reached for his gloves and earmuffs where he had put them on the back of his vehicle. He nodded to Lennie. "I will look into it and let you know when I find any, hmm, noise-generating... things."

Lennie seemed happy with this promise and sauntered off, turning back once to wave at Harry. Harry tipped his hat and got to work. Less than an hour later he was finished with the garden. He could now turn all his attention toward the unexplained nightly noises.

He stepped through the glass doors of the furniture shop into blissfully cool air. Although he had now gotten a report from the horse's mouth, it was a horse he did not altogether trust, and a second opinion from the tenants themselves would not go askew. However, neither the business owner nor Troy, the manager, was available and the only other staff member not currently occupied with a customer was a young girl with big eyes and too much make-up who didn't know and wasn't keen on hearing anything about any night-time goings-on. Harry shrugged.

"I'll just take a look around, okay?" he said.

The girl didn't seem interested in that either. She muttered something and turned away, reaching for the phone in her pocket.

Outside in the cloying heat again, Harry circled the building, looking for clues, though what he expected to find he would not have been able to tell. There was a long list of possible sources for the noises, both animate and inanimate. Animal, mineral, vegetable, so to speak. Unfortunately, Lennie's explanation of what the noises had sounded like had not been particularly useful. Harry had a few suspects in mind: animal (rats, possums or reptiles), human (juvenile delinquents or serious criminals) and elemental (tree branches, loose sheeting or anything else the wind could blow about).

Since there was basically no garden at the back of the building, Harry rarely went there. The ground surface that wasn't covered by concrete was a mixture of crusher dust and coarse blue gravel and although weeds did not mind growing in either, they were a small enough problem to be left to the occasional clean-up by the tenants themselves. The space was mostly occupied by a small delivery truck, three or four cars presumably belonging to staff members and a rusty outdoor table with three mismatched chairs under the only tree on the property, a bottlebrush covered in red flower puffs.

Some empty timber pallets were stacked neatly on one side of the building's rear roller door and on the other side bits of used packing material stuck out of a large skip bin like a dry and discarded bouquet. This seemed to be the most obvious place to search for the origin of the noises.

Harry looked over the edge of the bin and pushed aside some of the rubbish with his hands. He wasn't going to attempt a thorough search of the bin. He assumed it was being emptied regularly, which made it unlikely that unwelcome guests in the form of native fauna would choose it as a nesting place and if they did, the next bin collection would put an end to the problem.

The stack of pallets reached to shoulder height and Harry tried peering down through the slats. He couldn't see much. It was possible that something could have made a nest in the depths of dusty timber, a rat most likely. He gave the pallets a shake, not expecting anything, and indeed nothing happened. No rat came bounding out in fear; no snake struck out in anger.

He bent down to look at the gravelly soil around the pallets. It was hard and dry, with no signs of animal activity besides a row of hurrying ants and half an imprint of a shoe heel. A creeper weed had taken root at the edge of the pallets and he pulled it out with some effort.

Maybe it had been humans after all making the noises, some teenagers having a smoke or making out in the dark. That could as easily sound like 'something being there' as anything else he could imagine. How could you tell? How would you know that the noises recurred, anyway, unless you waited around after dark? Was it really something to worry about? He doubted it.

Harry walked back to the front of the building and went inside again. The girl with the big eyes was busy polishing a dining table and didn't look up. Another staff member, a young man with tattooed forearms and the shadow of a moustache, came to meet him. Harry had seen him around before but couldn't recall his name.

"Morning," the man said. "How can I help?"

"Yes, uh, morning," said Harry. "Troy still busy?"

"He's just on the phone," the man smiled, revealing uneven front teeth. "We have a big delivery due tomorrow. Anything I can help with?"

Harry explained about the noises that Lennie had reported. No-one at Homespun Furniture seemed to have heard anything themselves or suspected anything out of the ordinary.

"Not that you would be here during the night, though," said Harry.

"Of course," the salesman agreed. "But I mean, nothing's been damaged or anything. And there isn't anything to steal outside, really, unless you wanted some pallets." He laughed. "A lot of people use them for furniture, you know. Make tables out of them or benches or some such. My partner's always at me to take some home to make her a wall planter. I say it's easier to buy stuff for that."

Harry nodded. Nancy was forever showing him pictures of someone's ingenious use of old timber pallets for upcycled furniture and garden ornaments. Every time he went to dump green waste at the rubbish tip, the heaps of discarded pallets admonished him for his lack of creative carpenterial endeavour.

"Well, I had a look and I can't see anything wrong, either. Guess it could have been a once-off thing. We'll leave it at that then and I'll tell the guys next door I've looked into it. Let me know if you hear something."

Road trip

Cecily leant back in the seat, let out her breath in a long sigh and unclenched her hands. She entwined them on her lap, then put them palms down on her thighs, before finally settling into a relaxed posture with hands just touching in a cradle on her lap. She was tired out after the morning's crisis.

It had been a long time since she had had to deal with car problems—her Toyota was normally as reliable as the sun coming up each morning—and having to do so under the pressure of limited time had been stressful. There had been a moment, disappointment like a heavy boulder in her belly, when she had been tempted to call off the trip, or at least postpone it until Friday morning. But Michelle had been cheerily efficient and would not hear of defeat, and now they were on their way at last.

The landscape outside her window was rapidly changing as they cleared the outskirts of town and travelled northwest towards Mount Larcom and the Bruce Highway. The car had that plastic, impersonal smell of a new rental vehicle. Cecily longed for her own car with its worn seat covers and its smell of gardenia and sun, its mess of little things in the glove compartment and console, the extra packet of tissues and the half empty tube of hand lotion in the door storage. She still had that nagging feeling that she had forgotten something, but she had looked through the car twice and counted the items as Michelle had transferred them to the rental car. She patted the handbag at her feet in confirmation. Everything was here.

The conversation during the first fifteen minutes of the drive had been punctuated by frequent interruptions to give directions—turn here and take the next right and straight across at the traffic lights. Now the milestones were becoming less frequent. Soon they would be on the open road—miles and miles of uninterrupted highway north, with only the occasional turnoff or direction to keep them on track. She thought her mobile phone had some kind of satellite navigation that they could have used, but it was a straightforward journey to Bowen. Besides, her phone still had not resurfaced, even after she had gotten Michelle to ring the number while they stood listening all around the house and in the car.

Michelle slowed down behind a delivery truck and glanced over at Cecily with a quick smile. "You okay?" she asked.

Cecily nodded. "Straight across here," she said unnecessarily, as they neared the last roundabout.

The truck was turning left, and they sped up again, chasing the dark track of the road. Michelle turned the radio on, fiddling with the buttons to find a station. She settled for a regional station, playing a variety of popular music interspersed with much enthusiastic bantering by the presenters.

"It's strange to be back," she said. "All this," gesturing towards the radio, "the music, the accent, the lingo, the whole culture, I suppose."

"I'm sure. Did you miss it?"

"It's been so long; I had forgotten it existed. But yes, now I miss it, now that I'm back. Does that sound crazy?"

"No."

"I should have come back sooner. I'm sorry, I really am."

"Thank you, but it's not your sorry, Michelle. It's Anne's, really, isn't it?"

Michelle didn't reply and they drove on in silence for a while, the dry bush unevenly populated with eucalypts now slipping past outside. At the T-junction at Mount Larcom they unobtrusively joined the highway and sped on towards Rockhampton. After a while, Cecily turned in her seat to reach for the cool bag.

"Would you like a bite to eat? Or should we stop somewhere?" she asked.

"That sounds good, thanks. We can eat on the run. It saves time."

"Oh!" Cecily suddenly gasped. "Oh, I forgot to phone the hotel; I should let them know we'll be late."

"Of course."

"I don't think we're going to make it for tonight."

"No," said Michelle, glancing at the dashboard clock. "You're right. We'll have to stay over, probably in Mackay."

Cecily rummaged through her handbag and tsk-tsked. "Ah, my mobile. I keep forgetting. I don't know where I could have lost it."

"Use mine," Michelle said and pulled it out of the centre console.

Cecily took it from her and swept a finger across the screen to open it. She sat staring at it, momentarily lost in thought, then clicked on the Contacts icon. Michelle glanced at her.

"I don't have their number, Cecily," she explained gently. "You'll have to type it in. Do you...?"

"Oh, of course. I've got it in here," Cecily said, opening her handbag again. "Now where... It's not... My address book, it's not here."

"Are you sure?"

"Look," said Cecily and upended her handbag onto her lap. She returned the items one by one to the bag—her purse, a tube of lipstick, some loose coins, reading glasses, a pill container, two wrapped mint chews, a blue paperclip, her house keys, a small notebook, and a pen. No address book.

"I had it this morning, when I phoned the mechanics. And when I phoned you. It was... I must have left it in the house."

Michelle was silent, thinking. She glanced at the clock again, confirming what she already knew. They would not make it to Bowen, not today.

"Do you know the name?" she asked.

"Of the hotel? I think... Something... with a view or a beach... Beach View? No. I'm sorry. I don't remember."

"Okay, we should be able to get their name on the net, though. There can't be that many hotels in Bowen. I'll do it from my phone. Looks like we'll have to stop anyhow, so look out for a nice spot and we'll stop for lunch."

Travelling on

It was another fifteen minutes before they reached the service station at Marmor. They parked under a large gumtree at the edge of the parking area. There was a concrete picnic table barely covered by the shade and when they opened the doors on the sticky midday heat, Michelle was tempted to stay just where she was, in the car's air-conditioned interior. But Cecily was already getting out, taking the lunch bag and thermos with her.

While Cecily unpacked their lunch, Michelle searched the internet for the hotel. It wasn't easy. There were more hotels than any of them would have thought.

Michelle read them out—Beach Hotel, Queens Beach Hotel, Bay Hotel, Harbour Motel, Ocean View—but none of them seemed to ring a bell, and the more names she could not recognise, the more agitated Cecily became. It was no use. They would need to call every hotel to check which one they were booked into.

Cecily bit down on a cherry tomato. It popped in her mouth. When she swallowed, it tasted like tears.

"I'm sorry, Michelle," she sniffed. "I'm so sorry. I just cannot remember. How stupid of me!"

"No, not at all. It's not a problem. Let's just leave it, okay. It's not the end of the world. I'm sure they'll understand; they must get no-shows regularly. We'll just find something new tomorrow. Now, what have you got here? Quite a spread!"

They lunched in silence, while the heat and humidity pressed down. There was something in the air and a strange lethargy settled on Cecily. It was as if a giant hand was holding her down. She remembered a time as a child when she had lain in bed with a fever while her mother kept vigil and even her gentle hands had felt heavy on Cecily's skin. Michelle walked to the service station shop to buy bottled water, but she stayed behind, heavy and immovable as the concrete bench she was sitting on. A stone gathering moss.

Michelle came back with the water and two chocolate bars. "For later," she said. "My guilty secret."

"I'm sorry, I should have thought of it. Do you like chocolate?"

"I definitely do. By the way, the guy here says there's a storm coming. A cyclone? Do you know anything about it?"

"Yes, I remember hearing something. Wasn't it supposed to be near Cairns? I haven't kept track the last few days, to be honest."

"Will it be safe?" asked Michelle. "I mean, should we keep going?"

"We'll be alright," Cecily said. "It's far away from here."

They packed away the remaining food and set off again, refreshed. The afternoon slipped by outside their windows like a silent movie. An old song was playing on the radio and Cecily joined in.

"'I beg your pardon'," she sang, "'I never promised you a rose garden'. I love this song. Do you know..." Michelle shushed her as the news came on and turned up the volume.

"...as the weather intensifies," the radio presenter was saying. "Residents are urged to keep an eye on the latest forecasts and warnings. Continued heavy rainfall and possible flooding is expected in the following areas..."

Despite the best predictions of modern meteorologists, the cyclone circling down from the Coral Sea had made landfall much earlier and further south than expected. It curled heavily westward before proceeding south and spilled its guts over a stretch of sparsely inhabited coastline. The eye stormed through two campsites in a national park, sweeping the roof off the ablution facilities and stripping down large ironbark trees and quandongs as if they were weeds. Its swirling ends slowed down over the land, but kept travelling southwards across the east coast, trailing heavy rain like a whirling dervish.

Floodwaters swept through towns and over roads as it kept on raining without end. The State Emergency Service was on high alert and the Bureau of Meteorology kept updating its severe weather warnings. As the flooding spread and more roads were covered by water, businesses started closing their doors and children were sent home early or told to stay away from school or day care.

As Michelle and Cecily drove north through Rockhampton, the sky seemed to take on a hazy quality, like the breath of a sleeping dragon. It was nearly three o'clock. Between them and a bed in Mackay lay over 300 kilometres of endless highway. They were nearing the end and had just passed through the small town of Sarina, when they drove into the storm.

There was no gentle pattering, no apologies for what was to come. It was cyclonic rain from the start—heavy drops splattered onto the windscreen like juicy suicidal insects and within minutes they were enveloped in wet curtains. Michelle slowed down and flicked on her headlights.

"Shall we push on?" she asked. "To Mackay?"

Cecily nodded. "Of course. It's not far now."

"About thirty or forty kilometres, half an hour at the most."

It was not even that. It was much longer than that. The outside world became a muddled, churning pool, sliding past in a slow haze. The few other travellers daring to be out on the road loomed up as watery head or taillights, then disappeared again.

The rain drowned out the sound of the radio. Michelle turned the volume up and reset the frequency to a local station. Two or three songs, a string of advertisements, then a weather update. Cecily leaned forward in her seat, listening.

"... has now been down-graded to a category two tropical storm, but the Bureau of Meteorology has renewed warnings of flooding as heavy rain continues across the region. Strong winds with gusts of up to 90 kilometres per hour are predicted in the Central Coast, Capricornia and Wide Bay and Burnett districts. Flights into and out of several airports have been cancelled and there is concern that power supply and telecommunications may be interrupted in certain areas. In the meantime, a helicopter has been sent to rescue..."

Police at the door

It might appear, from our brief acquaintance with her, that Martha was a wispy little girl taken to much fantasy and free association concerning words and people and pets. And that might be so. After all, she was only five years old. She had a mother who got paint in places other mothers only got talcum powder or cookie dough. She had a father who killed garden pests manually, one by one, like a Nazi on happy gas.

But Martha was no village idiot and no innocent. She might fantasize a misguided teenager into a postman, but she knew a policeman when she saw one, even a friendly policeman with a big smile and a freckly face, or a lady policeman with pretty earrings.

"Well, hello there," the policeman smiled. "Is your daddy home?"

Martha shook her head.

"Mommy!" she called, without taking her big serious eyes off the man. "Mommy!" with more urgency.

"I'm coming, Martha. I'm coming. Oh. Hello. Officers."

"Mrs. Green? Good day to you, ma'am."

"Good morning. Is it still morning?" She looked at her watchless wrist. "Afternoon?"

There is something disconcerting about police at the door. It made one's stomach turn. Oh God, she thought, please let Harry be okay.

"I'm Constable Berkley from the Gladstone Police and this is Constable Susan Pritchard."

"Nancy Green. Pleased to meet you."

"Your husband, Harry Green, he's not at home?"

So, he hadn't been in an accident, at least. Or was that a rhetorical question?

"He works. He's at work. He..."

"Would you mind if we asked you a few questions, Nancy?" Berkley asked. Constable Pritchard had taken a small notebook from her pocket and stood ready to take down anything Nancy would say.

Nancy nodded and lifted her eyebrows into a question. Her throat had gone dry. She needlessly and nervously wiped her hands on the front of her dress. Martha, who had been hovering behind her, snuck a small hand into hers. It grounded her, but she had to let it go.

"Martha, love," she said, stroking the girl's hair. "I just need to hear what these people have to say, so why don't you go play with Blossom for a little while? In your room."

"It's Snail, Mommy."

"Snail? Yes. Oh. Well, you go and play with her while I chat with them, okay?"

"Okay, Mommy."

When Martha had disappeared, looking over her shoulder a couple of times to make sure that her mommy was still okay, Nancy nodded again. "Okay, what did you want to know?"

"Your husband is a gardener, am I right?"

"Yes. Actually... But yes, yes, he is."

"And where would he be working today?"

"Friday. Hmm. So, this week I think it's Atkinson, then Fred Holmes. The Blacks? And a property in Glen Eden – Eastman – he always does that on a Friday afternoon."

The policewoman wrote down all the names and read them back to Nancy to confirm.

"And do you know when he might be back?" she now joined the conversation. She had big brown eyes like a wombat and a gently neutral voice.

Nancy breathed deeply, thinking, then shrugged. "Four, five? It's never exact. You could give him a call on his mobile?"

"We could," Susan Pritchard said. "We will. Do you have the addresses of these people, his customers?"

"I do. Somewhere." She started to go back into the house, then turned back. "Excuse me, officers, could you tell me what this is all about? Has something happened? Why do you want to speak to Harry?"

And feeling reasonably sure of the fact that Harry couldn't be dead if they wanted to speak to him, she added with a scared grin, "No-one has died, have they?"

Constable Berkley looked flustered for a moment, a blush spreading up his freckly face. His colleague stepped forward and smiled confidently.

"No, Nancy," she soothed. "I apologise; we should have said. We're merely investigating a missing person. We believe your husband may have been the last one to see her."

"'You always take the weather with you'," muttered Michelle.

"What was that?" Cecily squinted at her over her reading glasses, a road atlas open on her lap.

"It's a song, from an Australian band. 'Everywhere you go, you always take the weather with you'," she sang.

"Ah, I see. It's not true, though."

"Well," grimaced Michelle, squinting into the rain to see the road. "We do seem to be stuck in this rain. When will it stop?"

"Oh, it will. It's going south now, isn't it? That's what the radio said."

"Hmm. It's taking its time. I'd thought it would have let up a bit by this morning, but it just keeps throwing it down. I don't think I've ever seen this much rain!"

"Doesn't it rain a lot in England? The British are always complaining about the weather."

"We're not! And we do get a lot of rain, but not like this, not buckets full for hours on end."

"It hasn't even been a day," Cecily mused. "It feels much longer. Are you hungry yet?"

"I'm fine, thanks. How about you?"

"I'm starting to feel like a cuppa. It's past ten already."

"Okay, we'll stop at the next petrol station. Service station."

"Servo."

"Servo, yes!" chuckled Michelle. "Oh, I miss the Aussie lingo, I really do."

The service station was a stranded ark next to the highway, its driveways ankle-deep in water. Michelle carefully manoeuvred the car onto the concrete slab between the fuel pumps and the building. The clamour of pelting raindrops slackened as they moved in under the roof. She motioned for Cecily to stay put and got out. Even here the water was flooding across the ground, splashing up as she walked.

She came back with two takeaway cups of coffee and thickly sliced roast beef sandwiches and handed them to Cecily through the window.

"I hope that's okay; they're a bit stale, I think. Apparently, some of the delivery trucks could not get through. The woman says many of the roads are flooded. Actually, I'll get us some water as well. Do you want anything else? Chocolate?"

They sat there in the car, sipping at the hot coffee, listening to the downpour and watching the world dissolve into wetness. Cecily felt absurdly happy in the tiny cocoon of the car with this woman, this young girl from the past. She licked the milk foam from her lip and bit a chunk out of the sandwich. It tasted of Sunday evening leftovers at a wooden kitchen table and summer breezes on the veranda.

Michelle smiled at her, indulgently and complicitly, a partner on an adventure. That smile was something you couldn't put into a letter or a phone call, not even a photo. Cecily nodded, as if it was a question she was answering, both to Michelle and to herself.

It had been an uneasy night, the rain thundering down without end, so they were stuck in the guesthouse they had booked into on the southern outskirts of Mackay. Most restaurants in town had closed early because of the weather and even take-aways proved near impossible to get. The guesthouse owner had offered to cook them a simple pasta dish for dinner and afterwards they had sat in their room barely talking, alternately listening to the storm and listening to news reports of the storm on television.

The latest report had shown a huddle of wet teenagers being rescued from a beach house and Cecily had stirred in her chair. The air had suddenly seemed heavy with memories, unbreathable.

"You okay?" Michelle had asked.

"Mmm."

"Memories?"

There was so much that Cecily had wanted to say, that she had been storing up for the past few months to discuss with Michelle. Truth be told, for the past twenty-plus years. And the previous day at the airport she would have been ready to spill it all into Michelle's lap. But now that Michelle had finally stirred the subject, a huge inertia had settled on her and whether from fatigue or sorrow, the words had escaped her. She had opened her mouth, but no sound would come out. So she had sat there, just listening and breathing, until it had been quite late and they had finally gone to bed.

"Ready?" Michelle asked now, when they had finished the food.

"Ready."

The rain stormed down on them again as they pulled out under the roof. They still had a hundred and fifty kilometres to go. It was going to be a wet journey. Cecily had remembered the name of the motel in Bowen where they were booked in, but when they had phoned, they had reached an answering service telling them that the motel had been temporarily closed because of the floods and giving a few names for alternative accommodation. They had then decided not to plan too far ahead for the coming night. There would be time enough to find accommodation once they got there. But doubt was seeping into their minds like rising moisture on a wall as they drove north into the storm.

"We'll be okay, though?" Michelle asked again. "I mean, you know more about these storms than I do, but it seems pretty wet. Shouldn't we have stayed in MacKay until the storm is over?"

"I think we'll be okay. We have to get to Bowen. I have to... We'll be okay, don't worry."

There was little traffic on the road. Two or three cars passed them travelling south, throwing up large sprays of water from their wheels. Rivulets of water beside the road were turning into muddy streams. Michelle was hunched over the steering wheel, peering through the walls of water, driving at a steady pace. She rolled her shoulders and stretched back in the seat.

"I could drive," Cecily said.

"Oh, that's okay. I'm the designated driver."

"It's tiring, though, this rain."

"Hmm. I'm okay."

They were silent for a while. Cecily turned the radio on, but the reception was shoddy and after unsuccessfully trying to tune in to a station she liked, she switched it off again.

"I should have brought some music."

"Hmm."

"Or we could sing?"

"Oh! You're on your own there, I'm afraid. I have a terrible voice. My mom always said I sang like a kookaburra with laryngitis!"

"Margaret?" Cecily protested. "She did not!"

"She did too."

"I miss her, you know. We weren't close, not like you and Anne, but I did miss her, and I still do."

"So do I. It's just... you and me, then."

Cecily sighed but didn't answer. "Would you like some water?"

"Sure, thanks."

Cecily reached around to the back seat but couldn't quite get hold of the water bottles. She relaxed her seat belt and tried again. The bottles had rolled over to the far side of the right back door and she grappled to get hold of them.

"Uh, should I..." Michelle started saying.

"I'm fine, I'll get it. Just a bit arthritic and not as supple as I used to be."

"No, I mean, does this look..."

The bottles were within reach now. Cecily had grabbed one in her right hand and was transferring it to her left, when the car suddenly slowed down. She plonked back into her seat as the other bottle rolled off and under the driver's seat.

"Oh. I got one," she said, holding it out to Michelle. Then she looked down at her feet. They were wet.

The car swayed gently at first, pounded by the floodwater, and then lost its grip on the road. The engine cut out. The women stared at each other, their minds flooding with panic.

"I didn't know," Michelle said. "I didn't..."

The road had only seemed to make a gentle downward dip. She had approached it cautiously, but not cautiously enough. The surroundings were obscured by sheets of rain and by the time she had noticed the flood markers on the side of the road, it was already too late.

"Oh. Oh my," Cecily said, trying to lift her feet clear of the water. She was still clutching at the water bottle. Absurdly, a line from a poem came to mind—'Water, water everywhere, nor any drop to drink'—and she unscrewed the bottle and took a swig, as if they were drifting on an ocean and it was a life-saving drop after great thirst.

The car was being swept across the road and into a gully towards a grove of trees. By now they were wet up to the ankles.

"Hold on," Michelle said. "We'll be okay. Hold on."

"But..."

"It's okay. We'll get out of here."

"My bag. I need..."

"Here, I'll get it. There you go. It's a bit wet; hold it against your chest."

"Michelle."

"Hold on, Cecily. We're going to bump into some trees, okay. Here we go."

There was a bump and a scraping noise as the nose of the floating car collided with a tree trunk. The water kept pushing at it. It turned sideways and bumped against another tree. It bobbed against the trunks, sinking lower in the water.

"I'll have to get out," Michelle said, unfastening her seatbelt. "We can't stay in the car while it's floating; it might get swept away."

"Won't it sink, anyway?"

"I don't know. I suppose it will. Don't worry, it's not deep here, I think. No, you stay put; I'm just going to have a look first. When I'm out, close the window again and switch off the car completely. Okay?"

Cecily nodded. Michelle turned the key in the ignition, just far enough to get the electronics working, and started opening her window. The rain streamed in, its downpour only vaguely stumped by the trees. She hoisted herself up onto the seat and then straightened awkwardly up and out through the window into the rain. She gave Cecily a thumbs up as she lowered herself into the knee-deep water. Then she disappeared from view as the window slowly went back up.

Greening the gardens

Thank God, Joseph Black had cancelled for today, Harry thought as he started on the last patch of Ben Eastman's lawn. "Patch" being a euphemism for nearly a hundred square metres of thick couch grass on a gentle slope that had in Harry's mind expanded to a football field on Mount Everest. Not that Mount Everest could ever, ever dream of being this hot. The amount of sweat that had poured out of him today could start a small deluge. Anybody still questioning global warming should try a spot of gardening on an average Queensland summer's day.

He turned the lawnmower around, pushing against gravity, friction and solar induced dehydration. What a day it had been!

His hopes of an early start at Mary Atkinson had been dashed when the lawnmower's pull cord broke. The nearest lawnmower shop only opened at eight, so he had to work for an hour, impatiently doing the edging and weeding, then drive to the shop to buy a new cord, then back (losing nearly an hour's prime work time), only to find Mrs. Atkinson waiting for him.

She was at her gossipy best behind a large mug of tea with a red comic book font asking *Have you hugged your grandma today?* She latched onto Harry, something he normally avoided through a strategy of perpetual motion.

Caught at a standstill with his hands in the mower's innards, he had to listen. It would have been impolite to yank the mower into roaring life while his client was extolling the latest academic achievements of her favourite grandson, of which there somehow seemed to be at least three. Not just three grandsons, but three *favourite* grandsons.

"He is the best, he's really such a blessing to his parents," Mary effused. "He's studying law, you know. And so handsome! He is just my favourite favourite."

Harry could have presented as evidence—if it pleases the jury—previous conversations in which Mary had proclaimed the economics student and the IT professional as her favourite favourites. Wasn't that the point of comparisons—being the best meant being better than others, so how could all three grandsons be the best at once? Nancy, being an honoured member of the grammar police, would have a field day with Mary Atkinson.

"He's sharing a flat with two of his mates in Brisbane. Not the cheapest option, I can tell you. The cost of accommodation these days—it will *literally* make your heart stop."

If only. Harry flinched at the thought. He wasn't being charitable at all this morning. But they were only thoughts. He held his tongue and stood his ground. When Mrs. Atkinson's diatribe was momentarily diverted to her one-eyed pug's morning toilet, Harry yanked away. The mower's noisy fumes blissfully drowned any further conversation.

The delay at Atkinson's put him back an hour on his schedule. Then, of course, there had been a missed call from Tanika, but when he had called back, the call had immediately gone to voicemail. He had left a brief message— "Hi, it's Harry. Looks like I missed you, so I'm just returning the favour." That was only mildly funny and absolutely ungrammatical, but he chuckled anyway. He had also called the Real Property office, but she hadn't been in and no-one could tell him her reason for phoning, so he had left it at that.

Nevertheless, the whole phone tag shebang had taken another fifteen minutes of his time. Not that his next customer would have cared.

The Holmes property was one of several rental properties for which Harry did the garden maintenance. The first tenants that he had encountered in Fred Holmes' house were an elderly couple who had been there for years. The husband had been doing the garden himself but had recently had a back operation that put him out of action, so Fred had called Harry in to take over.

Fred was an engineer, a large man with balding dark hair and size thirteen shoes, who now lived and worked somewhere in Bundaberg, two hour's drive further south on the Queensland Coast. He had moved away at the height of the big boom in town when property prices had soared to crazy heights and rental income could pay off your mortgage in two ticks. Yet from a comment or two he had let fall, Harry suspected that economics hadn't been Fred's sole reason for leaving. But how would he know? He was only a man, after all, and according to Nancy, too dull to pick up nuances in language and body language.

Within a liberal set of guidelines provided by Fred, Harry mowed, trimmed, edged, and weeded as he saw fit. At the end of each month, he sent an invoice that was duly paid within a few days. They only met on Fred's occasional visits to inspect his property, which could be anything from two to six months apart. Yet their working relationship was unshakable and constant and had been for three years or more.

When the old people had moved to a retirement home eighteen months ago, Harry had continued doing the gardening for a while until a new tenant moved in. Herbert Ainsley was single, thirty-something and had, besides his job as process technician at the local aluminium smelter, only one other interest—fishing. One of those fifteen percent of Queenslanders who fished regularly, according to the newspaper.

Herbert was more than willing to pay more rent if it meant no time wasted on mowing the lawn. His boat was a more or less permanent extension of his Mitsubishi Triton ute, the tinnie secured upside-down on the ute's flatbed with tie-down straps. If it wasn't on the ute or in the water, it got pride-of-place under the carport, while the vehicle stood outside.

As a shift worker, Herbert was on an eight-day rotating roster comprising two day shifts, two night shifts, and four days off. Harry could never remember his schedule and therefore never knew if he would find Herbert at home when he arrived and if so, whether Herbert would be just lazing around or catching some shut-eye before a night shift. When the Triton was parked under the carport or in the driveway, Harry always felt a twinge of guilt at the thought of disturbing Herbert's slumber, but neither Fred nor Herbert himself had ever complained or asked to have the gardening moved to a different time slot.

Harry had free access to the whole garden. In the front, the lawn on the footpath extended beyond a low timber fence to form a small patch of roughly three by eight meters. Around this a few garden-beds contained no-nonsense, low maintenance shrubs needing only the occasional trim, some perennials like chrysanthemums and geraniums that Harry sometimes had to replace with new plants once they started looking sad, and three foxtail palms. In a corner at the front door was an informal and uneven collection of pavers, on which a group of plant pots was arranged, overflowing with hardy agaves, bromeliads and succulents.

The back garden was an exaggeration of the same low maintenance principle, being mainly lawn, with only two trimmed shrubs along the boundary on the left. It was bigger than the front garden and sloped steeply up to the adjoining property. On the right side, halfway between the house and the back fence, was a small garden shed, looking as if it had been dumped onto the lawn with no consideration of functionality or design. A connecting strip of lawn ran from front to back on that side of the house, beside a paved pathway.

The sloping backyard had been a problem since Harry first started working here. With every significant downpour, the thin layer of topsoil under the lawn was eroded further. Grass tufts held on for dear life. The lawnmower kept going over the uneven, exposed ground, but the going was getting tough. Harry watched it with trepidation, like a vet would watch a dog with scabies getting balder by the week while the owner merely nodded and smiled and said "Sit, Rover. Stop scratching. Good boy, Rover."

The problem was not that Fred was ignoring the issue. He just could not make up his mind about the best solution. Did he want a formal retaining wall or just smaller terraces?

Would planting with enough natives and ground covers do the trick? Or was a rockery a better idea? Perhaps he just needed to add extra topsoil in the dry season. Every option presented a seemingly insurmountable problem—it cost too much, or it would take too long to establish or he didn't like the design. Whenever Harry mentioned the slope in an email or telephone conversation, Fred would give a figurative nod and change the subject.

The last rains had now pushed things to the edge. Soil was being eroded from under the back fence. With the next flood, the neighbours might end up in the backyard. In fact, after their bullterrier had tried to crawl through and been stuck under the fence for two hours some weeks ago, even the elusive Herbert was getting fidgety—the estate agent had sent out an urgent appeal for something to be done.

So finally Fred had decided on a retaining wall. Once the wall was built and backfilled, Harry would fill it with plants.

The excavations at the Holmes property had now started in all earnest. A couple of broken bricks propped open the small wooden gate on the side of the house and Harry walked through to find the back yard a shambles of soil, rocks and tools. Two men in yellow high-visibility shirts were busy with spade and spirit level in the excavated foundation trench. A mini digger had disturbed what was left of the back lawn and left muddy tracks all the way to the street.

"How're you doing?" the older man greeted Harry, smiling at the edge trimmer in his hands. "Messed up your lawn a bit, mate."

Harry shrugged. "It'll come good again. At least the run-off will be less."

"Sure will be. We're making it a metre high."

"When do you reckon you will be finished?"

"Middle of next week, I reckon. Yeah, I'd say we might even be done by Tuesday."

"Good. I have to put in some plants at the top, once you're done. You'll be back-filling with good soil?"

"Sure. Always do in a garden, mate. No use doing it with rubbish."

"Thanks, that sounds good," Harry said, although he had his reservations.

"And we bumped off a couple of toads for you; just popped them behind the wall. That okay?"

"No worries. Just dig them in deep enough, though. They tend to smell."

Harry detested the poisonous cane toads that seemed to invade every moist hidey-hole in a garden. Lift a log or push aside a stack of old pots, and they would sit there in all their warty ugliness. Killing snails gave him the satisfaction of clearing the garden of a pest, but killing a cane toad brought an extra gratification. It was the feeling he imagined teenage boys got shooting monsters in a video game. Die, you evil spawn of the devil! he imagined shouting.

"Good compost," the builder said and grinned. "Push up the daisies, they will."

"Indeed. Now I'd better get going in front then and leave you to it."

"Sure, sure. See ye."

Having substantially less lawn to mow here, Harry hoped that he would make up for lost time. It was already stuffily hot, and it would not get any better. But he was not about to be let off the hook. This time it was a bird that held him up. Birds, to be exact.

He started on the front lawn, trimming the edges and then moved around to the side of the house. Here there was a grated drainage channel that ran along the paving skirting the outer walls. A sturdy magpie chick, well out of the nest but still pestering its parents for food, had somehow gotten one foot stuck in the channel's grate. When Harry came around the corner with his edge trimmer like a cowboy with gun blazing, the chick restarted its efforts at escape with renewed enthusiasm. The parent bird squawked around in panic.

Harry shut off the edge trimmer. He contemplated the scene. Magpies could be aggressive parents. Their dive-bombing tactics on anyone venturing near a nest of chicks were legendary, enough to have the bravest pedestrian reaching for a hard hat. He had never considered whether their aggression extended beyond the nest to protect nest leavers, but he was not going to test it without due care.

The chick fluttered and pulled in desperation. The parent magpie fluttered and squawked in sympathy. Harry took a few careful steps nearer. Flutter, flutter. Squawk, squawk. Step. Step.

The next step was too close for comfort for the magpie. It hopped out of Harry's way. So much for continued aggressive avian parenting. He reached out with hands shielded in gardening gloves and took hold of the chick, softly but firmly, as he would do with the branches of a new shrub to be planted. Then, supporting the bird against his leg, he disentangled its foot from the grate. There was no perceptible damage.

"There you go, buddy."

It hopped out of his hands, still dazed and unsteady, like a drunken youngster pulled out of a bar fight. Its parent turned a beady and disapproving eye on both Harry and its offspring.

"Go on then, silly bird," Harry chuckled as he walked on with his edge trimmer. The engine's loud whir left no further doubt in the birds' minds that it was time to get out of there. Harry quickly trimmed the side-strip of lawn, then around to the back. He would not bother with mowing the damaged back lawn but would just trim the edge adjoining the house for now.

Near the back door was a corner of pavers on which some pot plants stood, similar to the front ones but with colourful pelargoniums that trailed over the edges. A few runners of grass had crept under the pavers and pushed their greenish white fingers along the wall. Harry usually just snipped them off with the edge trimmer, but today, despite being pushed for time, their straggly ends kept mocking him like hydra heads. He walked back to his ute to get a spade. He moved the pots out of the way, carefully lifted the edges of the pavers and cut off the wayward grass shoots with a satisfying push of the spade. Having pulled the severed runners out from under the pavers, he replaced the pots and continued with the trimming, then waved a last goodbye to the builders before leaving.

As he now battled his way back and forth over the last lawn of the day, he thought of Martha and how he would tell her the story of the magpies. She would probably want one as a pet. Goodness, what a fizzy little creature he and Nancy had bred! She was like those errant grass runners, determinedly pushing her way through life, up and over and everywhere. It took a lot of patience and love to guide her in the right direction and sometimes he had to curb the urge to sever her straggling shoots with one angry thrust. God knows, she needed a bit of trimming, but doing it in a painless way was not easy.

It was not something he ever discussed with Nancy anymore, but he did at times wonder how it would have been had she had siblings. Would a sibling or two have tamed her, worn off her uneven edges? Or would it have been trouble multiplied? Joy multiplied?

He gave a grunt as the lawnmower bumped over an uneven spot. He was halfway through Eastman's sloping patch of lawn when someone called him. At the top of the slope, where the lawn flattened out to meet the sidewalk, a man was waving, silhouetted against the light. Harry could hear and see him calling, but he had to turn off the lawnmower to make sense of the words.

"Mr Green! Harry! Can we have a word, please?"

Harry climbed the hill. It was only as he neared the top and his eyes adjusted to the light that he realised the man was in police uniform. There was a second officer in the police car, a woman. His first thoughts were that someone had complained about the noise, dirt or sloppy parking. Now *that* would make his day. He greeted the policeman politely and slightly out of breath.

"I am sorry to bother you. You are Harry Green?"

Harry nodded, neither admitting nor denying the inconvenience of the interruption. The policeman had a softly freckled face that seemed out of place on an officer of the law. He extended a hand in greeting.

"Constable Alec Berkley. Your wife mentioned that you might be here."

"My wife? How..."

"It's about one of your clients—Mrs. Cecily Stone."

"Yes?"

"I'm afraid that she has disappeared, Harry."

"Disappeared?"

"Missing."

"Ah. You're sure? I saw her only Wednesday and..."

"Exactly. We believe you might have been the last person to have seen her."

It sounded suspiciously like an unfinished sentence, Harry thought, as in "the last person to have seen her alive".

"But she was expecting a visitor."

"So we have been told. Do you know who it was and when they were coming?"

"A family friend, I think, a friend of her daughter's. I know it was this week, but I'm not sure of the date."

"Male or female?"

"Uh... female? Yes, it would have been a woman."

The policeman made a note of this while Harry waited. Having come to a stop after all the physical effort, he was steaming in his own sweat. He took off his hat and wiped his forehead with a corner of his shirt.

"Was she planning on going anywhere?"

"I think she was, but I don't know when."

"Do you know where to?"

"I don't know. North somewhere?"

"She didn't tell you?"

"I'm sorry, constable," Harry scoffed. "I'm just the gardener."

"Hmm."

"Look, are you sure she's really missing? It seems a bit soon to tell, just two days."

"We take any reports of missing persons seriously, especially with the elderly. And the storm coming."

"Hasn't she just gone sightseeing with her visitor? Maybe they're visiting the daughter. I think she lives in Perth. Or the Whitsundays."

Constable Berkley gave him a strange look, as if Harry had just suggested Cecily had flown to the moon for a tea party.

"You did Mrs. Stone's garden on Wednesday?"

"I did. As I've already told you."

"Indeed." Berkley tapped his pen against his notepad. "And she was there when you left?"

"Well, no, she wasn't."

"Ah, so she was already gone then?"

"Gone? I don't know. I imagine she must have gone out. It is not unusual for me not to see my clients when I'm working. Most people have jobs, though obviously not Cecily. I saw her in the morning, though."

"Did you notice anything unusual?"

"No, not really."

"Not really?"

Harry shrugged. "Well, she was dressed up more than usual, I suppose, but I'm not sure that qualifies as suspicious behaviour. Have you asked her neighbour, old whatshisname? He seems like he always keeps a look-out on the neighbourhood."

"We are questioning everyone who could help us with finding her. So how did you know she wasn't there when you left, Harry? Did you knock?"

"As a matter of fact, I did, which was pointless really and irrelevant anyway, since her car wasn't there. It would be strange if her car had gone and she was still in the house, don't you think? The case of the missing car?"

"That could be," Berkley said, rubbing his freckled forehead in perplexity. "But you see, her car is still there. It's Mrs. Stone who is missing."

Flooded and marooned

She remembered a summer when the girls had been small, an outing to the dam. They didn't have a boat then; Jack only bought his years later. They had borrowed or rented a canoe, mostly for the children's sake, but Cecily had also tried it. She remembered that now, the feeling when you pushed away from the shore, the mud gently scraping under the hull, then letting go as you became waterborne. For a few short minutes, the car was now like a canoe, afloat and swaying in the water, bumping against the trees where it had come to a stop, looking for a way out. There was a gap between two mature trees, with only a thin sapling barring the way, fighting the force of the water and the flotsam, of which the car was now a part.

She had closed the window and switched off the ignition as Michelle had instructed. The driver's seat was wet where the rain had poured in. It would smell mouldy by tomorrow. But that was the least of their concerns, a drop in the bucket. Her feet were wet through and cold. She shivered. She had brought a cardigan, but it was in her suitcase in the boot.

Michelle had moved around the front of the car. Squinting through the rain-besieged windscreen, Cecily could see her wading through the floodwater. She stumbled and put out a hand to steady herself against the car. It rocked and bumped. There was now a puddle of water at Cecily's feet.

Michelle kept walking around the car. Her hair and clothes were plastered against her body. Cecily shivered again, whether from her own cold or in sympathy with Michelle, she wasn't sure. The car moved again, sinking down onto solid ground. For a moment its rear end swayed out. It steadied, seemed to bob again, jarring its right back door against the sapling.

Turning in her seat to look backwards, Cecily could make out Michelle's form at the back of the car. She was pushing at it. Surely, she could not hope to push it back onto the road, not against the force of the water. Besides, the car had already run aground. It was a brave but foolhardy gesture and would only get her cold and wet. Cecily waved, trying to attract her attention.

There was another jar as Michelle shoved at the car. It rocked, an ungainly raft in the muddy water. For a moment it felt as if it was moving forward again, as if Michelle was indeed succeeding in pushing it along. But then there was a crack. The rear end swerved wildly as the sapling gave way and the car was again carried along on the water, further into the trees.

Alone in her drifting, drowning raft, Cecily gave a cry of dismay and hugged herself. She could not see Michelle anymore. Was this how it would end, their quest? What irony if they were to drown, so near their journey's end!

The car did not float far, however, before hitting more trees. And this time Cecily could feel another bump, a jerk as the car came to a stop. It was a definite stop, this time, like a canoe striking the shore again. You could not mistake the solidness of the earth.

Michelle appeared soon after, at the driver's door. She strained at the door, but it would not budge against the outside water pressure. Cecily leant over to switch the ignition back on and opened the window. Michelle climbed in and flopped back into her seat like a wet dog, closing the window again.

"Brrr!" she shivered. "Sorry about that. I was hoping to push it onto higher ground, back to the road. Are you okay?"

"I'm okay. Cold, but okay. But you... you're wet through!"

"I know!" The water dripped down her face from her hair and she tried to wipe it away with a wet forearm. "I think we're stranded now."

"Well, yes."

"We won't float away. But we're pretty much stuck here. Can we call anybody? Do you have an emergency number here, like 911?"

"Um. Triple zero."

Michelle reached over to the glove compartment for her phone. She dialled the number and held the phone to her ear. Nothing happened. She stared at the screen, its surface wet from where it had touched her ear.

"No service."

"It must be the weather," Cecily said, digging around in her handbag. "The lines are probably down. Try mine."

Michelle watched her with a wry smile without saying anything.

"Where is it? I'm sure... Oh. I forgot."

"It probably wouldn't have made a difference anyhow. We'll just have to wait it out."

Suspicions and suppositions

Harry had barely stepped into the house when Nancy was upon him. She hugged him like a prisoner set free, then suddenly let go.

"Phew! You're smelly."

"Hello, love. I'm smelly every day. You just never get near enough to appreciate it. Why the sudden affection?"

"I thought..." She smiled sheepishly. "The police. I thought... Well, actually I thought something might have happened to you; I thought you might have died!" She gave him another fervent hug.

"There, there. I'm here. Smelly but not quite dead. There now, love."

"And then," Nancy said and stood back. "Then Mrs. Stone is missing and the police are looking for you and you've still got the little doll and... and... and Martha calls her cat Snail!"

"Oh, that's something to cry about, all right. Snail? I thought we were past that danger. Wasn't it Blossom the last time?"

Nancy rolled her eyes. "Blossom, Patrick, Jupiter, Doggy... I don't know where she gets the names from." She followed him into the kitchen.

"Patrick? I thought it was a girl."

"It is."

"Hmm. Snail. I guess it will be okay, after a while. One could get used to a cat called Snail. There are worse things in life than cats with invertebrate nomenclature. Want a drink? No? Anything to nibble before tea?"

"Harry, we're going out to Jenny's, remember? And yes, there *are* worse things. Like the babysitter not showing up."

"Tell me about it," he scoffed.

"No, you tell me first. Did the police get you?"

"They didn't *get* me, Nancy. So, can I please just sit down and enjoy my beer before you also start interrogating me?" He looked at his watch. "There's still plenty of time to get ready."

He sank thankfully into the comfortable old couch, sighed and took a deep draught of his beer. Whatever the day brought, he thought, there's always home at the end. Something tickled his leg, and he instinctively swatted at it.

There was a soft rustle under the couch, then a more insistent tickle and the fairy touch of small fingers. A fluffy patchwork tail appeared and disappeared. A giggle was not quite smothered.

"Now where is our Martha?" Harry said. "She must have run off with that cat of hers. What is its name again? Flower? Kitty? I know, it's called Patches!"

"Not Patches, Daddy!" exclaimed the couch. "Snail! Snail!"

Snail reappeared, tail-end first, and was followed in slow motion by the squirming bits that made up a little girl—hands, arms, hair, face, body and the rest. Martha gave herself a little shake and then flung herself at her father with no consideration for the person. He staggered back into the couch, shielding his beer with both hands.

"Careful, Martha," Nancy warned.

"Boo, Daddy!"

"Hello, possum. Had a good day?'

"You must scare when I say boo, Daddy."

"Oh, I'm sorry." He widened his eyes and trembled in mock fright. "I'm scared. I'm very scared."

Martha giggled and then slid off the couch to pursue her kitten that had scampered under the dining table. Harry smiled and drank his beer.

"So?" Nancy prodded. "The police."

"The police. Well, apparently old Cecily Stone has gone missing."

"So I gathered. But you saw her on Wednesday."

"Yes, that's what I told them. It's two days ago. Do people go missing so quickly?"

"No, you mean..." Nancy pounced on his mistake.

"Sorry, I mean, can they be *reported* missing that soon?"

"I suppose so. I wonder who reported it."

"Probably her Bingo friends. They must be worried about the storm—the police, I mean, not her friends. Or maybe the friends are worried too. And according to the policeman..."

"Constable Berkley?"

"Exactly. As far as I could gather from the constable no-one has actually seen her since Wednesday. He insinuated that *I* was the last person to have seen her." He took a deep draught of his beer and swilled it around his mouth before swallowing. "I find that hard to believe. You know how neighbours can be—real sticky beaks, watching their neighbours' houses to see whether the lights come on at night, listening for their cars coming or going."

"I suppose you hear these stories about old people, don't you? She's not... dead somewhere in the house, is she?" Nancy asked. "You know, the way they find the old people days after they've died and the neighbours go round because of the smell."

"No, Nancy. I saw her on Wednesday. Really!"

"Yes, okay, I know. That's what I told the police. But later, you knocked and there was no answer."

"You told them that as well?"

"No, not about you knocking again. I just said that you'd seen her, so she must have been alive then."

"Okay. Well, I've thought of that, her being gone then already. But her car wasn't there and now it is. So, she must have come back and then disappeared again."

"Unless the murderer brought back her car to make it seem like she was still there."

"Murderer?! Hey, she's just missing. She's not dead!"

"Not yet," Nancy said defiantly.

"Not at all. Anyway, she could have taken a taxi to the airport perhaps, who knows. Perhaps she's gone to visit her daughter with the friend, that's what I told the police. But pretty decent of them to act so quickly.

"Wait, I know! Maybe the daughter is worried about the cyclone and phoned, but can't get hold of her. I guess that would get a daughter pretty worried, what with some airports closing down up north. We could be next."

"I'm sure. Imagine waiting for your mom of eighty-something..."

"Seventy-nine."

"Whatever. Imagine waiting for her to arrive, say at the airport, and she just doesn't pitch."

"But she didn't fly," said Harry.

"Says who? What if she had?"

"I don't think she did. The police would check flights, wouldn't they?"

"Maybe. Anyway, waiting for her car to arrive, then, and she doesn't come. I would imagine all kinds of tragedies. Can you imagine, my mom..." Nancy shivered at the idea.

"She can't have driven to Perth, though," said Harry. "It must be local. And with the weather. She probably left her mobile at home. She's not used to it like we are. They think differently, don't they?"

"They do," said Nancy. "Anyway. Martha, enough of that. Get out from under the table; you'll damage the chairs." She turned back to Harry. "And what, if I may ask, are you going to do with the Kewpie doll?"

Harry shook his head in mock-despair. "Good Lord, first my daughter thinks I'm a murderer and now my wife thinks I'm a thief! I'll give it back, don't worry. I'm not a criminal, whatever you may think."

The dangers of working

The babysitter, a library assistant that they had used a few times before to look after Martha, had broken her arm on the job and could not help them. They would either have to call off the outing or take Martha with them.

"We cannot *not* go," Nancy insisted. "We had to cancel last time, remember?"

"I do remember. But that was because of the cyclone, an act of God for which we could not be held responsible. If we wait long enough, we'll have another act of God to blame. That storm is turning pretty nasty, and it's headed this way over the weekend, they say."

"Exactly. Jenny would be devastated. She'll have made some special dish for the occasion."

"She's vegetarian."

"So? What has that got to do with anything?"

"Nothing. It was just a thought."

"She won't make a meat dish, if that's what you're thinking. She doesn't even serve meat in the café."

"Hmm."

"She eats fish, though, so strictly speaking she's not a vegetarian but a..."

"How do you break an arm in a library?" Harry suddenly wondered. He couldn't imagine a safer workplace.

"She fell."

"She fell? Just like that? I can't remember there being stairs in the library or loose carpets even."

"Don't they use steps to get to the top shelves?"

"You mean ladders? But wouldn't the readers then also have to use them?"

"Well..." Nancy tried to recall the height of the library shelves. An image came to mind of a prim bespectacled librarian in a Victorian dress, standing high on a ladder and pushing *Lady Chatterley's Lover* onto the top shelf, safely out of reach of any immorally minded readers. "I'm sure there's a perfectly good explanation, Harry. Now, I guess we'll take Martha along then."

Harry's eyebrows went up. He narrowed his eyes. His lips pouted and slid sideways as if he was chewing on something. Then he slowly smiled.

"I guess we'll take the missy along."

"Good. I'll just give Jenny a heads-up."

It was with some persuasion plus a degree of logical argumentation and social education and a hint of despotism that they convinced Martha that, although well-behaved children might be perfectly acceptable dinner guests, the same did not go for cats, however pretty, cute or "lovingable". Snail was to stay at home and no, she did not need a babysitter.

Despite a last-minute search for Priscilla, the pink elephant, who *was* allowed to attend the dinner, they arrived at Chris and Jenny's in good time. Martha was introduced to the aging Silky terrier, but neither showed much interest in the other. Martha thought the dog was smelly and its teeth snarled at her when it panted. The dog in return found Martha devoid of tasty treats and thus of less interest than the kitchen floor.

As the adults sat down with pre-dinner drinks Martha and her pink elephant found a spot between a set of nested tables and a decorative bird cage on a stand and proceeded to create their own private universe. Jenny's teenage son Alan was staying over with a friend.

"Have a bite." Jenny passed around a plate of assorted snacks artistically arranged on a blue ceramic platter. It matched the colour of her necklace, a string of small polished gemstones that Nancy thought must be sapphires.

Harry's hand hovered over the smorgasbord of pickles, crisps, stuffed baby peppers, dressed shrimps, assorted olives and dips. The social pressure of such chocolate box choices left him as indecisive as a chameleon on a pointillist painting.

"Come on, Harry," Chris teased. "It's all safe. The food tester passed it—no trace of any poisons." Then, as Harry picked some shrimp and bit down on a gherkin, he added, "Oh wait, what's that gagging sound I hear from the kitchen?"

Harry gagged on the gherkin, swallowed his laughter, coughed when Nancy whacked him on the back.

"Good God! Don't joke, Chris. If I don't get poisoned here, I will eventually at work. That's if Nancy doesn't kill me with a backhand first."

"Pooh! You don't break that easily, honey."

"Harry's made of strong stuff, is he, Nancy?" Jenny asked. "Here, have some more snacks. The guacamole is really good."

"He's not exactly stainless steel, but he's strong enough. Either that or he has an awesome guardian angel."

"I can imagine. Gardening is a dangerous job." Chris was an accountant and got his lean, tanned body from kayaking. It was with a fair bit of reluctance that he mowed his own lawn.

"Not as dangerous as working in a library."

They laughed and looked across at Martha, who was having a serious discussion with her elephant.

"How did that happen?" asked Chris.

Harry shrugged. "Books are dangerous things. They can trip you up."

"They can kill you," said Jenny.

"Oh, that's far-fetched, even for you, Jen."

"It's true!" she protested. "Books can poison you. Can't they, Nancy?"

"Literally."

"Literally?" queried Harry.

"Yes. Have you heard of *The Name of the Rose*? It's a book by Umberto Eco."

"And it was poisonous?"

"No. But in the book... You tell the story, Jenny."

"Okay," said Jenny. "So, in this book, in this story, these two travelling monks investigate the murders at a monastery. One guy is found dead in a vat of pig's blood and another drowns in a bath and I think someone suffocates as well. But they've all got these strange ink marks on their fingers, so the monks, the investigators—I can't remember their names, but in the movie Sean Connery plays the main guy. So Sean Connery thinks it could be poison. You probably wouldn't have been able to tell then; it's not like they had all the forensic stuff we have today, CSI and all that.

"Anyway, they somehow end up in the library looking for a book and the book has been stolen or hidden away, because it talks about the virtues of laughter and one of the monks—not the Sean Connery monks, one of the resident guys—is dead set against laughter. He thinks it's a big sin."

That would have been another book stashed away on a high shelf, next to *Lady Chatterley*, thought Nancy. Sex and laughter, too sinful to read.

"And in the end," Jenny continued, "it turns out this monk, the anti-laughter guy, has put poison on the book's pages. When the monks read the book, they lick their fingers to turn the pages and they get poison on their fingers. Then when they lick their fingers again to turn the next page, they get poisoned. So—poisonous books."

"Literally," admitted Harry. He stared at his fingers, sticky with salt and pickle sauce, wondering whether it was safe to lick them.

Later, during dinner—which was, to Harry's delight, not just a vegetable bake but a delicious paella—Harry told them about the disappearance of Cecily Stone and how the police had come looking for him.

"And? Are you a prime suspect?"

"I would imagine not, Chris. They have to go through the motions, fact gathering and that sort of thing. I probably won't hear from them again. If you ask me, considering the storm, they should be searching up north, collaborate with the emergency services around there. I don't know why they're bothering us. I suspect old Cecily will turn up yet, wet but well. She must have weathered quite a few storms at her age."

"How old is she?" asked Jenny.

"Eighty," said Nancy. "No..."

"Seventy-nine," said Harry. "She's a feisty old girl, all right. I don't think she's ready to keel over yet. She'll die in harness, picking a flower or swatting a spider."

"Swallowing a spider. 'There was an old lady who swallowed a fly'," Chris sang out.

"No, no, she'll die of a broken heart," said Nancy. "She's always been sweet on Harry."

"Ah! So it was *you* who knocked her off! The jealous wife getting rid of the competition."

"I think you've all got overactive imaginations," said Jenny. "You watch too much television."

"We don't have a television."

"Read too many books, then. Murder mysteries and what not."

"There you go," said Chris. "All those dangerous books. The pot calling the kettle black, isn't it, Jen?"

Martha, who had been sitting next to Nancy on a high stool, quietly chewing away at her food and following the conversation with watchful eyes, stabbed a runaway pea with her fork. "My daddy's a murderer," she said, before popping the pea into her mouth.

Harry coloured. He gave a little shake of his head and shrugged. "I kill garden snails. That makes me, what? A *petticide*, according to my daughter."

"Oh, oh!" Jenny exclaimed over the rim of her wineglass. "And I was going to make escargots for entrée!"

"What a faux pas that would have been," said Nancy. "Martha's got a new cat, you know. Tell Aunty Jenny what your cat is called, Martha."

"Her name is Snail, Aunty Jenny!"

"You see?"

"But you're a vegetarian," said Harry. "You don't eat snails, do you?"

"A pescatarian," said Jenny. "And yes, I do."

"Ahh..."

"They're not really meat, are they? They're molluscs, which are like mussels and oysters. Seafood, really."

"A pescatarian," mused Harry. "A pesticidal pescatarian. Yes?"

Shelter from the storm

After Michelle had been out in the rain for the second time, Cecily put a stop to it. Michelle was dripping wet again, soaking the car seat. She had walked a few hundred metres up and down the road, trying to find a signal on her phone, which she had wrapped in the clear plastic wrapping from their sandwiches. And she hoped that another traveller would pass by just at that time. Cecily knew the chances were slim. She also knew that it was better to stay with the car, their only shelter from the storm. Was that from a poem as well? A hymn?

"Look, they'll find us eventually," she said. "You're just making things worse, getting yourself chilled to the bone and the car wet."

"The car is already wet," Michelle shivered.

"Wetter, then."

"But what do we do, then?"

"We wait."

And so they waited.

Michelle climbed through to the back seat, from where she could reach the boot. Neither of them had packed any towels, but Cecily had a dressing gown of soft white towelling material. Screened by the curtains of rain around them and the windows now fogging up from inside, Michelle stripped down and used this to dry herself as best she could, before changing into dry clothes. There wasn't much in the line of warm clothes, but she found a jumper for herself and a cardigan for Cecily. She also pulled out a long skirt from her suitcase.

"We need to change places," she told Cecily.

"Why?"

"You can't sit there with your feet in the water. You have to get to the back seat."

"What about you?"

"I'll sit across both front seats. Now come on. Lower your seat way down."

It was a manoeuvre worthy of comedy, with much grunting and sighing, bits of anatomy in awkward positions and clothing getting caught on the seat and headrest. Cecily lost a shoe as she crawled over the seat back and with a final lunge landed next to Michelle, who had squeezed up against the back right door. Michelle then had to climb back to the front. When Cecily was sitting crosswise on the back seat, Michelle handed her the skirt to drape over her legs like a throw. They settled in for the wait.

They lost all sense of time in the murky wetness. Occasionally Michelle checked the time on her phone, but after a while it became too disheartening to watch the slow creep of minutes turning into hours. Eventually the darkness grew darker, and they knew it had to be night. The rain did not stop. There were two apples and half a chocolate bar left over from the morning's tea, which they munched on slowly, knowing it might be their last meal for some time.

"I've been thinking," said Cecily. "About this... trip."

Michelle was just an unseen presence in the dark, but she heard her shifting in her seat. There was no other response.

"I've been wondering why it has taken me so long to undertake."

"Hmm."

"I should have done this sooner. I'm wondering whether I've left it too long."

"Everybody has their own timeline for grief."

"Yes, but twenty-four years?"

"She was sixteen?"

"Just. Somewhere between her birthday and yours."

"I remember. A week before my birthday. Mom didn't tell me until after. I had a birthday party, and she didn't want to spoil it."

They were silent for a time, with just the rain's never-ending pounding outside. Now and then something would bump against the car, some flotsam swept away into the wet darkness.

"Was it a foolhardy decision then? This trip, I mean. For you to come all the way..."

"But I'm visiting you as well! It's not just for this I came. So even..."

"Even if we don't get to Bowen?"

"Even if we don't get there, I'm so glad I came."

Cecily reached out in the dark and touched one of Michelle's legs, stretched over the centre console with her feet on the passenger seat. Michelle's hand found hers and gave it a squeeze.

"You're cold," Michelle said.

"Hmm. But even if we do get there. I mean, what are we actually doing, Michelle? What am *I* doing?"

"Saying goodbye? Laying ghosts to rest."

"You don't think that's sentimental?"

"It's human. Human beings need ritual. Why else do we have funerals? It's for—and I hate to use the clichéd word—closure."

"That's why she buried the doll." Cecily's voice was soft as candlelight and she wiped at the tears on her cheeks. "Anne. She couldn't go to the funeral, so she buried the doll."

Storming south

All down the coast the towns waited with bated breath on the storm's southward track, stocking up on bread and milk and toilet paper, taking down shade sails and tying down hatches.

Early on Saturday morning, as Tanika rolled out of a bed that wasn't hers and reached for her discarded clothes, as Lennie dreamt of noises in the dark, and Gareth peered over his hedge into Cecily's yard while his dog peed against a fence post, the sun was still shining and only some wayward breezes tangled through the highest trees. After hours of aimless driving Fred had coursed north into a red dawn and was now heading into town with a sense of purpose fuelled by anger and resentment.

By noon, the sky was darkening significantly. The sea was grey and angry. But still the rain held off. Stubborn dog-walkers let their pooches off the leash on a last free run, before turning their backs on the beach and heading home to watch the endless live coverage of reporters lashed by wind and rain at the heart of the storm. A few curious townsfolk drove or even walked to lookout points at the harbour and river mouth to stare at the threatening horizon, chatting to strangers with the goodwill of a shared adventure, but the streets were emptying and by five o'clock when the first drops fell, the town tucked its head in and buckled down for the deluge.

After the storm

On Monday morning Harry woke from a dream of magpies pecking and clawing at his face and chest. He swatted at them in panic. A claw caught in the sheet and Snail pulled herself back up onto the bed with an indignant meow. She looked at him from her pretty patchy face, apparently decided that there lurked no real danger in his drowsy countenance and resumed her pawing and purring on his chest.

Harry groaned. He sighed in resignation. Next to him Nancy reached out a searching hand without opening her eyes and stroked the kitten. He watched her face.

"Smiling in your sleep, love?"

"Small fluffy things do that to me."

"I bet." He turned to snuggle into her neck, causing a rapid adjustment in Snail's positioning. "As they do to me. Mm..."

Their dawn cuddle was interrupted by another visitor to the pod, as Martha came padding in and threw herself at the tangle of sheet-wrapped bodies. Harry grunted from the force of her small body and Snail went flying to the floor. Nancy opened her eyes at Martha's smothered giggling.

"Another small fluffy thing," said Harry. "Peace disturbed, then. I'm getting up."

Martha gave him a quick hug, and then took his place, snuggling up against her mother. Nancy stroked the child's sleep-tousled head.

"Has the rain stopped? What do you have planned for today?" she asked Harry.

"Normal routine, I suppose, and some cleaning up. See what damage has been done. There might be some extra trimming to do at Jason's; I'll have to see. And poison at McMullen's."

"McMullen? Poison for what? Aren't they poison-free, as a rule?"

"They are, as a rule," he said, pulling on his work shirt. "And I truly appreciate that, but even after the last spell of rain everything was just growing wild and it will get worse now. The weeds have proliferated, I can't keep up with pulling them out and they won't allow me a few extra hours to catch up or spread mulch. So, poison it is, I'm afraid."

"Money talks."

"It does. Which is not a problem if something else talks louder. But with people like the McMullens eco-friendly is not exactly a voice shouting in the wilderness."

"Oh, but it is," Nancy said, sitting up. Martha curled into her lap. "It's shouting all right, but there's no-one nearby to hear it. They've all left the wilderness. Now all they hear is traffic."

"And money."

"And money."

"What about you girls? Anything exciting happening today?"

"I've got my art class this afternoon, all young ones, so I might take Martha along after kindy. And we have to take Snail to the vet, I suppose, but I don't know whether that will be today. Maybe next week."

Harry looked from his wife and daughter to the kitten that was now attacking the laces of his work boots and back. He harrumphed, scratching his head. He had the uncomfortable feeling that all his fears regarding the ownership of a cat would be well-founded. And with a name like that anything could happen.

"So it's going to stay Snail, is it?" he asked of no-one in particular or maybe of the great big universe who had fostered this on him. "That's the final name? No chance of a Poppy or Molly or Dolly? Well, God save your children one day, Martha. You'll probably name them Magpie or Crocodile."

Enough to poison a village

The three-by-five metre shed in the backyard was by its every fingerprint Geoffrey McMullen's territory. It could have been a shirt he wore daily, so imbued was it with his identity, his thoughts, his very odour. It was neither flashy nor poor, with just the right amount of tools and trinkets to make the space look used, but not cluttered.

A handful of screws, a rusted pipe coupling and two screwdrivers lay scattered on the otherwise neat work counter, like runes dropped from the hand of a Technology Age soothsayer. Several lidless glass jars were stuffed with pencils, pens, markers and used paintbrushes. From hooks on the roof and walls hung not only hammers, saws and other tools, but also bits of varnished driftwood and pebbles strung on cords. An old bicycle wheel served as a base for a mobile of washers and nuts.

The garden tools were bunched together against the wall between two shelving units on whose sides someone, presumably Geoffrey himself, had painted figures of Australian fauna in a quasi-Aboriginal style. On a slim shelf above them, out of reach of any presumably irresponsible youngsters, was stacked a plethora of poisons. This was contrary to what Harry would have expected of people who claimed to be virtually poison-free. Since he mostly used his own tools and chemicals, he had never been in Geoffrey's shed before to behold this stash.

He had to admit, though, that most of the containers seemed old and dusty, as if poisoning was something that belonged to a faraway regrettable past.

He reached over rakes, spade and garden fork and grasped a bottle between thumb and forefinger. He peered at the grubby label.

It was a pesticide for roses. Harry had never seen a rosebush in the McMullen garden in the three years he had been working here, so that had to be from a previous gardening phase. He put it back, pushing it to the side to reach for another bottle. This one was a sulphur-based pest spray for controlling fungi on fruit trees. There were no fruit trees in McMullen's current garden, either. He put that back as well.

The rest of the collection included a herbicide for nut grass, a specific tree killer containing triclopyr, snail and slug pellets, some more eco-friendly pyrethrum-based products and finally the weed killer he was looking for—a generic glyphosate that would kill anything remotely weedlike and a lot of other stuff besides.

On the pavement outside the shed, he now picked up his own safety gear from where he had piled them earlier. The gloves he was used to—he wore them every day. They had become an extension of his skin and fitted, well, like a glove. The safety goggles weren't too bad either, no worse than the reading glasses he had to slip on now and again these days. It was the mask that irritated him the most. It was stuffy and uncomfortable, creating a mini sauna around his mouth and nose and fogging up the glasses. But if he had to choose between temporary suffocation and chronic poisoning, there wasn't really any argument.

So donning the array of Personal Protective Equipment which made him feel like a medieval knight on his way to battle, Harry marched against the weeds.

An hour later he was done, his killing gear packed away, and the poison returned to its nook in McMullen's shed. He closed the shed's door behind him. There was a disturbing whiff of poison in the normally clear morning smell of greenery. He sniffed in disgust.

It ought to be illegal, collecting poisons like this. Maybe in fifty years it would be. In the meantime, he felt complicit in some undefined crime. He paused. Perhaps...

Harry turned around and went back into the shed. On one of the lower shelves, two rusted pruning shears stood in an otherwise empty cardboard box. He removed them from the box and arranged them neatly on the worktop. Then he packed all the poisons into the box. He left behind only two containers of what he judged to be lesser poisons. It was time to confront Mr. McMullen with his environmental conscience.

"Morning," Geoffrey McMullen greeted him as he came down the veranda steps toward Harry. He was a lean fifty-something with wispy grey hair and clear blue eyes that peered at the world from behind rimless spectacles. The lime green thongs on his feet seemed incongruous under the hems of khaki chinos.

"Hi, Geoff," Harry said. "Survived the storm?"

"We did, we did. A small leak in the garage, but otherwise we're good. I cleared away a lot of branches that came down with the wind. And the lawn was flooded, of course."

"Yes, I saw that. We had it too. It looked like a dam; you could have floated a tinny on it."

"Lot of damage further north, I hear."

"So they say. And it's still heading south; they reckon it could even get to Brisbane."

"Sure. All done, then?" Geoff asked, nodding at the poisons.

"I'm done, for sure. I hope your weeds are too."

"Nasty stuff, that poison, isn't it?"

Harry nodded and sniffed again. Maybe he should have left his mask in place until he was well clear of this place.

"More than nasty," he said. He lifted the box full of poisons towards Geoffrey like an offering. "You could kill a small village with these."

Geoffrey leaned away from the box and stuck his hands in the pockets of his chinos, as if to deny any association with its contents. After a moment's impasse Harry lowered his arms and put the box down at the foot of the steps. Both men stood looking down at it.

"Surely not a whole village," Geoffrey mused.

"Perhaps not. Maybe just a few village elders."

"Sickly ones."

"Weak and compromised."

"Dying from a long life of decadence and debauchery and..."

"And exposure to poisons."

"Hmmm. You win," said Geoffrey with a sigh. "I should throw it out, shouldn't I? Do my bit for the environment, that kind of thing."

"It's not just the environment, Geoff," said Harry. "Although that would be reason enough. This stuff is what it is—poisonous. To you and to me. A rose by any other name and so on. I'm getting to the stage where I'm just going to refuse to use poisons. I mean, if you insist on using this stuff, feel free. Go ahead. Just don't expect *me* to do it."

Geoffrey bent down and prodded at the collection of containers, tipping them sideways to read the labels. He picked one up and gave it a little shake, gauging the amount left.

"So what are you saying, Harry? Flush it all down the drain?"

"Goodness, no!"

"Just joking. How do I get rid of it? It's like nuclear waste, isn't it? Once you have it, there's no safe road to *not* having it."

"You're right there." Harry picked up the box again. "Leave it to me. I'll ask at the dump; they take chemicals like paint, so they might take poisons as well."

"Sure, thanks. So, I guess it's hard yakka from now on, just pulling them out by hand, the weeds?"

Harry nodded. It would be his hard yakka, unfortunately.

"There are some new eco-friendly stuff coming on the market, though I haven't tried any of it."

"Anyway, you'll be on top of it now. It's a good start."

"It is. See you next time, Geoff."

Harry carried the poisons box to his vehicle and stashed it securely among the tools on the back. He made sure that nothing could fall over or leak out. As he got in behind the steering wheel, he coughed. It was his imagination, but every time he used weedkiller, he felt adulterated. He could imagine himself glowing in the dark.

He supposed every job carried its own risks. Office workers could die young from sitting too much. Gardeners got poisoned or felled by a falling tree. Even housewives were exposed to exploding stoves or electrocution by faulty wiring in the vacuum cleaner. In the old days, painters got poisoning from the lead in their paint.

It was a case of choose your job, choose your poison.

Harried by Holmes

Harry suspected something was up from the moment he recognised Fred's number on his mobile phone. Given Fred's dithering nature, a last-minute change of plans was perhaps to be expected. Harry was in his vehicle on his way home from McMullen and considered ignoring the call—Fred could just leave a message like everybody else—but since he happened to be in a quiet street with abundant parking on the side of the road, he decided to stop and take the call. He drew up in a parking space and picked up his phone.

"How're you doing, Harry?"

"Hi, Fred. Not too bad, thanks. Yourself?"

"Could be better, could be worse." He coughed and cleared his throat. "I had a bit of flu last week, can you believe it?"

"Flu? In summer?" Harry asked. Fred didn't sound sick, but who was he to judge? No-one ever believed *him* when he had flu. Not even a jury of her peers could convince Nancy if Harry ever had double pneumonia and heart failure.

"Yeah, I know. A bugger, I can tell you. Had to spend the weekend in bed. But I'm more or less okay now, so for a Monday morning I guess it could be worse. Listen, Harry, when are you planting?"

"I've got it booked in for tomorrow."

"Have you talked to the tenant at all?"

"Er, no. Why? Is anything wrong?"

"No, no. You haven't seen him around, have you?"

"I haven't been back there since Friday. Is it about the wall? He's not still complaining, is he?"

"I... Yes, I wanted to know what he thought of the wall, how it had held up during the storm. How much rain did you get up there?"

"We measured 660mm at our place. Would have been much the same at yours, I suspect. How did you go down in Bundie?"

"Yeah, pretty wet, it was still dripping this morning. Some roads flooded, some stupid people got washed away in their cars, but I think they found everyone. Alive."

"People don't realise how dangerous it can be."

"No, they don't. So, listen Harry, you haven't seen Herbert, you say. Have you got the plants yet?"

"I've organised them, yes. They'll deliver tomorrow morning. Is there a problem?"

"No, no, I was just wondering whether I should have asked his opinion, you know? I mean, he's staying there, after all, not me."

"Er..." Harry knew something about Fred's statement made little sense, but it took him a while to harness his words into some semblance of a logical argument. "I don't know. You're the owner, Fred; surely you get to decide on what plants to put into your garden."

"Do I?"

"I would say so. After all, you're in control of the garden anyway, at least through me, that is. I think as long as you don't plant any objectionable plants, you get to decide."

"Objectionable?"

"Like cactuses, or poisonous plants that a child or a pet might chew on."

"You get poisonous plants that you can put in a garden?" Fred asked incredulously.

"O yes. Like oleander, for example, and foxglove. A lot of the lilies are poisonous as well. Of course, an adult is unlikely to chew on plants, but with children and pets you just never know." Harry could have told Fred a lot about kids and the unknowable. In his rear-view mirror he watched two bicycles approaching, a man moving smoothly and steadily along behind a young boy who every so often weaved erratically into the centre of the road.

"The point is, Fred, I don't think any of the plants we're putting in is likely to give offense to your tenant."

"Not objectionable, then?"

"Not in the least."

The bicycles moved past Harry, the boy so close that he could have touched him. A car coming from behind gave them all a wide berth.

"Hmm," Fred mused. "All the same, maybe we should just ask his opinion, don't you think? Just ask him. As a mark of ... oh, I don't know, benevolence or goodwill or something."

Harry thought not. He did not need any complications on this job. It would be upsetting if he had to change the plants now. He did not enjoy renegading on a done deal, whether he was on the paying or paid side of it. With such short notice, Paul at the nursery was not going to be too happy with a change of plants. Besides, he knew for a fact that Herbert would not give a damn about the choice of plants. But Fred seemed beyond persuasion. "Whatever you want, Fred."

"Thank you, Harry. So you'll ask him?"

"Wait, what? I'm not on site at the moment, Fred."

"Oh. Yes. Of course. But when you get a chance, later on. Will you let me know whether he is... what he decides? Will you check on him and let me know? And you can ask him about the wall as well. You know, whether he's happy with it."

"You could just call him yourself, Fred, couldn't you? Because I don't have his number."

"Oh, I don't have his number, either. Owner-tenant confidentiality, you know, or is that agent-tenant? Anyway, we only work through the agent. Couldn't you just ask him? In person, I mean."

"I don't even know if he'll be home today. Besides, I've scheduled the planting for tomorrow, which doesn't give us much time."

"But please, Harry, could you check?"

Harry thought this was asking a bit much. He couldn't be expected to go chasing around after tenants, when a simple phone call would work just as well.

"Just call him. Or get the agent to call or something."

Fred mumbled something else that Harry couldn't quite hear and ended the call. Harry sat looking at the phone for a while, contemplating his next move. He could just ignore Fred's call and go ahead with the planting as planned. If he knew anything about the average tenant and about Herbert in particular, he wouldn't even notice the plants Harry was about to put in. In his experience, most people on either side of a rental agreement would have preferred a garden comprising nothing but a flat expanse of lawn. After all, why complicate a relationship with more things that could go wrong?

On the other hand, if for some inexplicable reason—allergies perhaps or a mortal aversion to the smell of orange blossom— Herbert had issues with the choice of plants and Harry had not consulted him as directed by Fred, it could lead to all kinds of unsavoury and uncomfortable situations involving digging up freshly planted plants. It made him think of the exhumation of a body and sent a shiver down his back. Better stick to honesty and procedure, even if it meant a detour past the Holmes property on his way home.

His phone vibrated on the seat next to him as a text message came in, but he ignored it. Ten minutes later, just as he turned down Parkside Drive, his phone rang again. This time it was Tanika. Harry was only mildly surprised at her call, since he hadn't heard from her again after the Friday's missed calls. He was expecting more problems from his tenants or perhaps feedback on the night-time noises. He pulled up outside Herbert's house and left the engine running while he answered the phone.

"Harry," she greeted him. "Sorry to bother you."

"What's up? Not more noises, I hope?"

"No, it's not that. Did you find the cause, however?"

"Not yet. I think it was just a once-off. Probably a possum or a rat. I'll check again on Wednesday."

"Good. I have a favour to ask, Harry," she said.

"Sure. Shoot."

"I've just had a rather strange call from one of my owners; I gather you do his garden."

"Yes?"

"Fred Holmes."

"Wait, what? He's with you, is he? My God!"

"He's not with me!" She was vehement in her denial, like a teenager protesting her adoration for the boy next door.

"I mean, he's with your agency. He's one of your customers."

"He's with Real Property, yes. The house in Parkside Drive."

"Well, talk of the devil. I didn't know. I just spoke to him half an hour ago; I'm sitting outside the house as we speak. Is it about the plants?"

"Yes. I'm sorry, Harry. He can be... anyway, you're there now, are you?"

"I am," he said, switching off the engine and getting out. Herbert's Triton wasn't in the driveway.

"Do you think you could check with Herb... with the tenant? I've tried calling him, but there's no answer."

"He might be at work. His car isn't here."

"No," she said. "He's not working today. He said... I've been trying to call him since... You're sure he's not there?"

"Well, as I said, his ute is not here. Which doesn't mean he isn't. I have given up trying to keep track of his comings and goings. Even if he's not working, that doesn't mean he should be at home, does it?" Something about this argument seemed vaguely familiar to Harry. It was Cecily, of course, and the presence or absence of her car.

It was the question of whether the presence of a personal article should be assumed to mean the presence of the owner of that article. Assumption is the mother of all... uh... yes, and all that. If he came home and saw Nancy's bag in the bedroom, he could assume that Nancy would also be near. That bag was a Pandora's box of items apparently essential to life. If, on the other hand, it was only her mobile phone, she could be anywhere within a radius of ten kilometres.

"Oh, wait," he said, suddenly realising something. "His tinnie is gone. He must have gone fishing."

"Oh. Okay, then. Thank you, Harry."

"So, what happens now? Do I go ahead with the plants?"

"The what?"

"The plants. Wasn't that the whole point of me running after bloody Herbert?"

"Yes, of course. You'll have to ask Fred, I think. Bye, Harry."

It was at times like these that one missed the old phones, Harry had thought, where you could smash down the handset with a bang. Clicking on the red "end call" button just didn't have the same effect. He looked at the earlier message on his phone. It had been from Tanika – "Please call me urgently." The bloody arrogance!

He kicked at a weed emerging on the edge of the driveway. Damn the lot—owners and tenants and agents—he would just plant the bloody shrubs and get it over with. He walked to the front door and knocked, not expecting any answer and not getting any, then turned back to his own vehicle and drove home.

More than one way to get a doll

During her art studies, having taken English Literature as an elective module, Nancy had gone through an etymology craze. It was as if certain words had mutated so they glowed in the dark and sprang out of sentences to catch her eye. Her attention would drift away from conversations, books or studies, following a word back to its origin like a salmon up a river.

One thing this had taught her was that words could not always be trusted to wear the same characteristics they were born with. There were many false leads and unreliable revelations. Often what seemed like the most obvious explanation was the furthest from the truth.

She thinks of this every time she enters a library. Somewhere in the high mountains of language, in a time and place where even Latin had only been a trickle over pebbles, "liber" had been born. Or rather, conceived, and then born as twins. Etymological twins, they were called. By the time Nancy had stumbled upon them, the words had split and branched and twisted and procreated. It took a tiny electric flash in her brain's language centre to connect them again—liberty and library. Clever Romans, though, to link books and freedom. Oh hey, even Rome was one of a twin, Romulus and Remus brought up by a she-wolf.

There was no prim Victorian lady to greet Nancy and Martha as they stepped through the sliding doors into the air-conditioned library, nor any sight of Jessica, the injured babysitter. Martha's disappointment about Jessica's absence did not last long. She was mainly looking for an audience with whom to share the news of her cat and any moderately friendly adult would do.

It was now a week since Snail's arrival on their doorstep. Nancy and Martha had already paid two visits to the local pet shop. Nancy's last pet had been a sixteen-year-old spaniel who died four months after her wedding to Harry. Within weeks she had been ready to replace it with anything furry—a dog or a cat or even a pigmy goat, if need be. Martha's fascination with pets had after all not come out of thin air. But Harry had always voiced the same counterarguments. It was too expensive or too labour-intensive or unfair to keep an only pet and not big enough for two. Over the years his arguments hadn't changed, only Nancy's determination.

But having been out of the pet ownership business for so long, she was astounded at the size of the shop. Or, as a condescending staff member pointed out to her, the pet *warehouse*. Where-house, more likely. It was a wonder she hadn't lost Martha somewhere among the rows and rows of pet food, aquariums, hamster house accessories and bird cages. She imagined having to search behind each dog bed and among the colourful collars, jackets and toys for a little girl who could get lost in a wardrobe without too much effort.

Their list of essential cat accessories (litter box, food bowls, food) had expanded to include an igloo bed and a feathery toy supposedly simulating a stricken bird. Snail had been mildly amused by the toy, but preferred a ball of scrunched-up paper, as she preferred a corner of the couch to her new bed. She did like the assortment of foods they offered.

They could also get flea drops and worming pills at the pet store, but for a check-up and vaccination they needed to see a vet. The pet shop attendant had scared them with tales of cat flu and fatal viral infections. So, despite Nancy's plans to put it off for another week, the previous afternoon had been scheduled for a visit to the animal clinic.

They had gone home with a health-checked, vaccinated, micro-chipped, documented kitten and a nifty pet carrier, leaving behind a hundred odd dollars and a smitten vet nurse. The nurse's adulation, ignored by Snail, who mistrusted the whole outing, had gone to Martha's head. It was fifteen minutes of vicarious fame that she was determined to stretch as far as it would go.

While Martha described her cat's finer points of merit to a librarian, Nancy browsed the books. It might be easy to lose her daughter in a pet shop, but she reckoned a library was safe enough. There really were no steps or ladders in sight. As for herself, she would get lost in the books, but that was only metaphorical.

She chose a handful of novels, a new murder mystery from an author she liked, a book on sculptures and installations, and two cookbooks. For Martha, but for herself as well, she added a stack of picture books and a Pixar movie. As an illustrator, it paid to keep abreast of what was happening in a wide field. Then she added Martha, collected from in front of a poster of butterflies in the play corner, and headed for the check-out.

After the freedom of the library, they were bound for the supermarket. She would make a casserole for dinner. Harry had a busy day ahead planting the new retaining wall garden bed at Fred Holmes and would probably come home starving.

But they were not going to get away all that quickly. As they were leaving the library, a woman rushed out of one of the adjoining community rooms, leaving the door open to a wonderland Martha was not about to miss. She pushed the book she was carrying into Nancy's hands and made for the open door, beyond which was visible an embarrassment of riches. Nancy needed a few moments to regain her balance before rushing after Martha.

The Lions Club was organising a toy sale for the coming weekend, and this room was the depot. Toys of all sorts spilled out from boxes and bags or lay in heaps on trestle tables. Two elderly women were busy sorting through and organising the toys into categories, while a man looked on in confusion. He picked up a worn wooden locomotive and wheeled it back and forth. The wheels scraped and scratched on the table's surface.

Martha headed for an unguarded table where dolls had already been sorted into groups according to size or type. A floppy ragdoll lay at the bottom of a heap, embroidered eyes staring out of its flat face. Squashed under the stuffed bodies of several other dolls, it seemed in urgent need of rescuing. A teddy-bear on top of the adjacent heap was slowly sliding down. It bumped into the ragdoll with its scuffed leather feet. Martha pushed aside the teddy and reached for a baby doll that could in all political correctness only be described as "previously loved". It caused a minor landslide in the doll pile.

"Hey!" one of the women gasped. "Please..."

"Martha!"

The woman's appeal and Nancy's simultaneous reproval were snubbed by Martha's guiltily beseeching face, her eyes peering out over the dimpled patchwork of plastic and paint that was the baby doll's face. The doll was fitted out in someone's do-it-yourself idea of baby wear—an ill-fitting onesie of pink towelling, inexpertly embroidered with hearts.

"Please, Mommy?"

"Please, we're not open to the public yet, we're..."

"Please, Martha, just put the dolly back, okay?"

Nancy was only mildly surprised by Martha's total lack of consideration for what she considered the aesthetic appeal—or lack thereof—of the doll. True to the whimsies of her unadulterated heart, Martha wasn't one to judge people or any other creature, whether animate or inanimate, on mere appearances. Her adoration was as unpredictable as it was irrational. If Cupid's wayward arrows had sought out an ugly baby doll as the object of her affections, then that was whom she would love, no questions asked.

Nevertheless, at five years old one is little more than a pet on a leash, restrained and restricted. One had parents and they had to be obeyed. Martha vacillated between obedience and desire. Her grip on the doll tightened, but the resolve in her eyes was wavering. Before resolve turned to tears, Nancy moved in with a different tactic. Something on top of another heap had caught her interest.

"Look," she said. "Now just look at this."

Curiosity got the better of Martha as Nancy stood bent over a pile of small dolls, pointing at something with a finger. Still clutching the baby doll, she shuffled nearer to her mother. The other woman had abandoned her post and was now bearing down on them, her sneakers squeaking on the tiled floor.

"Excuse me," she tried. "This is a private meeting. We're still... you're not meant to... Excuse me?"

"Look, Martha, it's another Kewpie doll, like the one Daddy found. See?"

The name meant nothing to Martha, but the association meant a lot. Her daddy's find had been taken away from her after a short period of play. She had understood that it was an old lady's toy, even though old ladies did not play with toys anymore and this old lady did not even have a little child who could play with the doll. As far as Martha could put two and two together, the old lady had in fact disappeared and was being chased by the police, thus totally excluding her from ever needing a little doll. That her mother had now found another of these "cutie" dolls was a well-placed coincidence, God's way of giving Martha her very own toy.

As Nancy picked up the Kewpie doll from the pile, Martha turned around to the other woman, holding out the baby-doll.

"You can have this one," she said. "She's a very nice doll. Her name is... um... Judy. You can play with *her*, if you want to."

"Hmm, yes, thank you, but listen ..."

The woman took the doll and pointedly returned it to its category-coded table. She pushed the pile back into a semblance of order. Then she turned back to Nancy, intent on admonishing her instead. It wasn't for nothing that she had been a primary school teacher for forty-plus years. She firmly believed that children were the products of parenting, whether good or bad. Don't blame the little ones, was her prime philosophy. It was the parents who needed a talking to. But Nancy was one step ahead.

"Oh, I'm so sorry," she said, smiling apologetically at the woman while clutching her stack of books against her chest as if for protection. "She did like that doll, didn't she? Would it be okay if we took this little one instead?"

"We're not open yet," said the woman. "We're only just organising stuff today. It's not a free-for-all and children need to know that. *You* need to teach them that."

"I'm really sorry. She's usually quite obedient."

"That's what they all say."

"I'm sorry?"

"Parents. They always say that. Disobedient? Naughty? Disruptive? Not *my* little brat!"

Martha pushed up against Nancy, her cheek on the skirt that smelled of crushed flowers, but didn't let go of the Kewpie doll. Behind her big green eyes, she was trying to gauge the threat from this stern old lady. She looked like her grandmother, with her grey hair in curls and her glasses and her wrinkles, her best nanna who knitted blankets and smelled like cookies and had a yellow pet bird in a cage and the bird could sing.

Nancy sighed and patted her daughter's head. "She *is* my little brat, you're right. But I love her. We all just try our best, you know? Are you a teacher?"

"Was." The woman shrugged. "Am. Always will be, I suppose."

Her stern look was dissolving at the edges as she looked down at Martha and Nancy pushed the advantage. "She doesn't have a lot of dolls; we prefer not to spoil her. So this is like a kid in a candy store, I'm afraid." She gestured at the room full of toys.

"We have another doll like this," she continued, not altogether untruthfully. "In fact, I think it's exactly the same. They could have been twins. Such synchronicity—you never see these anymore and now, within a couple of weeks, to have two. A strange world, isn't it?"

"Twins, yes. 'It's a strange, strange world we live in, Master Jack'," the woman murmured. Her face relaxed, a flush rising in her cheeks. Then suddenly her eyes were tearing up. Nancy reached out in concern, placing her hand lightly upon the woman's arm.

"I'm sorry. What is the matter? What did I say? Please, are you alright?"

The woman shook her head lightly, as if to deny her melancholy. She smiled and swallowed back the tears.

"Oh, it's nothing. Nothing, really. I'm fine. Memories. When you get to my age," she shrugged and wiped the back of one hand across her eyes, "there's so much to remember."

"I can imagine," Nancy sympathised. The woman didn't look all that old, in her early seventies at most. Her hair was a dark grey, and she had what could be called a well-preserved face, with dark eyebrows drawn in where her natural ones were thinning or had been plucked into non-existence. There was a small mole at the left corner of her mouth and wrinkles on her cheeks that deepened into dimples when she smiled.

Nancy's own mother was a touch younger than that and in no way old, as far as Nancy could see. She even scoffed at the idea of being classified as a senior citizen. Mind you, these days you were classified as "senior" once you reached fifty-five and got treated to an annual Seniors Week with free movie screenings, yoga classes and technology workshops.

"Sad memories?" she asked.

"Yes and no. But even happy memories make me cry these days."

"I'm so sorry to have intruded here. I apologise. I'm afraid my daughter is a wild one with a mind of her own. We'll go."

"No, please," the woman said, reaching out a hand to stop Nancy. "You don't have to go. You have a beautiful daughter. But there are rules, I'm afraid, and they should be for everybody."

"That's alright. You... do you have children?"

"I do."

"A daughter?"

"No. No, I have four sons. I tried." She gave a half-hearted chuckle.

"Grandchildren?"

"Three boys."

"Oh, goodness!"

"Yes, I know. I'm getting a little girl though. My one daughter-in-law is pregnant with twins and they think at least one will be a girl." The woman brightened, laughter lines crinkling her face.

"That's wonderful. Maybe both will be girls! Will you get her a doll from here?" Nancy asked.

"I did consider it. But you know how parents are these days; only the best and newest toys are good enough. And my son's wife... Well..." Her voice had become teary again, but there was an edge of anger. "Do you know to whom we sell the most toys? Take a guess."

"Well, I would have thought people with children. No? Poorer people? Kids themselves?"

"Old people like myself."

"Really? But why?"

"Nostalgia. Oh, you get some interest from young families or the odd collector looking for a find, but mostly it's old people. Look at me. I'm just an old woman crying for the past. We're all here for the memories."

She nodded her head towards where the others were still sorting toys. The man had put down the locomotive and was now gathering a selection of Dinky toy cars. The woman was staring down at the knitted teddy-bear she held with a rapturous face.

"Emilia was an only child with hundreds of toys that her parents just kept on recycling for new ones. But she remembers one doll she got for a birthday or Christmas just after her cat died. It disappeared along with the others and she's never gotten over it. Alfred says he's just volunteering, no hidden agenda, but he wants to get something special for his grandson. I think if he finds something, he'll just keep it himself. The grandson won't want it, anyway. It's all old. Like us."

"That is so sad," Nancy said.

"Growing old *is* sad."

"No, I meant..." What did she mean? Was it sad that people yearned for the past? But nostalgia—yearning for the good old days—didn't mean that the present was really worse. In fact, one tended to look at the past through rose-coloured spectacles. Was it sad that a girl had lost her treasured doll or that her cat had died? Of course it was and yet that also wasn't what she had meant. Perhaps the sadness lay in people's inability to gauge the real worth of things, or rather the value of human relationships compared to mere things. Yes, that was the real tragedy and in the end, people had to hold on to symbols of previous happiness—dolls, teddy-bears, toy cars—to sooth their anguished hearts.

Even as she thought it, Nancy knew it to be a cliché—anguished heart, indeed. But you could die from heartache—that was certain. Not too many centuries ago, nostalgia was considered a disease and could even prove fatal. And there was that strange mutation of words again. Nostalgia, from the Greek *nostos* (homecoming) and *algos* (grief), was a disease, while at the same time in German and Old English the word siblings of *nostos* meant "to heal". Healing by coming home. Not so sad, after all.

"I don't think kids care all that much if toys are old, really," she said. "Not inherently. They must get it from the parents. Just one moment. Martha, you can't sit on the floor, possum, it's dirty. Come, get up. No, get up. There's a chair over there. You go and sit there and play with the doll for a bit, while I have a chat with the lady, alright?" She pushed Martha towards some empty stack chairs against the wall and then turned back to the woman. "There. By the way, I'm Nancy."

"Pleased to meet you, Nancy. I'm Dorothy."

"Hi, Dorothy. Nice to meet you too. And I'm truly sorry for barging in here today. Is there any way we could buy the little Kewpie? Not today, perhaps, but could we reserve it in some way? Put our name to it?"

"I'll see what I can do," Dorothy said, turning away towards where the other woman was now sitting down at the main table, pouring coffee from a flask into three mugs and opening a container of biscuits. Someone had returned the teddy-bear to its heap.

Nancy watched as they talked, occasionally looking in their direction. The other woman shrugged and nodded, shook her head, nodded again. When Dorothy returned, she held a small invoice book and was smiling brightly.

"You can have it today. It's probably worth more, but you can have it for fifteen dollars. Is that okay?"

"Oh, that's wonderful. Thank you so much. We really have another one at home."

Nancy paid her and wished her all the best with the upcoming toy sale. She collected Martha, who was slightly surprised that her mother did not insist on taking away her doll again, but wasn't going to object. Then they said goodbye, gathered up their books again and left.

Putting in the plants

The three gardens scheduled for the morning were routine mowing jobs, boring to the extreme, with not even the diversion of weeding or shrub trimming. Up and down Harry went with the lawnmower, up and down. The owners all worked during the day, which meant he seldom saw them. There was no small talk to brighten the prospect of the work at hand.

The time was coming, and sooner rather than later, when he would get an assistant to do these mind-numbing tasks and focus on more interesting things himself, things that asked for insight, planning and creativity, even if only a drop thereof. At least today there was the planting at Fred Holmes to look forward to.

He took a lunch break at noon, choosing the shade of a large Moreton Bay fig in a park on the way there. He shuffled in among the leaf litter and dropped onto the ground, leaning his back against the tree's smooth trunk. On the lawn in front of him a willy wagtail was cheerily hunting for grubs. Now this was what he called "being grounded". Give him a sturdy tree and a bit of wildlife any day and you could keep the air-conditioned coffee shops with their generic décor and franchised food. He bit into a peanut butter sandwich as if to prove the point.

A good old no-fuss sanga, that's all he wanted. Nancy could go on about quinoa salads and shredded pork wraps and gluten-free veggie muffins all she liked, he still preferred a thick slice of bread with real butter, a good spread of crunchy peanut butter and a touch of honey. Honey was healthy, wasn't it? He took a long draft from his water bottle to wash it down. Ahh! Now on to Fred's place.

The builders had been as good as their word and Holmes' retaining wall was completed. It stood proud, bisecting the backyard into the now smaller remaining lawn and a new raised garden bed along the back fence. This last covered an area of about one and a half metres wide by twenty metres long. The surface was neatly levelled. What lay beneath, despite their assurances of "good soil", was anybody's guess. Harry, tasked with filling the space with suitable plants, would find out soon enough.

Fred Holmes had with characteristic shoulder shrug left the design and choice of plants to Harry. There were pros and cons to this attitude. He loved the freedom it gave him to play with colour, form and texture. On the other hand, being spoilt for choice meant the decision and its inherent consequences were his responsibility. Not that there was too much that could go wrong. Few plants truly had invasive root systems or uncontrollable growth habits, and Harry knew to stay away from them in restricted spaces such as these.

He had chosen a mixture of mock orange and lily pillies to form a hedge-like backdrop against the fence, with a selection of smaller cheerful plants in front. He had had a good working relationship with the local nursery for some years now, and the owner, Paul, had been more than happy to deliver the plants. Fred's call the previous day had nearly upset the apple cart.

Neither Fred nor Tanika had called him again and, sorry for them, but it was too late now. He had confirmed the plant order with Paul, to be delivered this morning, and asked for a load of woodchip mulch as well.

"My ute's going to be full of mowers and tools and stuff. And I might not be there until after lunch, so could you just stack the plants at the back if I'm not there? There's a pad of concrete next to the driveway. You can drop the mulch on that."

Which was exactly what Paul had done. The woodchip mulch formed a neat heap in the front. There was still no vehicle in the driveway, Herbert either back at work or still out fishing.

In the back, the forty odd plants huddled in a corner, a spot of fresh and promising green against the turned-up lawn and the raw soil behind the retaining wall. They were healthy plants, and probably the biggest specimens for their pot size, if he knew Paul at all.

Paul had also delivered a few large bags of compost, so Harry would give them the best start he could. If he didn't see Holmes on the weekend, he would phone to negotiate some extra time during his visits for the next two months, to water the plants. He had hopes of convincing Holmes of the need for an irrigation system, but given his tendency for indecision, it would probably take a nation-wide drought to convince him. The recent cyclonic soaking would not help.

The retaining wall had done the job it was built for and more, holding up against the torrential rain. Tenant and neighbour should both be happy and relieved now.

Harry collected the necessary equipment from his vehicle— gloves, garden fork, pruners for trimming away any damaged branches, and posthole digger, a tool that looked like a giant scissor-like salad spoon, for removing dirt from small holes. Then he started marking out where the plants were to go. He would do a few quick probes with the spade to gauge the quality of the soil.

The spade was not among the tools he had offloaded, but neither could Harry find it on his ute. He did a thorough search among the boxes, empty garden rubbish bags, fuel canisters and lawn mowing equipment. The box of poisons from McMullen was still there. He had forgotten about it and made a mental note to dispose of it properly. But he could not find his spade. He even walked away and came back to search again, in case it was a case of a 'man search', as Nancy liked to call it. Still no spade. He could not remember when he had used it the last time. It must have been at Cecily's the previous week.

He had a rusty long-handled spade that he sometimes used for moving large quantities of soil or sand. It would be uncomfortable to dig with, but short of driving out to buy a new one, it was the only option he had. There might have been some tools in the shed, but he wasn't about to go fossicking in there. Although the property and buildings belonged to Fred

Holmes, the privacy thereof was solely that of the tenant and Harry meant to respect that. He picked up the long spade and returned to the garden bed to push its blade into the soft new soil.

His probing gave a mixed result. Yes, there was a fair layer of good garden soil added in most places, but it definitely wasn't thickly and evenly spread all over. Getting holes that were big enough for the plants was going to take some work. While the weekend's rain had truly drenched the soil, digging into rain-heavy clay and splintered rocks would still not be an easy job.

As he started with some serious hole digging, holding onto the spade's long handle as onto a medieval lance, there was a faint whiff in the air of something rotten. At first Harry blamed the builders. Had someone thrown in their half-eaten MacDonald's lunch as extra organic material? Or had the neighbour's cat left the remains of its prey nearby? Then he remembered the cane toads the builders had killed last week. Now *he* had to contend with the stink of their rotting remains. Killing was one thing; getting rid of the body was a whole new kettle of fish and a smelly one at that.

His shoulders jarred when digging deeper he struck the occasional rock or unsolicited building material, but there were no other surprises and Harry kept going at a fair pace, ensuring enough space in the holes for the plants to spread their roots comfortably. A good dose of compost and a handful of gypsum added to the backfill mix, and you had a cosy hole for planting. Once he got into a rhythm, he could let his mind go. By the end of the afternoon he had all the plants in the ground. All the garden needed now was water and a thick layer of mulch and he could go home to a well-deserved rest and some watering and feeding for himself.

It was near six o'clock by the time he had finished, the day still muggy and hot, but with the promise of a cooling breeze by sunset. He gave the new garden one last satisfied look, then gathered his tools and headed home.

Home smelled divinely of chicken curry. He got a peck on the cheek from Nancy, her hands red from shredding beetroot for a salad. Martha was more lavish with her affection, latching onto his leg like a leech. When he had shaken her off and collected a stubby from the fridge, he collapsed into a chair in the lounge.

Martha ran out of the room and soon came back, her hands behind her back. She then brought both hands forward and thrust her clenched fists at Harry, inexpertly trying to conceal something.

"You have to choose one, Daddy."

"Hmm... Let's see." He stabbed at her fists with a forefinger. "Eeny, meeny, miny, moe, what has Martha got to show?"

"Choose one! Choose one!" she cried, unable to keep her excitement at bay.

Harry brought his finger to a halt on her right hand. She opened both hands with a shout of glee, revealing a Kewpie doll in each. Harry blinked.

"Two?"

"Unbelievable, isn't it?" said Nancy, stepping out of the kitchen and drying her hands on a tea towel.

Harry inspected the two small dolls, while Martha jumped up and down next to him like a jack-in-the-box. It was incredible. The dolls were nearly identical. If it hadn't been for the patchy eye, it would have been hard to tell which one was Cecily's.

"Where did you find it?"

"In the library."

"The library?" Harry was beginning to think he had misjudged the range of activities to be found in a library. Clearly it wasn't just about books anymore. Not only were there steps and ladders and a serious possibility of physical injury, it also boasted a second-hand toy collection dating back to the mid-twentieth century.

"Yes. Well, no, but... Next door. They had some toys there and, well, voila, we found another Kewpie doll."

"So..."

"So, now Martha can keep the new one and you can take the other one back to Cecily. It's like having your cake and eating it."

"Nancy, I will. I will take it back, okay?"

"Good. I'm glad we've solved that problem then."

"It never was a problem."

"But we don't want it to become one. Hungry? Let's eat, then."

Breathing space

She was drowning, gasping for air, but all there was to breathe was water. Water, water everywhere. Her hands flailed in panic, catching on something cold and metallic. And then, a hand. She opened her eyes.

"Cecily." A woman's concerned voice. Blond hair and eyes so blue they must have been made from water themselves.

"Anne?"

"No, Cecily. It's me. It's Michelle."

"Michelle?" And then she remembered. Her sigh was full of sadness.

"I'm sorry, Cecily."

"No, no, don't be." She tried to sit up, struggling against the sheets. There were tubes attached to her hands. Looking down her nose, she could see a pipe on her cheek, a knobbly thing at one nostril.

"Do you want to sit up? Should I get a nurse?" Michelle asked.

When the nurse had been to adjust Cecily's bed, checked her intravenous fluids and made some notes on the hospital sheet, she leaned back, exhausted from even this small amount of activity.

"How are you feeling?" Michelle asked.

"Tired."

"I'm sorry," she said again. "If I hadn't gotten us stranded..."

"Don't be. I..." Cecily coughed, reached for the glass of water beside her bed, and took a small sip. "I should have warned you. I should have known better; I'm the local."

"The responsible adult," Michelle smiled.

"Yes. And look at me now."

"You scared us all. But the doctors say you're going to be fine; you're so much better already. Yesterday they thought...I could only get through this morning."

"Yesterday? What day is it, then?"

"Tuesday."

They had spent a long, uncomfortable night in the stranded car, falling asleep from boredom and exhaustion in equal measure. Cecily had woken a few times. With no way to tell the time and no discernible sound other than the rain and Michelle's soft breathing, she had felt lost, disoriented and floating in the darkness. She was cold under the meagre protection of her jumper and Michelle's skirt, her hands and feet like blocks of ice. And then she was hot again, yet shivering.

Morning had seeped in with no change in the weather, but around nine the rain had stopped for a while and the clouds thinned. The water level around them had dropped overnight. By some miracle the car's electronics were still working and Michelle had again ventured out through a window, like the dove from Noah's ark. This time she found dry land. She came splashing through the water with a big smile like a child through a puddle.

"I've found someone," she said, leaning in through the window. "A local farmer. He's got a big pickup, a ute. He'll get us out."

He was a young bloke, tanned and muscled, with dark curly hair and a wispy moustache. He stomped around the car in gumboots before leaning in through the still open front window. He nodded at Cecily.

"Morning. You alright?"

"Morning. I'm okay. Cold. I'm cold."

"Right. I'll get you back to the house first, warm you up, and then come back for the car. By the way, my name's Matt."

"Hi, Matt. I'm Cecily. But how are you going to get this old lady out of here?"

Even with the lower water level, they had been unable to open the doors.

"If you can hoist yourself onto the window frame, I'll take you from there."

It hadn't been easy. She had never felt her age like she did then—old and stiff and sore in all her joints. But she had made it to the window and with some assistance from Michelle, Matt had picked her up and carried her to the vehicle. She had relaxed against him, breathing in his warmth and the smell of animals and stock feed from his jacket.

He had driven them to his house, ten kilometres further on the road they had been travelling, and left them in the care of his wife Emily. He then went back, and with the help of a neighbour had pulled the rented car back onto the road and towed it to his home. By then they had had several cups of hot tea and the warmth was slowly returning to Cecily's limbs. After a warm bath, a change of clothes and a meal of steaming soup, she felt much better yet could not stop shivering.

Many of the roads to the towns were still flooded, so they were going to have to stay with Matt and Emily until they could get through. But Cecily became feverish overnight, and it was a rescue team from the State Emergency Service that picked her up on Sunday morning. She remembered being carried across a wide expanse of water at a dip in the road. She thought it was Matt again, but this man was older, more solid, and he was in SES uniform. He was knee-deep in the water with two men on either side steadying him as he bore her across.

The rest was vague. She didn't know whether they were memories or dreams. She remembered Anne, wet hair plastered against her head, reaching out to her. But of course, that had to have been a dream. Michelle—*she* was real.

Petticide

Harry stood in his bare feet at the front door looking out onto the garden. It was barely seven and already the day was shimmering with murderous intent—humidity and heat turned up to the maximum. Summer was such an intense season here, nothing done in half measures. If it wasn't the sun burning the life juices out of everything and everyone, it was a storm throwing down buckets of rain. You had to dig in and hang on or you'd be washed away. He watched as a blue-faced honeyeater snatched at insects among the leaves. God might be merciful, but nature wasn't.

It was Thursday again, and he was looking forward to a quiet day of minding his own business. His initial enthusiasm for doing the gardens at his own properties on a weekly basis had quickly waned. Perfection was fine, but it took an indecent amount of energy to maintain. Good enough was good enough and that meant a fortnightly service and nothing sooner.

He could use the day to catch up on paperwork, get some quotes on landscaping materials for an upcoming project, and find out about the disposal of McMullen's poisons. In any case, he would spend some time with Nancy and Martha, perhaps even convince his daughter to help with another snail hunt later in the afternoon. They had made quite a dent in the snail population, he thought. Well, he had. Martha was there only for moral support and comic relief.

An arm sneaked around his middle and Nancy laid her chin between his shoulder blades, hugging him from behind. He leaned into her.

"Off day today?"

"Hmm."

"Planning anything?"

"This and that."

"Do you think you could drop Martha off at kindy for me?"

"I might consider it." He turned around to kiss her. "What is her mommy going to do?"

"Her mommy has a dentist appointment at nine and then she needs to get her bum on a chair and draw some pretty pictures."

"Then her daddy will take her to kindy. I might go on to Cecily afterwards."

"Cecily? Is she back then? You didn't tell me."

"I haven't heard anything. No, I think I left my spade there last week. I was looking for it the other day at Fred's."

"Taking back the doll, then?" Nancy asked.

"Back where? If there's no-one there..."

"It's not yours, you know."

"Of course I know. But what do you want me to do with it? Stick it back in the ground? I'm not stealing it. When—if—Cecily returns, I'll give it back to her. It's not as if it's very valuable. It's a doll, not a... not a diamond!"

"I'm just saying. At least put it back in the box and take it along today, just in case. She might be back already."

After dropping Martha off at the kindergarten—dropping-off being a euphemism for the ten minutes it took to gather Martha, her backpack, her hat and Priscilla the pink elephant from the vehicle, arrange it all into a socially acceptable unit and walk her through the throng of other little people attached in varying degrees to the hands or clothes or general auras of parents, to be handed over in due time to the care of a teacher or teacher's aide, before retracing his steps through nods and greetings to the safety of his ute—Harry headed for Cecily's place.

When he had originally thought of going there, it had been with the sole intention of looking for his missing spade. A crazy thought flitted across his consciousness. Had Cecily's garden suddenly become the local Bermuda's Triangle from where things just disappeared without rhyme or reason? First Cecily and now his spade. He smiled at his own thoughts. How absurd! There might not always be a rhyme for everything, but a reason there had to be. And just to complicate life, there was often more than one reason for something. It was the way the world worked.

So even if he could not return the doll yet, this could be a multi-purpose visit. Besides getting his spade, he could check on the new plants. Watering would not have been a worry, even without the weekend's rain, thanks to Cecily's irrigation system. But it was always a good idea to look in on any new plantings and he would be able to see how they had weathered the storm.

It was like a surgeon checking in on his patients after an operation, he liked to think. Even if it had been quite a routine procedure—say, a tonsillectomy or the removal of a skin tag—the doctor probably felt reassured by seeing that his patient was doing fine.

Harry himself had had a few sun blemishes freeze-burnt from his face and scalp not too long ago. They were sore, much more painful than they looked, which was probably why Nancy hadn't been all too sympathetic. Women seemed to think they had the prerogative on pain, always quoting the agony of childbirth at you. His wounds had scabbed over and healed quickly and he hadn't really thought it necessary for the doctor to see him again. Still, he had made another appointment and waited for nearly an hour in the aptly named waiting room, just for Dr Maddison to take a look at them, nod his head enthusiastically, and mutter "Very good, very good, yes, yes", before sending him away again with a smugly satisfied grin.

He was also curious about Cecily. Since his conversation with the police, he had heard nothing regarding her disappearance. And then there was the doll. He ground his teeth. He had brought the tin along with the doll inside, just in case, but he would not leave it here, no matter what Nancy said, unless he could put it directly into Cecily's hands. It had seemed such a simple and logical act to take it home with him when he could not find Cecily. Now the world had shifted and unless he buried it again where he had found it, there would be too many complicating and uncomfortable questions to answer if he just left it on the doorstep.

He parked in the driveway, as he had done every fortnight for the past five and a half years. Everything still looked the same. There was the large golden penda tree next to her mailbox that had shaken down its usual batch of leaves for Harry to tidy. The lawn was lush but not yet in need of a trim. A few weeds had popped up in the flower beds, sticking through the thinning mulch. Even Cecily's old blue Toyota was parked in the carport as usual. The driving rain had washed off the dust, but a passing bird had left its visiting card in a splash of white against a back door. It all looked so normal that Harry could have assumed that Cecily was back or had never even been away in the first place. But leaf debris had washed up against the car's wheels during the storm—it had obviously not been moved for a while.

He got out and walked to the front door, leaving the tinned doll in his vehicle. He almost expected Cecily to appear behind the lounge window, waving a friendly hand at him. There was no sign of police activity. But what had he expected—crime scene tape around the property?

He knocked on the door. There was no answer. It didn't surprise him. He shrugged and walked around to where he had put in the new plants.

They were flourishing. Already delicate new leaves had appeared on the shrubs. A tiny brown honeyeater flitted from its perch near a grevillea flower head, trilling in song as it flew away. Harry looked closely but could not see any threat of grasshoppers or caterpillars and there didn't seem to be any damage from the rain. However, there was also no sign of his spade.

He searched among the shrubs and against the wall and everywhere else he could think of passing by, but the spade was nowhere to be seen. Only Cecily's old spade still leaned against the wall where he had placed it. Since he did not believe in mystery disappearances, that only meant that he had left his spade somewhere else. It was probably gone by now. He would just have to get a new one.

Before leaving, he knocked on Cecily's door again. Then it suddenly occurred to him that he should phone her. He tried the home number and could hear it ringing inside before switching over to an answering machine. It was strange hearing Cecily's voice. He hung up and dialled her mobile number. This time it immediately went to voicemail. He listened to her voice again, deliberating whether he should leave a message. The voicemail beeped. Harry took a deep breath but couldn't think of anything to say and hung up after a moment's silence. If Cecily still had her phone with her, at least she would see that he had called.

As he was returning his phone to his pocket, it rang in his hand. It was Troy from Homespun Furniture. As Fred had so superciliously pointed out a few days ago, officially tenant and landlord were supposed to work through the agent if there were any concerns about the property, but because Harry was also involved with the general maintenance, he had a more relaxed relationship with his own tenants. It was no true friendship, though, so the call could only be business related, meaning Harry's quiet day had just disappeared into thin air. Bermuda Triangle, he thought wryly; it swallows everything.

"Sorry to have missed you last week, Harry," Troy began.

"You're a busy man. That makes me happy."

"True, true. So, I think we've found the source of the noises."

"You have? That's news. I couldn't find anything. What were they? Rats?"

"Cats."

This was surprising. Harry had suspected a lot of things, but cats had not been on the list. It had not seemed like a particularly cat-friendly environment, though he imagined a once-off rendezvous could happen anywhere. It still seemed unlikely that any feline passing through would hang around to be discovered in the morning.

"Cats? You're sure? Last night?"

"Oh, we're sure, alright, and no, this morning. A whole nest of them, mom and three bubs. We were moving the pallets with a forklift this morning and they kind of got in the way. Mom-cat copped it and left her babies behind."

"She ran away?"

"No, mate. She didn't have any running left in her. The forklift caught her in the side. It wasn't a pretty sight, but she's dead now. Did you want to come by?"

Harry grimaced. How awful! The cat must have been torn between running for her life and protecting her kittens. He wished he could have prevented it, somehow found the cat and scared her off earlier. At least it was a feral and not somebody's pet, but death was still death. And no, he didn't really want to come by.

"Yes, I'll come," he said. "What about the kittens?"

"I reckon they're only a few days old, maybe a week. Their eyes are still closed. I can't see them surviving, really, ugly scraggly little things, so don't worry."

"Okay, hang on. I'll come now, won't be long."

On the way to Hanson Road Harry made a quick detour to get a sample of decorative pebbles from a landscaping supplier but it took him less than half an hour to get there. He parked in the street and went straight to the backyard. A forklift stood to one side with the timber pallets neatly picked up in the arms of its lift like a man holding a stack of crates. No-one was around. He walked back to the front and went inside.

Troy stood at the front desk with a cup of take-away coffee, talking to the young salesman Harry had met the previous time. He beamed when he saw Harry and pushed himself away from the counter, extending a hand in greeting.

"Harry! Good morning, nice to see you."

"Morning, Troy." He shook his head. "Cats, hey? I wouldn't have thought it."

"Yeah. It wasn't pretty, I can tell you," he said, still smiling. "Ask Stan here. Just blood and guts, hey Stan? He's the one who drove the forklift."

"I'm sorry, Stan. It must have been terrible." The image of a squashed hamster body flitted across Harry's mind and he pushed it away.

"That's okay. Actually..." Stan said.

"Actually..." Troy said.

"What did you do with her?" asked Harry. "And what about the kittens?"

Troy lowered his voice. "Rubbish bin."

"What?!"

"Bin collection is tomorrow. They'll hold till then, I think."

"But what about the kittens? You can't just dump them like that. They'll die!"

"Relax, Harry," Troy said, eyeing Harry over the rim of his coffee cup. "That's the idea, isn't it? Getting rid of them?"

"Getting rid of them? Meaning what?"

"Oh, come on, we killed them, okay? They weren't going to survive anyway. Stan drowned them in a bucket."

"You drowned them?" Harry stared at Stan, taking in his crooked smirk and the large hands capable of drowning three newborn kittens. Of course, you didn't need big hands for that.

Stan shrugged. "No big deal. My dad used to drown them when I was a kid. We lived on property, out at Calliope, and there were always heaps of feral cats hanging about and having litters. Dad would just dump them in the trough. It doesn't take long."

"Really, you should have seen them," said Troy. "They were tiny, not even the size of a rat. You'd kill a rat, wouldn't you? Set out a trap or bait? So what's the big difference?"

"But they're pets," Harry protested, yet even as he said it, he knew it was a flimsy argument.

"No, they're not. They're feral. That mother cat would have torn you to pieces if you tried to touch her. She'd never be a pet."

"The kittens could have been. Someone's pets."

"So could the poddies out on grass," countered Troy. "Or the piglets. But now they're killed and turned into tucker. Feed them up, slit their throats and slap them on the barbeque. Isn't that wrong, then? Who gets to decide?"

Harry was silent. Who gets to decide? Now there was a question that could turn your guts upside down and inside out. When is it okay to kill—leaving people out of it for the moment, because that gets really tricky—but when is it okay to kill an animal? Didn't he kill animals on a more or less daily basis? There had to be a line between pesticide and petticide, to borrow a word from Martha. Or was he indeed a murderer for the killing of snails and grasshoppers? Wasn't his protest about the killed kittens a bit hypocritical?

"You see?" said Troy.

"It's not that easy."

"Exactly."

"But still—kittens?"

"We did what we had to do. Now, if you'll excuse me. Good to see you again, Harry. Have a good one."

"Goodbye, Troy. You too." But Harry knew the chances of him now having a good day were severely diminished. He gave Stan a silent nod and walked back to his ute.

Missing person

When Harry did a follow-up visit at Fred's the next day, he was happy to see the plants looking well. It was a pleasing end to what had been an altogether pleasurable day. A brief thunderstorm the previous evening had followed up on the storm's downpour, keeping things moist and steamy. The extra rain had been soft enough to soak into the sodden soil without causing more damage. Weeds let go their hold on the wet soil like rotten teeth pulled from their sockets, coming away in his hands with a satisfying slurp. During the day he had also clinched two more jobs which included advising on, designing and planting new gardens, generally more satisfying than routine garden maintenance.

Fred's plants didn't need more water than what the rain had provided and a quick check-up on their condition was enough. Harry was curious to know what the tenant thought about the improvement. He had to be happier now that the wall was up, even if he had no interest in the plants. He himself was quite pleased with the result. It didn't look half bad. Fred would hopefully come past over the weekend and Harry expected a pat on the shoulder for a job well done.

He was no heart surgeon or successful entrepreneur, no suit-and-tie businessman or renowned intellectual and at forty-two he often wondered whether he shouldn't be doing more with his life than mowing lawns and planting trees. A gardener couldn't exactly be counted among the world's movers and shakers. Yet there was some basic satisfaction in any job well done and though he did at times envy other men their air-conditioned cocoons, even the physicality of his job brought its own fulfilment. As a tradie he belonged to an unofficial club of men and women who went through life getting down and dirty and ready to kick adversity in the guts with their steel capped work boots. He was still smiling with smug satisfaction when he got home.

Nancy was vigorously wiping the dinner table with a tea towel, while Martha methodically dropped a bunch of scrap papers one by one into the kitchen recycling bin. They were the day's detritus of Nancy's creative efforts. Martha examined each with the intensity of a university art professor appraising her students' efforts and finding them lacking, before dropping them into the bin with measured gravitas.

Harry deposited his lunchbox and water bottle on the kitchen counter and gave Nancy a kiss on the cheek. He ruffled Martha's hair.

"Had a productive day?" he asked, reaching into the fridge for a beer.

Neither answered. Harry stalled.

"Not?"

"I've had better ones, thank you."

"How so?" Harry asked, his mood starting to deflate a little.

"Nothing worked. I made a ton of drawings and just nothing worked. It was like digging a big hole and then filling it up again."

"That could be productive, you know. You just have to put in a tree before you fill the hole again. I can offer you a job?"

"Thanks, but no thanks."

"I had a good day," he declared, settling down in a lounge chair. "Thanks for asking."

Martha, having dropped the last of the failed drawings in the bin, ran over to Harry. "Hello, Daddy!" she cried, bumping into his legs.

"And now it's even better. Hello, Martha. Did *you* have a good day?"

"I made a dragon. He lives in a tree."

"A dragon?"

"Yes. He has big wings," she said, demonstrating with her arms out. She flapped them up and down and twirled around. "And he loves cats. He loves Snail."

"Oh, I hope he won't eat her. You'll have to be careful that he doesn't fry her to a crisp. Is he a friendly dragon?"

"He's super friendly, super super friendly. Daddy, what is fry to a crisp?"

"It's like when your mommy roasts meat in the oven and it comes out all crackly."

"I like Mommy's crackly meat," she said, turning around to smile at Nancy, who had come to stand behind her, twirling the tea towel in her hands.

"So do I, possum, so do I." He sniffed the air. "What's for dinner?"

"Casserole and..." Nancy's answer was cut short by retching noises from behind the couch and a sudden shriek as she dropped the tea towel. She glanced around the room in a panic, grabbed a newspaper from the coffee table and launched herself toward the retching. There was a small interlude of scuffling, rustling and subdued meowing, and snippets of Nancy's backside appearing and disappearing behind the couch, but before Harry could even get up to investigate, Nancy reappeared, looking smug. Martha stood frozen in action beside Harry, a look of anticipatory delight on her face.

"What?!" Harry gasped, sinking back into his chair with a sigh.

"Got it," Nancy said. He gave her a blank look. "The cat. Snail. She was vomiting."

"Aha."

"I caught it, on the newspaper."

He glanced at the table where the newspaper had been. A puff of disappointment exploded from his lips. "Today's?"

"Yes. Um... Sorry."

"Back page?" he asked hopefully.

"Sorry. Front page. I could..."

"No, no, no. Martha? Martha! Come here, missy. Nancy, will you... She's got... Martha!"

"I'm coming, Daddy," was the muffled reply from behind the couch.

"Good Lord! What is everybody doing behind the furniture today?"

"Daddy, look!" It was Martha's turn to make a reappearance. In one hand she carried Harry's newspaper, a soggy yellowish blotch smeared over the front page. In the other hand, she held the bunched-up tea towel, slightly more soggy and yellow. Her triumphant approach was enhanced by an entourage of the kitten, playfully swiping at her legs.

When Martha had been relieved of her vomit-drenched tea towel—the vomit pronounced by Nancy to have contained mainly bile and fragmented bits of what had once been a cockroach—and set to help lay the table for dinner, Harry tried to rescue his newspaper. A further blotting with paper towel contained the damage. He sniffed, trying to blot the sharp smell from his mind, and settled back to scan the headlines.

The front page was given to a clash between the Council and a community group regarding a planned upgrade to a local park and the subsequent removal of three large eucalypts. The accompanying photo showed a councillor in front of an angry, gesticulating crowd around one of the trees. Harry felt sorry for the poor man, all the more so now that his countenance was worsened by a bilious blot, but his own sympathies lay with the trees. He turned the damp page, taking care not to tear its sodden heart out.

Two advertisements claimed half of the next page, which also held a weather report (hot and sunny with still more rain expected after the weekend) and a few small news flashes about local events and incidents – an increase in illegal dumping near the river, a school's fortieth anniversary, and the upcoming appearance of a celebrity singer at the entertainment centre. The photo of Herbert Ainsley was on the third page and it took Harry half a minute before he realised why the man looked familiar.

The picture was of a smiling Herbert in high-visibility working clothes. One could see that it had been cropped and enlarged from an original group photo—it was low resolution and showed bits of shoulders and arms of other people who had been in the original. But after his initial confusion, Harry had no problem in recognising the red hair and beard of Fred's tenant. "Missing technician" was the caption in bold underneath.

There wasn't much more to the report. It simply stated that local technician Herbert Ainsley (32) was missing. He had not been seen since the end of his last work shift at the aluminium smelter on the previous Friday morning. Anybody with any information was asked to contact the local police or Missing Persons Unit at the given number.

Problem lists

Weekends were family time, or so popular opinion would have it. As far as Harry was concerned, this was flawed reasoning in the same way that considering Sunday as God's day was. If you couldn't find some time for God during the rest of the week, what was the point? If you couldn't find time for your family during the rest of the week, what was the point?

It seemed to him that too many people regarded their spouses and children as members of some social club with whom they had to spend time on the days that could not be used for making a livelihood. Harry argued that his family was infused into his life like water poured into a cup of sand, unobtrusively filling the empty spaces. Weekends were just as much or as little family time as any other day of the week, which meant no special obligations should be expected of him just because the day had a different name.

When Fred called on Saturday morning to say that he was in town and asking if they could meet, Harry had no qualms about leaving Nancy and Martha to their own devices while he nipped out for "work". They seemed to be knee deep in plotting some kind of messy business anyway, all giggly and whispering, opening cupboard doors and drawers, arranging containers and food stuffs on the kitchen counter with intent. There were a few small bottles that looked to Harry suspiciously like food-colouring.

"I won't be long, girls," he said, planting a kiss on Nancy's cheek. She nodded absentmindedly. Martha squirmed out of his embrace. "We'll catch more snails when I get back, poppet."

Martha looked at him, considering the proposition. There was a new meaning attached to that word—snail—and the world had to be rearranged accordingly. While she could not yet pursue a rational, logical or perhaps philosophical argument why snail-catching might now be out of bounds to one who owned a cat of that nomenclature, she felt a sudden reluctance to pursue her previous appointment as pesticide accomplice. She could not put this into words, so she merely scrunched up her face at her father in disagreement and turned her attention back to her mother's less controversial activities.

In their brief telephone conversation Fred had not seemed agitated, nor had he mentioned anything to Harry about his missing tenant. Maybe he didn't yet know or maybe Herbert had since shown up and the mystery of his disappearance cleared up. The question of Herbert's approval of the choice of plants wasn't mentioned either. Fred's call was ostensibly only to discuss the new garden, and Harry did not expect any other potential worries.

As Harry turned into Parkside Drive, a police car rolled past in the other direction. Its quiet passing left Harry queasy. The mere potential of what it could turn into—a wailing, speeding instrument of justice—reminded him of a muzzled guard dog, just waiting to be turned loose on any unsuspecting petty criminal or homebody dreaming of revenge on a pesky neighbour. The sight of Fred in his driveway dispelled any belief that the car's presence was merely a coincidence. The poor man looked lost, pacing up and down like a senile dog.

Harry parked in the street behind what he suspected was Fred's car, a white Kia sedan. There was still no sign of Herbert's ute. Fred looked up as Harry approached and shed his look of consternation for a more controlled one of worry and concern.

"Harry," he said, gripping Harry's hand firmly.

"Morning, Fred. How are you?"

Fred blew out a sigh as momentous as a whale's. He drew a hand through his dark hair and sighed again.

"I've been better, thank you. Bloody tenant's gone missing. The police have been here the whole morning."

"Yes. I know. They haven't found him yet?"

"You know?"

"I read about it in the paper yesterday, last night actually."

"I told them he probably went fishing."

"His ute's gone, with the boat."

"My point exactly. But no, he's now a missing person. I'm telling you, I'm through with renting, Harry. I don't know; I've just had enough."

Harry nodded but didn't answer. There wasn't much to say. He could empathise with Fred's rental woes; he had after all had some himself. There was the time a tenant broke three door handles within as many months. Once a whole carpet had to be replaced due to multiple cigarette burns. He even had one couple who let a flock of chickens run loose in the backyard, so that when they left after two years, the garden was essentially ruined. It was not unlike an arranged marriage—no matter what the agreement on paper was, you never quite knew what you were letting yourself in for.

He had, however, never had a tenant going AWOL. And if the police were hanging around, did that mean that Fred was somehow implicated in Herbert's disappearance? He decided to stick to the things he knew.

"Have you had a look at the wall, Fred?" he asked.

"The wall? Oh, yes, the wall. Yes, sure, I did. Thank you, Harry. Let's go around to the back. At least I have not been warned off my own property yet, though I've been forbidden to go inside." He scoffed. "As if I'd just walk in while Herbert's gone. You're supposed to give twenty-four hours' notice to the tenant. Did you know that? Of course you did. You have tenants yourself. Come."

They walked through the side gate to the back garden. Fred kicked tentatively at the gate frame and the low timber fence.

"Needs a coat of oil again, I suppose," he murmured. "It just never ends."

"Maintenance," Harry agreed.

"Do you do stuff like that? I might ask you... Oh, I don't know, never mind, it'll do for a while."

They stopped in front of the new raised garden bed. Fred leaned with extended fingers on the top of the wall and gazed at the plants. The mock-oranges were covered in small buds, waiting to burst into flower. Soon it would be a sweet-scented mass, scattering white confetti onto the ground. Harry pushed away some mulch to stick a finger into the soil. It was deeply satisfyingly damp.

"Looks good. You've done well, Harry."

"Thanks, Fred. The soil isn't the best all round, what with the building and so on, but I made sure the holes are big and there's a lot of compost worked in. I think they should be okay. I never got to ask Herbert about the plants, but I guess they'll be right."

"Of course they will. I'm not worried about that. It's just... I don't know. God!" He kicked at the base of the wall and rubbed at his forehead with a knuckle, then rolled his eyes. "Tenants, plants, walls, the fence, the shed has a leak, and now Herbert is missing. I'm over it, Harry. I'm just bloody well over it."

Well, thought Harry, did you want to hear my list? A snail plague, an unsolicited pet, a missing client, a missing spade, noises in the dark, a whole nest of dead cat and kittens, and—did I mention it?—another missing client! Talk about being over it. He glanced at Fred's face, tense with misery and despair, then took a deep breath of the humid morning air and tried on a smile.

"It's a good wall, though. At least you've solved that problem."

"Yes. Yes, I suppose you're right. And it is a good wall. They sent me some photos, the builders, but it looks even better for real. We've solved the problem, for what it's worth. But bloody Herbert! Can you believe it? Just gone. You haven't seen him? No, of course not. He was still... Anyway, I'll be thinking of selling soon, I can tell you that, tenant or no tenant."

"Are you sure? What's the market like, though? For selling? I know the tenants are pushing for lower fees everywhere."

"Pfft," he shrugged. "I just don't care. I've had enough, you know, more than enough."

"Well, I guess even if you're selling, you would have had to do the wall, anyway."

"You're right. What's done is done. Thank you, Harry, and thanks for coming over on your Saturday. I know it wasn't really necessary, but I was hoping you might have spoken to Herbert or seen him. I don't know. The police haven't questioned you, have they? No, of course not. Anyway, you somehow make me feel better about the whole affair. Must be your handsome face." He clapped Harry on the back and laughed not altogether insincerely. "Better get back home now. I'll make your payment as soon as I can."

Phone calls

Still there was no news from Cecily. Harry wondered whether the police would have contacted him if they did have news. If Cecily had been found, dead or alive, one would not expect them to inform everybody or anybody. Harry was merely the gardener, an innocent bystander who had been called in for questioning because he might have been the last person to see Cecily before her disappearance. He liked to think she herself would have phoned him to report her return. Did she even know that she was missing?

If she had not yet been found, there was again no reason anyone, police or otherwise, would inform him. It had now been nearly two weeks since he had done her garden. It was due for another service this week. Since Wednesday was the only day he could meet with the excavation guys regarding a property where he was putting in sixty-five plants plus an irrigation system, he would have to do Cecily's today. Another call to both her home phone and mobile had proven unsuccessful. Should he just carry on as normal, as if she was still around, expecting him to arrive?

"The grass is still growing," he meditated over breakfast.

"Life goes on," said Nancy, getting up from the table and gathering the empty cereal bowls.

"It does, doesn't it? I can't say whether that is good or bad, really. I think I'll go, anyway, and just do the basics. I'll check on her plants again, as well, although they were doing well last time. And look for my spade again."

Nancy nodded. She poured another cup of coffee and placed it before him. Martha wriggled in her chair, kicking her legs. Nancy could just see Snail's tail between the chair legs, a fluff of speckled colour appearing and disappearing.

"You may get up, Martha, please. And take your cat with you," Nancy told her and turned her attention back to Harry.

"So, just Cecily today? Are you coming home for lunch or should I pack you something?"

"If you don't mind, Nance. I've got a few things to follow up afterwards. There's a job coming up at Harbour Square that I'll look into. And I'll go to Bunnings then to get a new spade. Unfortunately, I really need one. If I could just remember where I left the bloody thing."

"Calling a spade a spade, are you?" she asked with raised eyebrows and a quick glance at Martha, who was now lying on the floor while Snail played with her hair. "The walls have ears."

"There are worse words."

"Well, don't start using them, please. Oh, and Harry, so what about the doll?"

"What about it?"

"You'll try again to take it back?"

"Damnit, Nancy!" He banged a hand on the table, spilling the coffee. "Stop nagging me about the bloody doll. Of course I'll take it back. I never intended to take it away. If she'd been there..."

"Only saying," she whispered under her breath and reached for a cloth to wipe the spilt coffee.

Harry, with the tinned doll again sitting on the seat beside him, drove to Cecily's. Not much had changed. There was a new layer of dust on the car and a cat's footprints showed up on the bonnet and front windscreen. He walked to the door again and knocked. No-one came.

The whole place now had an empty feel about it. He sniffed, hoping for a whiff of gardenia. Then he shrugged. He had been employed to do the garden every two weeks and as far as he was concerned, that was what he would do, until such time as somebody officially told him not to. Whether he would get paid for his work was beside the point. It had become a labour of love.

He got down to work as he did every fortnight, mowing and weeding and tidying the garden. As he worked, he pondered Cecily's disappearance for the umpteenth time. How could someone just vanish into thin air without leaving a trace behind? If she had been twenty years younger, he might have thought it more likely—a still handsome and independent woman going off on a jaunt. Or twenty years older, when the fog of dementia could make someone do the strangest things. But Cecily was no fool. Her mind was still as bright as a berry. She would not just wander off. She would not disappear without telling anyone, without making plans. Or would she?

What did he really know about Cecily, even after five years? He knew she had been married and that her husband had been a property developer or building contractor. He knew she had a daughter, whom he for some or other reason thought lived in Perth, but it could just as well be Alice Springs or Wagga Wagga. He knew she belonged to an oldies club who assembled every second Tuesday of the month. He knew she sometimes volunteered at the local information centre. And that, besides her love of gardening, was the sum of his knowledge about Cecily.

It seemed a shame to have known her for so long without really knowing anything about her. We brush past so many known faces every day—the postman, the cashier, the saleslady, even the neighbour—with no insight into their lives. Harry wondered whether this was something to be sad about or merely philosophical.

The small amount of garden waste from Cecily's garden did not yet warrant a trip to the refuse tip but he needed to get rid of McMullen's poisons, which had been travelling in the back of his ute for the past week. However, he had to drive past Harbour Square to get to the tip, so he changed his plans and decided to have a look at that site first, before dumping the poisons and then setting off to buy a new spade. It was a proposed revamp of the shopping centre gardens that he was hoping to quote on. They had to send him a document with the requirements, measurements, regulations and other bureaucratic intricacies, but he wanted to see the whole thing for real, to get a four-dimensional feel of the place. Virtual reality was fine, but nothing could replace the real thing.

It did not take long to walk around the centre, pinpointing the relevant areas as set out on the site map. He noted the way the sun would be blocked off in certain areas during summer or winter and the flow of people around obstacles such as pillars and rubbish bins. By the time he had finished, it was going on lunch time.

Harry stood beside his ute in the parking lot weighing up the options. There were at least half a dozen shops within his line of sight that could yield a fair lunch, from coffee shops and franchisees to a Chinese take-away and a bakery. The smells of freshly baked bread, fried chicken and chips swooned on the noon breeze, making his mouth water. Even someone who liked his sandwiches could not always be immune to the temptation of fast food. But he had asked Nancy to make him lunch and shunning that for the allure of a quick bite from someone else's kitchen would be tantamount to betrayal, if not adultery.

Just across the street was a park with well-kept lawns, large trees and palms, and a bench or two in the shade. It was cool and green and free, and it would leave his conscience intact, so Harry turned towards its welcoming familiarity with his lunchbox in hand. After all, he did love peanut butter sandwiches and egg and bacon muffins.

After lunch he was tempted to stretch out on the green lawn. It was something he would have done had he been accompanied by Martha or Nancy, but he could not quite allow himself the freedom. How enviable the uninhibitedness of children and artists, he thought. Those two made cookies out of life's mud. He would not be without them.

He shook the languor from his limbs and returned to his ute. Now that he had completed the day's main work, he was in no hurry. The man at the refuse tip accepted his box full of poisons without comment. It was all in a day's work for him. Then Harry headed to the Bunnings warehouse.

Without any further tasks for the day, he had a rare opportunity to amble up and down the aisles. The pleasure of a kid in a candy store. There was always the chance of coming upon some new tool or gadget that, though not strictly necessary, would in time become an invaluable addition to his collection, making work (and therefore life) just so much more interesting, comfortable and, yes, fun.

He was looking at a digital tape measure, turning it over in his hand to read the specifications in fine print on the box, squinting, indecisive about whether he should struggle on to bring the letters into focus or fish around in his pocket for his spectacles. His phone rang just as he put a hand in his pocket. He looked at the screen. Impossible.

"Cecily?"

"Uh... Hello?" A woman's voice, tentative, young. Not Cecily. "Who's speaking, please?"

"Oh. I'm Harry. Who is this?"

"Harry," she repeated, sounding relieved. "I'm Ella."

"Ella? Are you her daughter?"

"Daughter?" She laughed. "Whose daughter?"

"Cecily's."

"I don't know any Cecily."

"You're calling from her phone."

"I am? Oh, I see. No, I found this phone, see, I don't know whose it is, I just found it in the car park outside the Coffee Club, and it had your number on it. I mean, it has a lot of numbers, but yours was the last one and I thought I have to start somewhere, I might as well start at the beginning. So, you know whose phone it is? I'd like to give it back to her, of course. I'm not a thief or anything, but I couldn't just leave it there. It was gonna rain, like. It did rain!" She chuckled.

It had rained, twice, was the fact in this jumble that Harry's brain latched on to. He wondered whether she meant the big storm or the follow-up rain. Any rain except the merest drizzle would be enough to damage a phone beyond repair. He knew this from experience, considering a sprinkler system was a good enough approximation of rain. His previous phone had spent a good twenty minutes being soaked when he had left it on a deck next to an irrigation system he was installing. His pleasure at the successful completion of a difficult job had been severely dampened (literally) by the loss of his phone.

He remembered this as if in a dream, as his conscious mind tried to make sense of the woman's call. She wasn't Cecily. She wasn't Cecily's daughter. She didn't even know Cecily. She didn't know him, either; he was just a name on a list, the first one (or the last one, if hairs had to be split). She had found a phone outside a café. Before the rain.

If it was Cecily's phone, and he saw no reason to doubt this, it would have run out of battery long before any rain, assuming it had gone missing at the same time as Cecily, which was now almost a fortnight ago. If it hadn't, did that mean Cecily was still around, perhaps wandering the streets in a daze, losing things like phones and memories as she went along? If, on the other hand, the phone had been lying unclaimed in a parking lot for a week or more, how had this woman – Ella – been able to revive it and trace it to Harry, of all people? And why only now, when she had already come across the phone at least four days ago?

Harry, equally guilty of picking up and holding onto things belonging to other people—ahem—was not going to throw stones. He also judged that a Q-and-A session with Ella over the phone would be protracted and confusing, and not something he wanted to start while hanging around in an aisle in Bunnings. The answers would come, but now was not the ideal time to ask them.

"I see," he said.

"And you know this woman? Cecily, was it? It's a nice enough phone. Not an iPhone or anything, but good I suppose.

I was thinking of getting my nanna one of those. I reckon it must be quite new; it doesn't have a lot of stuff on. I mean, a bunch of numbers and some texts, but not really photos or anything."

"Yes, I see," said Harry, imagining scrolling through the numbers and texts and photos on a stranger's phone. It made him uncomfortable just thinking about it.

He wondered whether Ella would be prone to hysterics if he told her the phone had belonged to a missing person. Of course, it might just make her day. Something to tell all her friends, to post all over social media. However it may be, he did not really have a choice. As far as he knew, Cecily was still missing. It was his civil duty.

"So, where are you, Harry? Should I bring the phone to you, do you think? I can take it to... to... Cecily? I can take it back myself, if you like."

"Thank you, Ella. And thank you for phoning. I'm afraid you'll need to hand it in to the police. Cecily has gone missing."

The silence on the line did not bode well. Harry waited for the sobs, the hysteria, the gasps.

"Oh. Oh, wow. Wow! Really?"

"Yes, really."

"That's amazing."

"Would you be able to hand it in, Ella? To the police? Just tell them it's Cecily's. Cecily Stone, they'll know about the case."

But Ella's excitement had suddenly waned. While she had been willing to hand it over either to Harry or to the original owner, taking it to the police had checked her spirits a bit. She hummed and hawed and made a big case for not having the time or opportunity to go around looking for police stations, though she would be willing to bring it to Harry, wherever he happened to be. As it turned out, she was not too far away from Bunnings and agreed to meet him outside the store in ten minutes.

"I'm blond and I'm wearing a blue top. You can't miss me," she laughed.

Harry put the tape measure back on the shelf. Somehow, his interest in shopping had disappeared. He would buy the spade, get Cecily's phone, hand it in to the police and just go home.

Ella—blond in a blue top—was easy to spot. She was a big woman, straining against the confines of her clothing. There was a menagerie of butterflies, dragons and other unidentifiable creatures scrabbling for a hold on her tattooed arms and a row of piercings along the curve of one ear. But she was no girl with a dragon tattoo—her smile was pure youthful innocence as she waved the found mobile phone at Harry.

"Harry!" she cried, as if meeting up with an old friend.

For a terrifying moment it seemed to Harry as if she would hug him. But she came to a stop in front of him in a fume of sweet perfume and cigarette smoke and handed over the phone with a flourish.

"Ta-da!"

He thanked her. She repeated her statement of having found the phone before the rain, the big storm where everything got flooded, lying in the strip garden of the parking lot of a shopping centre, dead as a doornail next to a half-dead croton bush, until she had been able to find a charger capable of charging it and could scan the information it contained. It hadn't been locked. There were lots of numbers, messages and missed calls, with Harry's the last to arrive. She did not want to leave him her own number, nor her last name, and no amount of charm and honey-mouthed threats could convince her otherwise. There was nothing more to be said. Ella shrugged, smiled, and turned away.

The nearest police station was just a short detour from Harry's usual route home. It took him five minutes to hand in the phone, explaining its context and leaving his own mobile number. They would be sure to call him again. Not only was he apparently the last person to have seen Cecily alive, he was now also the most recent number called from her phone. Putting two and two together and adding some speculation and deduction to fill the gaps, someone would inevitably get an answer of nine or ten, enough to quicken their interest in his involvement.

On the drive home, Harry's phone did indeed ring. Not once but three times. First Nancy, then an unknown caller and then Fred. He glanced at the lit-up screen with every call but left it to ring. There was a reason phones had voicemail. He would not be bludgeoned into 24/7 availability. He was a gardener, not an emergency service. No-one left any messages. He shrugged. As far as he was concerned, calling back was thus optional. He might have returned Nancy's call, but he was heading home anyway and would see her in fifteen minutes.

When he arrived home, however, her car was not there. He phoned her. It was his turn to reach the recorded voice of a mailbox. He left a brief message telling her he was home. Then he unlocked the front door and shouldered it open, his hands and arms filled with phone, lunchbox, water bottle, appointment diary and for the umpteenth time the tin box containing the Kewpie doll.

The house was quiet. The refrigerator hummed gently, getting on with its refrigeration, and on the veranda a wind chime tinkled in the breeze. On the patch of lawn in the back garden a magpie was foraging, pecking noiselessly at grubs. It all seemed so peaceful.

Harry sighed, reaching into the fridge for a beer. It wasn't often that he was home alone. Most of the time, when he was home, so was Nancy or Martha or both. Even the cat seemed to have disappeared today, probably sleeping somewhere in a cosy spot. Curled up like a snail in its shell. The more he thought about it, the more appropriate it seemed for a cat to be called Snail. You had to hand it to children—they were endlessly inventive and creative, wonderfully free from convention. The trick was to turn them into socially acceptable human beings without squashing the free spirit out of them.

Harry had quaffed a glass of cold water and was halfway through his beer, when Nancy called back. Her voice sounded strained. There were noises in the background—people talking, a phone ringing. A dog barking?

"I called you earlier. We're at the vet with Snail." Was that anger in her voice? As if Harry was to blame for not being available in a moment of crisis. Maybe he was an emergency service, after all.

"I'm sorry. I was driving. What happened? Is she okay?"

"No. She's not okay."

"Are you okay?"

"She's hurt her tail," she said and explained how Martha and Snail had been playing, racing around the house, around and over and under the furniture. Martha had tied a piece of string around an empty toilet roll and was pulling it along behind her, while Snail followed, pouncing on the make-believe prey. Nancy, busy sketching flowers on the veranda, had heard a door slam and then the most awful howl, followed by Martha's screaming.

God knows how it had happened; she still hadn't been able to figure it out, but Martha's bedroom door had slammed shut on the kitten's tail. It was a mess. Nancy had had to comfort her crying daughter and extricate the traumatised kitten from under Martha's bed. She had not looked too closely at the tail—it seemed limp and bloodied—but had stuffed Snail into a carrier and tried to phone Harry, before rushing off to the vet.

"And? What does he say?"

"She. She hasn't seen us yet. We've just arrived. Oh, wait, that's us. I have to go now; I'll talk to you later."

She rang off before he could reply. I told you so, he could have said. Cats that need to be boarded when we go away. Cats that get pregnant or run-over or cat flu. Cats that get their tails caught in a door and need to be rushed to the vet. Case in point. But even if Nancy had still been on the line, Harry knew he would never say that, not anymore, not ever, because a part of him was still feeling shocked at the too-easy death of three kittens. And the other part had become just the tiniest bit attached to that cat called Snail.

A spadeful of mystery

Waking later than usual on Wednesday morning, Harry nevertheless felt drained, as if he had just recovered from a long illness or returned home after a reunion party with an old friend. He almost expected a headache, but there was no pain. Just emptiness and relief. Relief, yes, that was the feeling.

He left Nancy sleeping, made himself a cup of coffee and took it out to the veranda. He watched a pair of rainbow lorikeets chattering away in the bottle brush like talking flowers. They watched him with beady eyes while clambering around in the tree, bending down bottoms-up or swinging from a slender branch to get to the sweet nectar.

There was a gentle scraping noise, a soft bump as the cat flap swung open and shut. The lorikeets flew off, protesting loudly. Snail padded up to Harry and nudged at his leg with her head framed by the plastic cone attached to her collar.

She was already getting used to it. Harry grinned. The poor midget did not look her best at the moment.

Her altercation with the slamming door on Monday had broken her tail and damaged the skin so much that they could not salvage it. After a night on medication at the veterinary hospital, her tail had been amputated mid-length and thickly bandaged. To add insult to injury, she would have to wear the head cone for a week or more to prevent her from pulling at the bandage or stitches. The whole episode had cost them a pretty penny.

The kitten now launched herself and scrambled onto Harry's lap, digging sharp claws into his legs. He scratched her chin. She half-closed her eyes and started purring. Cats were such easy things to love.

The problem with love, thought Harry, was that it had such sharp claws. It just dug them into your soul, lay down in your lap and purred away and no getting rid of it from there on. No wonder half of the world's stories had love at its centre, in some form or another. Politics, war, murder and mayhem—wasn't it all somehow connected to love or the lack thereof? It was love, not money, which made the world go around. The face that launched a thousand ships and all that. Not that that was wrong in any way.

As if the universe was giving him a nod, Nancy at that moment pushed open the door and looked at him through sleepy eyes. He lifted his coffee cup towards her in a silent toast. She smiled.

"Your phone rang," she said. "I didn't get to it in time."

"Thanks, love. Bring it out to me, will you? I can't move. I've got a cat on my lap."

She brought him the phone and went back inside to make her own coffee. The missed call was from an unfamiliar mobile number and the caller had left a voice message.

Harry listened to the message twice, his brow furrowing, then phoned back. After a short conversation, he rang off.

Nancy had come out with her coffee. She sat down opposite him, causing Snail to dig her nails into Harry's legs again as she jumped from his lap. He flinched. The cat bumped against the table leg with her cone and clawed her way onto Nancy's lap instead.

"What was that about?" Nancy asked through a sip of coffee, stroking the cat. "Something about your spade. Have you found it?"

"I'm not sure, actually. It's all a bit of a mystery. It was a neighbour. Fred's house, you know? Or Herbert's, the missing tenant."

"Fred's neighbour? The one who complained about the slope?"

"No, not the neighbour behind him. One to the side, in Parkside Drive, it must be on the left; I know they have small children."

"What does children have to do with it?" Nancy asked, perplexed.

"Well, he says – the neighbour – he found the spade in his shed. Yes, I know, can you believe it? Apparently, his son found it in their garden last weekend. I've seen the boys a few times; I guess they're about five or six."

"Five or six? That's a handful. No, that's positively martyrdom."

"Years. Five or six years, not boys. I think there are two of them."

"Still a handful."

"Yes, well, how would you... Anyway, the son found it lying in the garden and put it away in their shed. I got the idea the dad is a bit of a stickler for things being looked after, put back in their place after being used and so on. He's obviously drilled it into his sons. The boy also knew there was rain coming, so he must have thought he'd win some brownie points for putting the spade away."

"Just a pity it wasn't theirs to put away."

"Exactly." Harry paused and glanced at Nancy to see if there was a hidden agenda in her comment. She looked squarely back, so he continued. "And he forgot to tell his dad. So the dad finds it yesterday when he's looking for something in his shed and of course it's got my name on it."

"Literally."

"Indeed. Green Gardens, as plain as day. Probably a bit cracked and scratched but still legible. The neighbour knows I do Fred's garden, that's why he phoned me. He'll put it under Fred's carport and I'll pick it up later."

"But how did it get there? In the neighbour's garden. You didn't drop it over the fence, I presume."

"No. I must have left it at Fred's two weeks ago, *after* the planting at Cecily. Bless me if I knew how it got across the fence, but I'll be glad to have it back, anyway."

"Hmm. Talking of tenants. What happened to the noises at Hanson Road? Did you find the problem?"

"Cats," Harry said, trying to sound casual. He did not want to explain the situation to Nancy. Even if it wasn't his fault, he felt somehow responsible.

"Ah, cats. Mating?" Nancy scrunched up her face in disgust. Mating cats made an awful but unmistakable sound. The same could probably be said for humans. She looked down at the purring kitten in her lap and stroked the colourful coat. No other way of making kittens, though.

Harry shrugged. "I suppose." He crossed his fingers under the table. It wasn't too far from the truth.

"They're gone now. That's another thing I'll check again. Looks like I might be busy tomorrow." He looked at his watch again. "I guess I should get moving. I'm meeting the excavation bloke at ten and I still have to research a few things."

Conversations at the hair salon

The hairdresser adjusted the cape over Nancy's shoulders with a wan smile and turned away, leaving her to her own reflexion in the mirror. Her hair had been dampened with a spray, combed back from her forehead and clipped up on either side with small brightly coloured hair clips. She stared at her reflexion. One always looked, and felt, at your most vulnerable when draped in a pastel-coloured sheet or gown, whether in a medical institution or a hairdressing salon, she thought. She looked like a rabbit on a rainy night caught in the headlights of a car. Behind her and to the side she could for a moment also see Martha's reflexion, the curled blond hair against the curve of her neck. Then the hairdresser returned and blocked her view.

Bringing Martha along to the salon had been one of those unplanned and unintended situations that seemed to plague her life as a working mother these days. Correction—a stay-at-home mom, as her very successful, very fecund physiotherapist sister-in-law Catherine liked to remind her. Because art wasn't really work, was it? Not when you compared it to health services, which actually meant something and made the world a better place.

It was a discussion that Nancy often had with herself, especially when income-generating projects were few and far between. The question was whether art made the world a better place as well, or whether it was just a private indulgence for weird people who had no other appreciable talents. Even after decades of dedicated art practice, she had not come to a definite and unwavering conclusion.

These days there were more and more studies that proved how art—not just the creating thereof, but also its enjoyment and appreciation—benefited your mental health. But in a world running on money and an education system dedicated to science, technology, engineering and mathematics, art was such a small word. Artists, it seemed, would always be outsiders. Even hairdressers were more esteemed.

Norma, to whom Nancy normally entrusted her hair, had suddenly come down with a tummy bug, so that Nancy had been relegated to her assistant, Blair. Nancy hadn't minded. It did not require great artistry to snip her straight tresses into shape. Until she turned twenty, it had been something her mother always took care of, and after twenty years she had deviated little from that style.

Nancy had met Blair before, and she had seemed confident and efficient enough with other customers' hair. What Nancy had not reckoned with was the girl's insistence on making small talk, something she and Norma had moved beyond a long time ago.

Blair was thin and pale, from her formless legs in black tights and her flat chest to her small hands and the ash-blond hair streaked with even paler highlights. A tiny diamond glinted in the flare of one nostril. Her eyes were the colour of a rainy winter sky and she had a voice to match—the breathy piping of a reed flute barely distinguishable from the general noise of air conditioners, hairdryers and bluesy background music. Wispy tattoos peeped out from under her shirt sleeves, slipping back again when she moved, like furtive animals.

"Planning much for the day?" she asked, having already exhausted the subjects of Nancy's wellbeing, Norma's illness and the general downturn in hairdressing business. She reached for the spray bottle half filled with water and gave Nancy's hair another spritz.

Nancy gave the question some thought. Was she planning much? Of course she was. There was the parcel of prints to be sent off to a buyer in Brisbane. Then she had to visit the supermarket for a quick top-up buy of milk, bananas and kitty litter. She also hoped to cash in (or was it cash out?) the collection of coins, courtesy of Harry's trouser pockets over the past three months. That, with the hair appointment, would more or less account for the morning. At home there would be a list of routine five- or ten-minute tasks and before she knew it, the day would be gone, snatched from under the point of her paintbrush like a paper blown away by the wind.

By the time Nancy had run this through in her mind, Blair's question had grown cold as congealed egg yolk. What did she really care about Nancy's domestic schedule, anyway? It was just all so many words up in the air. Nancy shrugged.

"This and that," she said.

"Hmm," said Blair, pulling a comb gently through Nancy's hair and considering the ends before snipping them off. "Hot out there?"

"Not too bad," said Nancy, although suddenly she could not recall what the weather was like outside. What did the outside temperature matter to Blair? These senseless comments about the weather irritated her in the same way as the insistence of telemarketers in asking about your wellbeing. She understood that communication wasn't confined to the literal meaning of the words; it was all about establishing a connection, if the linguists and sociologists were to be believed. But surely there were more creative ways of connecting than "how's your day been?" and "nice rain we've had".

There was a lull in the conversation, if conversation was what this was, as Blair flicked and snipped with her scissors, while Nancy tried to avoid her reflected image in the mirror. Behind her various parts of Martha's anatomy came into view and disappeared again. She was the easiest child to keep entertained, lost in her own little world of make-believe.

Two chairs on, a woman of Nancy's age waited with strips of foil and other hardware tacked to her russet brown hair. She put down the magazine she had been perusing and picked up her mobile phone. She was several minutes into a muted conversation of which Nancy could only make out the odd word and phrase when Blair resumed her attempt at small talk.

"So, you only have the one, then?" she asked, rolling her eyes to indicate Martha.

"Yes, she's the only one."

"Yeah, I'm an only child as well. People think you'd be lonely, but it never bothered me."

It bothered Nancy, but she said, "She's got friends. At kindy."

Snip, snip, went the scissors next to Nancy's ear. The woman on the phone nodded vigorously in response to some inaudible remark. The foil in her hair glinted like Christmas decorations.

"Oh, I had friends too," Blair said. "Mom tried for more. But it wasn't going to happen, was it? She lost the bubs before they got halfway, most of the time. Had a set of twins the last time. I must have been about five. That really got her. The boys, she called them. Still does. You want a bit more off in front?"

"I..." Nancy swallowed. "It's fine. Thank you."

"Yeah?"

"Yes, thank you."

"All done, then. You're good to go." She whipped the cape off with the flourish of a dignitary revealing a memorial plaque. Then she leant forward and left a last snippet of whispered gossip in Nancy's ear. "Now her," she nodded towards the other woman. "They've adopted. No end of trouble."

She caught Nancy's eye in the mirror and smiled knowingly. Nancy blinked but didn't reply. Her throat had constricted around a deep pool of tears she dared not let out.

The world was full of stories, every life a pattern of branching paths, of roads taken or not taken, of doubling back and reorientation. Your own story met up with those of others like the crisscrossing of animal trails at a waterhole. Mostly it was a fleeting contact, sometimes separated by space and time. Only a few stories ran parallel with your own, zigzagging in the same general direction.

But sometimes a line of prints—footprints, paw prints, hooves—caught your eye. A curve, a pattern, the way the light caught the edges of depressions and ridges or the way the prints fitted into yours. For a moment in time something would resonate and then it was gone.

Nancy paid for her haircut and made an appointment for the next time, when hopefully Norma would have recovered from her indisposition. She dragged Martha back from the fairy tale world she had created around the people who populated the fashion pages, gathering the magazines back into neat stacks.

"But can we come again, Mommy?" Martha asked, reluctantly letting go of the last Women's Weekly. And she had thought bringing her daughter along to something as boring as a hair salon was an unfortunate result of bad parental planning. Something, for example, that Catherine would frown upon. Never underestimate the power of a child's imagination. Now for the rest of the chores.

They were standing in line at the supermarket cashier, when Nancy remembered the incident with the Lion's Club woman, Dorothy. Martha, ignoring the enticements of diminutive Minions toys and Kinder chocolate eggs on the counter, had separated the bananas from their bunch and was arranging them in an upright position in the basket, keeping up a commentary on their familial positions.

This one was the daddy banana and that one was the mommy. Another one was an aunty in a spotted leopard dress. The three kids were being admonished not to quarrel. The lonely lemon had transformed into a dog.

Nancy smiled. Martha could make a toy out of anything, it seemed. She loved her small collection of bought toys, chief among these Priscilla the pink elephant, but a bunch of bananas would also do. Nevertheless, Nancy was glad she had bought her the little Kewpie doll. There was something special about it.

Her thoughts returned to Dorothy. There had been such sadness about her, a deep melancholy seemingly out of proportion to her lack. Was it only because she didn't have a daughter? Four sons, three grandsons—that seemed like rich pickings to Nancy. She came from a large family herself, with a brother and two sisters who had peopled the land (or island, in the case of her Tasmanian-based elder sister) with progeny, a total of eleven at the last count. Five of those were due to the combined efforts of her brother and sister-in-law, although Catherine would of course like to pretend that all the credit was hers.

Compared to them Nancy's single offspring probably seemed lean and lonely. Was Martha lonely? She seemed happy enough, surrounded not only by her friends from kindergarten but also surrounded by a never-ending corps de ballet of imaginary characters. And now she had a cat.

A cat or a sibling. Nancy had not been entirely honest with Harry—it was a choice she would never have held him to. But she knew that the kitten was a band-aid solution more for herself than for Martha. While Martha wouldn't feel the loss of siblings she had never known, Nancy could still recall the ache of two babies lost before term. Two years on, she was still coming to terms with it. Come to terms—oh, what a cruel irony of expression!

The boys, Blair had said of her unborn siblings. My boys, Nancy called them in her mind. Hers had not been twins, but the heartache was no less. Now there would be no siblings for Martha from *her* womb and adoption or fostering were such complicated, twisted attempts at restitution that they had finally given up on those dreams.

Twins. That was what she suddenly remembered Dorothy saying. And yet, there had been no further mention of twins in their conversation. It had been a comment made in passing to which Nancy had given no further thought and yet here it was, popping up in her consciousness again. Such was life, such were words. Synchronicity—twins entwined like a running thread in the border of cognizance. Perhaps she would ask Dorothy about it if ever she saw her again.

Calling a spade a spade

If asked to be character witnesses for Harry, most of his friends, family and acquaintances would describe him as caring, hardworking and honest. Some might call him unambitious or even unimaginative, while his brother-in-law thought him a "stubborn bloody do-gooder". Mary Atkinson liked to think of him as a vague green presence, someone undefined and unrefined by professional training, but harmless enough. Harry wouldn't hurt a fly, she liked to think, on the rare occasions she thought about him. She would have been aghast at his snail killing tactics.

A short temper was not something ever mentioned in the same sentence as Harry's name. But then again, if you only look at the sky when the sun is shining, you'll never believe in thunder and lightning, and few people ever saw Harry when his sun wasn't shining. Real deep anger was for him as infrequent an occurrence as a large comet passing earth, but that comet was now fast approaching.

The small irritations of the past few weeks were steadily conglomerating into something big in Harry's atmosphere and the business with his spade was approaching flammability. He had thought the issue resolved after the previous day's phone call from Herbert's neighbour, even though the mystery of its initial disappearance had remained, along with some annoyance at the unnecessary trouble to search for the old and then to buy a new spade.

His first stop early this morning had been to Parkside Drive to collect his spade from Fred's carport, where the neighbour had promised to leave it. There was no sight of the spade. Harry had even gone to the trouble of looking in Fred's shed, with some trepidation at trespassing but without success.

He had then knocked on the neighbour's door. He had been correct in surmising that it had been the neighbour on the left. One of the small boys Harry had previously seen around had opened the door. His school uniform was a size or two too large, bought with the growth spurts of small boys and the cost of school clothes in mind.

He gave Harry a gap-toothed smile and explained that his dad was already at work. His mom too, yes. Aaron, presumably his brother, was brushing his teeth and then they would walk to school. He had found the spade, yes (smile widening proudly), and had returned it the previous day. He had personally put it in Fred's (Herbert's) carport, while his dad had watched.

"Perhaps that other man took it," he said.

"What other man?"

The boy shrugged and looked over his shoulder. Harry could hear a shuffling somewhere in the house.

"The one who stays here? Herbert? Have you seen him?"

"My dad says he's missing. The police were here."

"They were, yes, I know. But you didn't see him?"

The boy shook his head. Then his brother appeared, slightly older and weighed down by a schoolbag. He frowned at Harry as he pushed his brother out the door, closed it behind them and they scampered off down the street without another word.

Harry groaned. His spade had once again gone AWOL. He felt like a cat chasing a spot of reflected light across the floor – just as he thought he had it, the light would become intangible in his hands or disappear completely, only to reappear just out of reach somewhere else. It was enough to provoke the ire of the most placid of pets. He felt like swiping at something or someone.

Well, no better cure for maladies of the mind than hard physical labour. At least, that was what he had always believed. Depressed? Bored? Confused? Angry? Get out there and dig a hole or mow the lawn or chop up a tree. Climb a mountain. Sweat out your misery.

There was no shortage of sweat-inducing work for Harry today and even if looking after his own properties didn't bring in any money, at least it prevented any money from going out. By the same token, he could argue that working up a sweat saved him the expenses of doctors, psychiatrists and gyms. For Nancy, running a household which included a five-year-old and a (currently injured) kitten, while trying to hold on to a career as a freelance illustrator, probably served the same purpose. Life's checks and balances were seldom as clear-cut as the physical taking and giving of money.

The two residential properties that Harry had inherited were within two kilometres of each other in what had once been the South and West suburbs. The nomenclature had remained even as the town spread like an ink stain on wet paper, leaving these suburbs behind to east and north. A few years ago there seemed to be no stopping the development. Now the bubble had burst.

Even in the short distance he travelled between his properties, there were "For Sale" signs everywhere. They reminded Harry of pins stuck in a map of war, indicating battles lost or troops fallen. Outbreaks of hopelessness as jobs disappeared and homeowners were forced to sell. At least he had not hit that rock-bottom yet. Although his income from the rentals had dramatically decreased, he could still hang on and wait for better days.

There was nothing special about either the houses or gardens of his properties. They featured only the basics— lawns to mow and edge-trim, and the occasional shrub to shape. Here at least Harry had kept on top of the weeds with thick layers of mulch.

Today he could exorcise his frustration by a vigorous mowing, his curses drowned by the lawnmower's drone. As he left the houses and headed to Hanson Road, the drowned kittens flashed through his mind again. For a terrible instant he imagined Snail being drowned in a tub of water, but he shoved the thought away with an angry groan. He was a gardener today, that was all. He would garden and for a few hours shrug off the stress of complicated responsibilities like a bag full of green waste dumped at the tip.

At the furniture warehouse he pushed the lawnmower to the end of the strip of lawn, its roar muted to a low drone by his earmuffs. At the end he pushed it back and forth a couple of times to cover the curve of the lawn and then maneuvered it around to face the other way. He nearly jumped out of his skin at the sight of the man standing just beside him.

"Bloody hell!" he gasped.

It was Lennie, the Salvation Army volunteer. He had graduated to a proper printed name tag, pinned to his blue shirt, and stood there smiling at Harry like a dog waiting for treats. Harry flicked off the mower and slipped the protectors from his ears. He was in no mood for small talk or some self-centred nonsense, least of all from Lennie. The last thing he needed was any reminders of the existence of the kittens. Correction—non-existence.

"Morning, Harry," Lennie said cheerily.

"Yes, Lennie. Thanks for scaring the crap out of me."

"Oh. I'm sorry. How are you doing?"

Harry shrugged. "I'm good. What is it?"

"Did you kill them, then?"

"What? I..." Harry went cold, as if someone had dropped a block of ice into his stomach.

"The rats. They were rats, weren't they? That's what Troy told me. Leonore said she thought they would be possums, on account of the scratch marks, but I told her rats can scratch pretty good too, can't they? Yeah. Good job, Harry."

"Um, yes. So they're gone, the noises? You haven't had any more problems?"

"All gone, Harry. Thanks, mate."

It served no purpose to explain to Lennie that it had been neither rats nor possums. The noises were gone, and that was enough. No need to lie, either. It was merely a case of withholding information and letting assumption do the rest.

"You're welcome. Now, if you'll excuse me."

Lennie nodded curtly. He gave a small wave and walked away, still smiling. Harry took a deep breath, put his earmuffs back on and returned to the mowing. But his temporary state of calm was now broken, shattered by Lennie's innocent mention of dead rats.

He finished the mowing. The irises needed a trim, but he wasn't in the mood to do that today. He did a quick clean-up of the fallen palm fronds, ripped out the most obvious weeds, and packed everything away.

But before leaving, he could not resist walking around to the back of Homespun Furniture. Revisiting the scene of the crime. He grimaced.

There was nothing to be seen. The stack of wooden pallets had now been completely removed, and the forklift parked empty-handed in a corner near the door. Only the indentation and tread marks were visible where their weight had pushed down into the mud. Pale grass tendrils were spreading out over the bare soil. Harry bent down to pull out a few weeds. How quick they were to move in! Nature abhors a vacuum— how true.

He looked closely at the building. There were indeed faint scratch marks on the guttering and on a loose piece of timber fastened next to it, although he doubted that cats had made them. It seemed more likely they were older marks from previous animal inhabitants. His gaze travelled up to the roof and beyond to the clear sky. Barely a week had passed since the last rain and already the soil was crying out for water. He kicked at a buried stone with his boot and walked back to his ute.

He had already started the engine and was about to pull out into the traffic, when his phone rang. It was a private number. The last thing he needed now was for some smooth-talking tele-salesman to stir up his smouldering wrath. He ignored the phone, watching the traffic in his side-mirror. A small tipper truck rushed past, followed by two cars. The phone kept ringing, fell silent, and started up again.

Damn it! Harry leaned back against the headrest, closing his eyes. He took a deep breath like a dragon preparing to incinerate something. Then he switched off the engine and picked up his phone.

"Hello," he said gruffly.

"Good morning. Is that Harry Green?" a male voice said. "This is Constable Alec Berkley. We spoke a couple of weeks ago regarding the disappearance of Cecily Stone. I was hoping we could meet for another chat."

When he had ended the call, Harry leant forward, resting his forehead against the steering wheel. It was warm and firm and real. He could feel it pressing into his skin and imagined the mark it would leave, the small indentations in the rubber creating a mirror image of indentations in his skin. The mark of Cain, he thought. Ha! Was he a murderer after all, as Martha insisted? What *had* happened to Cecily and why were the police after him again? *Were* they after him?

He jumped when someone knocked on the passenger window, hitting his elbow against the door frame.

"Shit!" he cried.

A woman's face withdrew from the window, then peered back in. It was Tanika. Her eyes were wide and for a moment Harry thought she had been crying. Her pretty face was a muddle of anxious apology. She tried a tiny smile and a wave. Harry let down the window.

"Um... sorry, Harry. I didn't mean to scare you," she said.

He waved it away and drew a palm over his face as if to wipe out his troubles.

"I was just passing by," she said, gesturing towards a closed business across the road with a Real Property "For Sale" sign in the window. It had a small photo of Tanika in one corner, as if to entice prospective buyers. Harry had always wondered why real estate agents liked having their portraits displayed like this, but he had to admit that in Tanika's case it might work. He did not think Helen's homely countenance would have been good for business, notwithstanding her actual efficiency at the job. The world was a tangled place, if one could induce someone to buy a house by displaying a photo of an attractive woman. It was supposed to work with cars, but houses?

"I saw your car," Tanika continued.

Harry nodded and grunted a greeting. Tanika had one hand in the open window, leaning forward to talk. The neckline of her work blouse fell forward as well and Harry looked away in embarrassment.

"You've sorted the noises?"

"Yes."

"Good. Um, yes...You know... You know Fred Holmes' tenant is missing?" Her voice thinned.

"Herbert, yes. It was in last week's papers. Fred seemed rather upset. He seemed to think Herbert must have gone fishing in the storm."

"They've found the boat."

"They have? Oh, that's probably not good news, then. No Herbert? Poor man. He was really passionate about his fishing."

"Yes, he was," Tanika said with what sounded to Harry suspiciously like a sob.

"Passion can kill you, can't it?" he said softly.

"Hmm. Harry, I... Fred, the owner... Fred told me the police want to dig up the new garden."

"What?!" he flared up, suddenly alert again. "Why on earth?"

"I know. They're getting a warrant, apparently. I don't know what's going on, Harry."

"Are they looking for... for Herbert? A body? Holy cow! But why? If they've found his boat, he must have drowned. Do they think he's been... killed? My garden!"

She was definitely sobbing now. She had retreated from the window and Harry could see her chest heaving with little gasps between her crying. It surprised him Herbert's disappearance should upset Tanika. He was, after all, only a tenant, in the same way that Harry was to her only a property owner. He had not taken her for such a sensitive person. He pushed aside any imaginings of Tanika crying over *his* disappearance, should that ever happen.

"I'm really sorry, Tanika," he said, trying to sound as rational and comforting as he could. His head was set to burst with anger and frustration. He wondered whether this had anything to do with the police calling him in again. Surely not. That was all about Cecily, not Herbert. Wasn't it? The constable hadn't actually said. "I'm sorry, but I'll have to go now. By God! Dig up the new garden. Why would they want to do that?"

As he started the engine again, she leaned in a last time, smiling meekly through her tears. "I don't know why, Harry. I don't think I was really listening. Fred said... something about a spade?"

End of a journey

As if the universe was endorsing the moment, there wasn't a cloud in the sky. Cecily looked up, turning a circle towards the land and then back again to the sea. It was as blue a day as anyone could have hoped for. Across the bay to the south-east the sun was blazing at half-mast, another hot day in the making, and beyond the peaks of the Whitsunday Islands poked out of the ocean like ridges on a crocodile's back. Nearer, a stone's throw away, lay North Head Island. She took a deep breath, appreciating the dry air in her lungs.

"Champagne," said Michelle, with a wide smile.

"Yes. It's a beautiful morning, isn't it? Absolutely sparkling."

"Yes, but I was thinking more literally. I hope you don't mind, but I thought we could have a champagne breakfast. To celebrate."

"Celebrate?"

"Yes. Because we are here. You are well again. We made it through the storm, and we are here."

"I don't know. Is it a celebration?"

"Oh," she said, sobering. "I'm sorry. Was that insensitive of me?"

Cecily stared across at the island. The sea was calm and shining, a translucent turquoise near the beach. It seemed so innocuous, this stretch of water not even a kilometre wide. Sometimes in winter during low tide, it was so shallow that you could walk across. And yet, what secrets lay in its every drop.

It was a secret the ocean had kept for twenty-four years and it would stay a secret. No-one would ever know the truth of that night. But it was good to face it at last and find that whatever the truth was, she was facing it and letting it go.

She shrugged, turning to Michelle. "That's alright. But... could we just sit here for a moment?"

They sank down onto the sand. Around them the morning shimmered, oblivious. It was now nearly a fortnight since the storm had passed through here and nature was settled into its usual course again. A few trees had been blown down and the curve of the beach altered. The jetty had suffered moderate damage, but that was all man-made and insignificant. The ocean swelled in and out as if breathing. Along the shore, a small sand plover scampered, picking at invisible snails.

After a while Michelle went back to the car. While Cecily had been recovering in hospital, the rental company had had the car repaired and cleaned. It still had a vaguely mouldy smell. She opened her suitcase and removed a small package wrapped in tissue paper, collected a picnic hamper from the back seat, and carried them down to the beach. Cecily smiled up at her.

"Here, I've brought it anyway," Michelle said. "We don't have to drink the champagne. I have coffee. I've brought a picnic blanket as well; I think it should be large enough to sit on."

She unpacked the meal of muffins, cheese and spreads, but left the champagne bottle standing like a sentinel in the soft sand. They ate in silence. The simple meal took on an almost sacred significance. Halfway through, Cecily shrugged as if shedding a heavy coat from her shoulders. She fixed Michelle in a contemplative stare.

"What?"

"Oh heck, let's drink the champagne, shall we?"

"Okay. Are you sure?"

"I am. We *are* here to celebrate. I think Anne would have wanted it."

"She would. I know she would."

Michelle poured the champagne. They clinked the plastic picnic glasses.

"No, wait," she said. "We have to do this properly. Give me your glass. Stand up. Okay, now you hold the glasses."

She bent down to pick up the parcel she had brought and started to unwrap it. It was a rough timber box with a hinged lid. She opened it to show Cecily. Inside, on a bed of shredded paper like a baby in a manger, lay a tiny doll.

They walked to the water's edge and lay the closed box gently in the water. The sea lapped at it but would not take it. It trembled in the shimmering shallows. Michelle nudged it further in and then, as the waves drew it away, they clinked their glasses again, smiling through teary eyes as they sipped at the champagne.

Twins

Nancy quickly realised that if she was going to survive the next two weeks of looking after a collared and bandaged kitten, or more accurately the child companion of a collared and bandaged kitten, she would need some extra creative inspiration. And she would have to keep up with or surpass the creative inspiration of said child companion.

Snail had quickly adapted to the transparent plastic cone she wore around her neck and was now wearing it with the royal flair appropriate to the Elizabethan collar for which it was named. For Martha, however, it held the enduring fascination of a weird new toy. She could not leave it alone. Which was why Harry came home to a double set of collared creatures.

It had taken Nancy more than an hour of trial and error, leaving off-cuts of paper, cardboard and string in her wake, to make Martha a collar like her cat's. They had threaded it with a yellow ribbon and Martha now confronted her father looking even more like an extra-terrestrial than her pet.

"My, my, Martha, what have you got there?" he asked. "You look like..."

"I look like Snail, Daddy. It's my snail hat," Martha said, holding her hands on either side of the cone like a child playing a sunflower in a school concert. Snail herself wasn't far behind, scurrying across the floor towards them. Because of the restricting cone, she could no longer fit easily under the furniture and Harry was already having nightmares of the kitten getting stuck under a chair and having to be rushed off to the vet again. As if he needed any further complications in his life.

"I see. Do you have a bandage as well?"

"No, Daddy! I don't have a tail."

"Sometimes I wonder, Martha," he said, walking to the kitchen to unload his lunchbox and water bottles. Martha had latched onto his arm and bumped into his side with her cone as they walked.

"I don't have a tail!"

"No, you don't. Thank God for that. Only snails have tails."

She let go of his arm to contemplate this. It kept her quiet for about two minutes. Harry stepped out onto the veranda, looking for Nancy. She wasn't there, and he came back inside.

"Do snails have tails, Daddy?"

"Hmm," he said. "Let me see. Snail has a tail."

"But she's not a snail!"

"She's not? Snail is not a snail?"

"No-o-o. She's a kitty."

"Ah. So Snail has a tail, but she's not a snail. And Martha doesn't have a tail, but she isn't a snail, either. And snails..." He stuck his head into the bedroom. "Nancy?"

"Snails have hats."

"Hats?"

"To hide under. Snails have hats that they carry with them, so things don't fall on their heads."

"They do, do they? Hats? Nancy!"

"Mommy's not here, Daddy."

"What? Where is she, then?"

Martha made a serious face and shrugged her shoulders. Harry was about to get worried when he heard footsteps outside. Martha giggled.

"She's hiding, under her hat!" she cried and dashed off to meet Nancy at the front door, in the process denting her cardboard collar against the security screen.

Nancy was slightly out of breath as she greeted Harry. She adjusted her daughter's collar and patted her shoulder.

"All good?"

"More or less. Where have you been?"

"I wasn't away for long, just had a quick chat with Tracy; she was showing me something in her garden. I waved when you drove past, but you didn't see me."

"Sorry. Long walk?" He smiled wearily. Tracy stayed half a block away, at the bottom of the street, and the uphill walk back to the Greens' house was steep enough to get you puffing if you took it at a fast pace. "So what does Tracy say?"

"This and that. She knows about Cecily."

"She does? Does she know her?"

"Cecily's cleaner also does Tracy's daughter's house. She says she has a key to her house and we might use it."

"Wait. Who said who has a key to whose house? And why would we want to use it?"

"Tracy says her daughter's cleaner has a key to Cecily's house."

"And?"

"We could get into the house. To return the doll."

Harry felt like banging his head against the wall. Mind you, it didn't have to be his own head. He pushed the heels of his hands against his eyes and took a deep breath. He opened his mouth to speak and closed it again. Nancy eyed him like a cat eyeing a puppy pushing the boundaries.

"What?" she asked. "What?"

"Nancy," Harry said and, taking her by the arm, led her to the couch and pulled her down beside him. "Now listen. I did not steal the doll, okay? I found it in the garden, I dug it up, and I could not bury it again. Cecily is not there."

And that is the least of my problems, he thought. Cecily's disappearance had paled somewhat in the light of the farce around the missing Herbert. In fact, the subject of Cecily hadn't even been raised in the conversation he had just had with Detective Inspector Brian Parker, Constable Berkley's boss.

"I have been back twice, you know that," he continued. "I have absolutely no intention of keeping it—it's a stupid bloody doll, for goodness' sake! Plus, we now have another one. So, would you please stop badgering me about it?!"

"Why does it have to be such an issue, Harry?"

"You're asking *me* that?! I'm not the one with the issue!"

"So, we take it back."

"By breaking into Cecily's house?"

"We've got a key; that's not breaking in."

"Unlawful trespassing. I don't need any more hassles from the police, I really don't."

"But you haven't done anything wrong."

"I haven't? No? Then what is this all about?"

She shrugged, her mouth set in an obstinate pout. Like mother like daughter, Harry thought. "They only questioned you because you're the gardener. Everybody always suspects the gardener."

"They do?" This was news to Harry. If only he could have been a suspect in Cecily's and Herbert's disappearances merely by virtue of being their gardener! That would have been an immense relief. Of course, he now knew it wasn't as simple as that, but if Nancy wanted to believe that, he wouldn't disenchant her.

"In the stories they do. The gardener or the stable boy. Anyway, that's nearly three weeks ago; surely you're not under suspicion anymore?"

"Hmm. Not the cleaner?" he diverted the question.

"No. The police did question her, Tracy says, but only for form's sake, and they used her key to have a look inside the house. Obviously, she's not doing the house until Cecily gets back; it's not like a garden with things that grow. And apparently, she knows you, or knows about you."

Harry considered this. His initial involvement had only been as an innocent bystander, the last person to have seen Cecily and therefore the first to be questioned. No guilt had been implied in that first questioning. It was, as Nancy said, only for form's sake, police protocol. He wondered whether withholding the truth could be grounds for prosecution. "They don't know about the doll."

Nancy broke into a victorious smile. "So you do feel guilty!"

"I..." What a turncoat! Suddenly there was just too much to explain. He did feel guilty, but the doll wasn't the big issue here. And yet it was just enough to niggle at his conscience.

If you were dishonest in the small things, did that make you a likelier suspect in the bigger matters? Did his innocent taking of the doll implicate him in Cecily's disappearance, as if the doll was an avatar for the woman? Could the fact that he killed snails and grasshoppers and hamsters, and was party to the killing of kittens, somehow make him a more likely murder suspect? Wasn't that what lawyers always did in court cases—throw suspicion on the character of an accused to hint at the predisposition to commit a crime?

Although there was as yet no evidence that Cecily had been murdered or had even died, this was not the case with Herbert. Worse, though, could one be implicated in killing someone just because the murder weapon belonged to you and was, however irrationally and inexplicably, found at the site of disappearance? He sighed and surrendered to the lesser condemnation.

"Okay, then. You win. We'll take the doll back."

Nancy planted a kiss on his mouth. He smiled and drew her into a hug. Such a small surrender, such a big reward.

"When?" she asked, pushing her advantage.

"When can you get the key?"

"Tonight?"

"No way. Tomorrow."

"Tomorrow then. I'll talk to Tracy. What does your day look like? Shall we go after work?"

"Done."

Digging it up

He could have told Nancy that his day did not look good at all. Black Friday did not half describe his feelings about the day. He was mildly surprised that it wasn't the thirteenth as well. It would have been just his luck.

Before he could report to Parkside Drive, where the police had probably already started digging up the retaining wall garden, where all those lovely mock oranges and lily pillies were just settling in after the stress of transplanting, there were at least two gardens needing their regular maintenance visits. It was with even less of his usual lack of enthusiasm that Harry unloaded his mower outside Mary Atkinson's house. His body felt heavy, his muscles like a team of unwilling draft horses that had to be coaxed into cooperation. No hard physical labour was going to cure his distress today. At least there was no sign of Mary yet, but—oh God!—perhaps she had also disappeared! Wouldn't that be just the end of him!

The prospect of Mrs. Atkinson's disappearance brought a brief interlude of comic relief to Harry's morning. As he pushed the roaring mower to and fro, he imagined the various ways in which she could vanish.

Perhaps she would fly away on a broomstick with her pug in tow. But no, she was no evil witch, merely annoying. Would she slip down a rabbit hole like Alice and meet up with the Red Queen? Off with her head! Would her heart burst with pride (literally!) when her favourite grandson won the Nobel Prize for Science or Economics? Maybe she would choke on a saucy piece of gossip or just run out of things to say and keel over.

By the time Harry had swopped the mower for the edge trimmer, he had run out of imaginary endings to his client's existence and was even beginning to feel slightly worried. His worry was, however, unfounded. Soon the screen door squeaked open, and the pug came out snorting and sniffling, followed by its owner, the words already spilling from her mouth. Harry returned her greeting but kept going. For the last half an hour of his visit, she stood outside, talking non-stop about the recent storm and the dearth of tomatoes and the cost of holiday accommodation in Sydney and her friend's new Labradoodle puppy, apparently not in the least concerned that her audience was a moving target and her voice dampened by his ear muffs. She did not seem to need any acknowledgement of her comments, only the knowledge that someone was within earshot. She would have made a great radio presenter, Harry thought. He packed away his gear and left her mid-sentence, holding forth on the subject of cruise ships.

The pondering about Mary Atkinson kept his mind from visiting more distressing subjects, but on the drive to his next job—Joseph Black's garden maintenance—the potential gravity of the situation struck him again and he gasped as if from a physical assault.

As annoying as the previous day's call from the police had seemed at first, Harry's conversation with Tanika had stirred up deeper worries. The prospect of another interview with more pointless questions about Cecily had not been appetising. Besides the niggling question of the doll, which surely could in no way be connected with her disappearance, Harry had already told them all he possibly could about his client. The possibility that his summons this time could be about something else of a more serious nature had gnawed at Harry all the way to the police station.

How had the innocent if mysterious disappearance of Herbert and his suspected drowning during a storm suddenly taken such a drastic turn, to the extent that the police were apparently suspecting foul play and were ready to dig up a garden to look for a body? Could the spade that Tanika had mentioned possibly be Harry's and if so, by what sleight of hand had it shown up in the neighbour's garden? And what on earth did that have to do with anything? Was it connected to Cecily's disappearance or to Herbert's, or perhaps to both?

At the station Constable Alec Berkley had greeted him with an anxious friendliness that Harry found disconcerting. He had then introduced him to Detective Inspector Brian Parker. It seemed the investigation had been cranked up a notch since Harry's interview on the heights outside Ben Eastman's garden.

Parker was a serious man who kept stroking his balding head as if looking for his missing hair. He had not minced his words.

"Harry *Green*," he had said with a sarcastic emphasis. "Your business is called Green Gardens, is that correct?"

"Yes."

"Now Harry – do you mind if I call you Harry? Good. So, Harry, do you recognise this?" the detective had asked, laying a photo on the table and sliding it over towards Harry. It was a clear photo of a garden spade and, as Harry had previously told Nancy, despite the scratches, the name stencilled on its side undeniably identified it as his. It had felt strangely unreal to see it like that. Whoever took photos of spades? The police, obviously.

He had nodded at Brian Parker, still unsure where this was going.

"It's my spade. Where did you...?"

"Good," Parker had interrupted him. "Could you tell me when was the last time you saw it?"

"Um... I don't know."

"You don't know?"

Harry had shrugged and smiled sheepishly. "I'm sorry, but yes, I really don't know. I've been looking for the spade for more than a week now, but it could have been missing for longer. The last time I clearly remember using it was in Cecily's garden—Mrs. Stone—when I put in her plants. So, Wednesday before last, the day she went missing. I've been looking for it ever since. You can ask my wife."

"Your wife?"

"Yes, Nancy. Your officers interviewed her after Cecily's disappearance."

"Ah, yes. But I'm afraid Mrs. Green could not be regarded as an unbiased witness in this instance."

Harry had bristled at this. "Witness? Who's talking about witnesses? What is this, a trial? What exactly is it you think I've done?"

"Now settle down, Harry. This is not a trial. You're not under arrest. This is a voluntary interview. If you could just confirm – when was the last time you can remember seeing or using this spade?" He had poked a finger at the photo in emphasis.

"I have already told you, Detective. In Cecily Stone's garden two weeks ago."

"What about Fred Holmes' garden in Parkside Drive? You recently planted some new plants there, didn't you?"

"I did and I had to do it with a long-handled spade because I couldn't find this one. By the way, about that garden," he had wanted to confirm Tanika's news about digging up Fred's plants, but the policeman had not given him the chance.

"I see. So, by..." Parker had consulted his notebook. "... by Tuesday last, that is the eighteenth of October, the spade was definitely missing."

"Yes."

"I see. And you haven't seen it since?"

"No. I've been looking for it everywhere. I had to buy a new one in the end. And then two days ago a guy phoned, Fred's—Herbert's—neighbour, saying he'd found it in his shed and he would leave it in the carport, but when I went to pick it up this morning, it was gone!"

Parker had stared at Harry in silence, chewing his lip before looking down at his notebook again. He had seemed to contemplate an issue and started to say something, but then he had just shrugged and smiled at him.

"Well, thank you, Harry. That is all for today."

Harry had been flabbergasted. "It is?"

"Yes, thank you for coming in. You may go now." He had stood up and waited for Harry to do the same before turning towards the door.

"But my spade... and the garden, are you going to..."

"I'm afraid the spade is evidence, but you will have it back..."

"Yes, alright, but where did you find it?"

"...as soon as we're finished at the Holmes property."

"Which you are going to dig up? Is that true? Really?"

Detective Parker had sighed and looked at Harry over his shoulder. He had not answered, not in as many words, but Harry had read his reply in the twitch of his mouth and the way he stared guiltily into space for a moment before shrugging and disappearing through the opened door. They were going to dig up Fred's new garden bed; no, they were going to dig up *Harry's* new garden bed!

A different kind of digging

After a month of inattention and two good rain showers, the lawn at Joseph Black's house was lush and long. It was a crowded property in the older part of town, with a thankfully small patch of buffalo grass between multiple garden beds, pathways and hedges, but after the mowing and edge trimming Harry still had to spend a good two hours attacking the weeds that were flourishing in every nook and cranny. Despite the soft soil, he had to dig in with a hand tool to get at the roots of dandelion and clover.

His shoulders and back ached as he bent down to get at the pernicious plants. People like the McMullens were getting more and more environmentally conscious, but many others still clung as stubbornly to poison as the only solution for keeping their gardens weed-free. He could understand the attraction of a quick spray versus the mind-numbing business of manual weeding. Today, urgent to get back to Parkside Drive, he would have given anything for an easy solution. He had even momentarily regretted dumping Geoff McMullen's poison. It would have come in handy and the Blacks would not have minded in the least.

But Harry had marked the borders of his own principles like lines in the sand and he would not cross them without serious deliberation. A gentleman might have been defined as someone who uses the butterknife even when no-one is looking. Harry used his weeding tools in the same way—to get rid of weeds even when no-one was looking. To do otherwise would have been hypocritical.

Besides, even for the environmentally apathetic, there were consequences to chemical killing. Poison killed the organisms, but it did not remove the evidence. After the weeds had died, you still had to dig up or rake away the dried debris. Like the dead cane toads, you were left with a body to dispose of. Which was probably exactly what the police were thinking when they decided to dig up Fred's garden.

People, dead or alive, did not simply disappear, although drowning at sea during a cyclone was probably as near to disappearing as one could get. Harry did not understand why the police could not just accept the obvious—Herbert, his fishing passion possibly fuelled by a drink or two, had taken his tinnie out to sea and met a watery end. Five fathoms deep and all that. But no, they had to go chasing after imaginary demons just because of the sudden and inexplicable appearance of a spade. There had to be something they weren't telling him and today, police tape or no police tape, he was going to find out.

He stabbed at a last patch of weeds, dislodged their roots and, shaking off the loose soil, thrust them in the sturdy garden bag beside him. Then he heaved it onto the back of his ute, packed away his tools and headed for the Holmes property.

Harry had expected a scene reminiscent of a crime movie, the street filled with cars and flashing lights, and the house tied up in fluorescent police tape like a giant Christmas present. What he found instead was decidedly low key. Except for one marked police car, only the number of vehicles parked in the driveway and the street hinted at any unusual activity. It could have been a social gathering. If there were any nosy neighbours around, they did not show themselves.

He found a parking spot on the opposite side of the road and casually walked up to Fred's house. He stopped at the timber side gate, his way barred by a single band of striped yellow tape stirring in the breeze. *Police—Do Not Cross*, he read upside down. There was no-one guarding the entrance. The part of the new garden bed that he could see from here was as yet undisturbed, but he could hear something going on around the corner of the house—people talking and the odd grunt or thud.

He softly let his hand lie on the tape, just feeling the plastic resistance under his skin. Should he call out first? Should he just duck under the tape? Or would that be (literally) crossing a line?

"Arnie!" someone called. "Give us a hand with this one, would you?"

"Sure," a man (presumably Arnie) answered. "Where do you want it?"

"Careful," someone else said, and Harry recognised the voice of DI Parker. "It's a tree you're digging up, not a bloody lamppost. And you should be out front, Sergeant Arnold, we don't want the neighbours walking in on this."

"Not much of a tree, Parker."

"Not when you're done with it, no. Here, put it with that other one."

"Hello?" Harry called out.

"That you, Alec?" Parker asked, but before Harry could reply, he came into view around the corner. "Hey, what are you doing here?!"

"Good day, Detective. I'm the gardener, remember."

"Don't get smart with me, Harry. You can't be here."

"I've got a job to do."

"Not today, you don't. This is a crime scene." He nodded toward the police tape. "And *I* have a job to do. Now get out of here."

From the back garden, the sounds of digging continued. Something thudded against the timber fence. Arnie swore. Harry winced.

"It's my garden," he said, lamely. He didn't know anymore whose garden it really was. It was Fred's because he owned it and was paying for its upkeep and improvement. It was also Herbert's, who rented the property and inhabited the space, or had until recently. But Harry did the maintenance, and the garden was thus also his, linguistically, if not literally, in the sense that he could speak of "one of my gardens". Was it now Brian Parker's as well? It was a quandary for the likes of King Solomon the Wise.

Detective Parker smiled at him with squinted eyes. "I think not. Go now. But don't go too far," he grinned.

Harry hesitated, then turned around and slowly walked away, Parker's eyes on his back. Another police vehicle turned into Fred's driveway, double-parking behind the first one. He watched as Constable Alec Berkley got out and with only a nod of greeting walked hastily up to Parker.

Harry crossed the road to his ute, slumping into the seat. His window was open and he could hear the conversation between the police officers, without being able to make out the words. He saw Parker's expression waver between disappointment and satisfaction. Parker glanced at him. For a moment it seemed as if he would come over, but he just nodded and turned away.

A key, a doll and a plan

There was a time, when he had just started doing garden maintenance so many years ago, that Harry had felt uncomfortable entering the properties of his clients while they were not there. He never entered the houses and very seldom had access to any sheds or other outbuildings, but he couldn't shake the feeling of trespassing. A garden could still be a very private thing and a reflexion of so much of the owner's life and character that it made a voyeur of even the most casually observant gardener.

People's lives spilled out of their houses into the outside spaces of their yards. Shoes were left outside a door and empty mugs were forgotten on a garden table next to empty cigarette packets. The cardboard boxes from purchases—a new dishwasher, a box of wine, a delivery from an online pharmacy or clothes store—accumulated in a corner of the patio for weeks before being disposed of. Children's toys, odd socks and dog beds populated the immediate vicinity of the back door, as did brooms, mops and buckets. Washing lines, broken crockery, cars, bicycles, the residues of barbeques or parties—these were all such immediate testimonies of lives lived that Harry had to consciously shake off a feeling of awkwardness.

After nine years in the business, this seldom bothered him anymore. He felt at home in the gardens of his regular clients and had developed an imperturbable professional nonchalance when entering any new property in much the same way as a doctor learned to approach the private fleshly properties of his patients. But with every return to Cecily's garden after her disappearance, his unease was growing. And now, no matter how much Nancy tried to deny it, they would really be trespassing. Given his current standing with the police, this was not a good thing, but without revealing his new status as prime suspect for another crime, he could not convince Nancy of the inappropriateness of their visit. That he was keeping yet another secret from her made him extremely uncomfortable.

Nancy had had no trouble getting the key to Cecily's house from her cleaner Clare, who had had neither cause to visit the house in the past three weeks nor scruples to lend out her access key to a friend's friend's friend, so to speak. She knew of Harry's existence as Cecily's gardener but they had never met. It made Harry doubt the trustworthiness of Clare in particular and cleaners in general. Nancy's apparent belief that cleaners were never suspected, at least not in the stories that crossed her path, seemed to him dubious to say the least. Nevertheless, here they were, parked in Cecily's driveway on a Friday afternoon with a key, a doll and a plan.

After the fruitless visit to the Holmes property, he had lost all enthusiasm for work. There was still Eastman to do, but he had fabricated an excuse about an incapacitated vehicle and promised to do the garden after the weekend.

Nancy had never accompanied him to Cecily's place before, but she did a perfect imitation of belonging. No-one watching would have had reason to suspect her of even the mildest illegal activity. She merely walked up to the door with the key, gave a perfunctory knock and then proceeded to unlock the door, leaving him to hasten after her with the tinned doll clutched in his hand like a door-knocking preacher holding a Bible.

The entrance door swung open into a spacious living room. As Harry followed Nancy into the room, he immediately caught the lingering gardenia scent of Cecily's perfume. The late afternoon light shone through the lace curtains at the side window like spilt gold.

As far as Harry knew, Cecily had been adequately well off but never flashy. The restrained décor of her house attested to this. The furniture was unremarkable—a beige lounge set comprising a couch and two chairs brightened with a few embroidered scatter cushions and a neatly folded green lacy throw over the back of one chair, a glass-topped coffee table with magazines and an empty flower vase, two overflowing book cases against opposite walls, and a corner table with a large television set. The walls were decorated with a few nondescript landscape paintings and a collection of framed photos. A set of double doors to the left led into a dining room, while to the right Harry could see through a doorway into the kitchen.

Harry's only purpose in entering Cecily's house was to return the Kewpie doll. He therefore immediately started looking for an appropriate surface on which to deposit it. He headed for the coffee table and placed the tin containing the doll next to the flower vase.

"There," he said. "Happy? Can we go now?"

Nancy, who was contemplating the photos on the wall, nodded in a way that Harry knew could not necessarily be interpreted as assent. It was the nonverbal equivalent of the mumble one uttered when cornered by a persistent and persistently boring guest at a function. It wasn't a yes as much as an attempt to stay civil while trying to follow the very interesting conversation in the adjoining group.

"Nancy," he said. "We can go now."

"Hmm," she said. "Just a moment."

Harry stepped closer to see what she was looking at. There was nothing unusual about the photos. They were the run-of-the-mill photos one found in most homes, usually single or group portraits of family and friends, displayed with that strange mixture of reticence, obligation and pride one felt when offering something private for the perusal of others. Harry was neither interested in them nor inclined to extend the intrusion into Cecily's private space, and *he* at least knew her. Nancy would not even be able to identify her on any of the photos.

"That's Cecily," he said, leaning over Nancy's shoulder to point at a picture of a smiling woman with her arm around a young girl.

He recognised the background as a spot in the garden where a climbing jasmine burst into flower each spring. The photo must have been taken many years ago. Cecily was younger, with brown hair to her shoulders and pinned up on one side, but she was still recognisable as his elderly client. It was obvious that the women were related, although he could not immediately pinpoint the resemblance to a specific feature like noses or eyes or mouths. Judging from their age differences, Harry guessed that the girl might be Cecily's daughter. She was a handsome blonde, her hair tied back from her face, which had a haunted look despite her smile.

"Yes," said Nancy and pointed at the girl. "And her daughter? I wonder if it was *her* doll."

"Well, we've brought it back now."

"Yes. Thanks, Harry."

Nancy did not move away, however, but kept looking at the photos with the interest of a viewer at an art exhibition. Cecily appeared in only two other photos—a charming black and white wedding photo and a very recent photo with a group of elderly ladies—but her presumed daughter was everywhere. There was a snap of her wrapped in a scarf and jacket against a snowy urban landscape, a photo with two boys at a formal function and one as a gangly teenager in bathing costume, holding a spaniel in her lap.

"They're all old photos," said Nancy.

"They are?" Nancy was right. In none of the photos did the daughter look any older than about seventeen. Harry shrugged. "So what? Let's just go."

"Wouldn't you expect more recent photos?"

"People don't print photos anymore; they have it all on their phones or computers."

"I don't agree."

"How many framed photos of Martha do we have? And when was the latest one taken, a year ago? Two years?"

"That's different. She's only five. But, yes, you might have a point. Still."

"Well, I'm going," Harry declared and turned away towards the front door.

"Okay," Nancy said at last. "Where did you put the doll?"

He gestured towards the coffee table. Nancy nodded, this time in true agreement, and turned to follow him, lingering only for a quick glance at a framed photo on top of one of the bookcases. Harry was already at the door, when suddenly the phone rang. It echoed loudly through the house.

They both jumped. Nancy, standing next to the bookcase, jerked her arms in fright, knocking over a pile of unshelved books next to the photo frame. They fell onto the floor with a thud.

"Good Lord!" she gasped, grabbing at her chest. "My heart!"

Harry could not but smirk at this. Nancy was also jumpy, enough evidence that he was not the only one with a guilty conscience. The phone had now stopped ringing, and he squatted next to her, gathering up the fallen books.

"Serves us right," he said. "Come now, we've got to go."

He picked up the last book, a hardcover novel from which the dust cover had come undone, and patted it into place. As he made to put it back, something detached from the back of the cover and fell to the floor. It was another photo and Nancy immediately latched on to it.

"Look," she said, standing up.

All hope of an immediate departure fled. Harry sighed and glanced at the photo. It was black and white and worn at the edges. Two blond girls in school uniforms were smiling at the camera with real delight, as if the photographer had just uttered something truly funny. Behind them a dark-haired woman in spectacles stood with a hand on the shoulder of each girl. She too was smiling, her cheeks charmingly dimpled.

It took a moment for Harry to realise that *both* girls looked like even younger versions of the blond girl in the other photos, whom they had presumed to be Cecily's daughter. They were apparently the same age and looked similar, so he wondered whether they were twins. But Cecily had only ever mentioned one daughter. In fact, the girl on the left had a finer, more delicate face. Perhaps they were cousins. Both girls were holding something in their hands and Harry leaned in closer to see, but Nancy was stabbing a finger at the woman.

"It's... it's..." she said.

"Not Cecily, but I think..."

"No, no. It's... Dorothy! It's Dorothy, I'm sure."

"Dorothy? Whatever. But look at this, Nancy."

"I'm sure it's Dorothy. The mouth... she has a mole just there, do you see? And she was a teacher, so..." Their heads were touching as they both now stared closely at the photo. Nancy gasped. "My god! The dolls!"

"Exactly, my dear Watson."

"Kewpie dolls." And so they were. Even on the small scale of the photo it was clear that the girls each held a Kewpie doll in her hand. Nancy turned the photo over, looking for explanations, but there was nothing written on the back.

"Mystery solved, then." Harry smiled contentedly.

"Yes and no," said Nancy.

"Well, we can assume that the doll belonged to Cecily's daughter."

"And? We still don't know where Cecily has gone."

"Excuse me," said Harry. "I thought we were just returning the doll. If anyone is going to find Cecily, it will be the police."

"What do *they* know? They don't know about the doll."

"But what could the doll possibly have to do with Cecily's disappearance?"

Nancy shrugged. "I don't know. Yet. But I'll have to find Dorothy again. Come, let's go."

Harry cast one last glance at the cookie tin with its strange contents sitting so innocently on the coffee table, before following Nancy outside. He pulled the door closed behind him and waited for Nancy to lock it. They walked back to his vehicle in silence. The relief he had expected to feel was slow in coming and necessarily only partial. They had returned the doll and that would get Nancy off his back. But extricating himself from the complications being dug up by the police was going to be harder.

He slid into the driver's seat and reversed out of the driveway. Beside him Nancy sat smiling smugly, lost in her own thoughts. She did not speak again until they had stopped at Tracy's to drop off the house keys for Cecily's cleaner.

"Did you know," she asked dreamily, "that the word 'doll' was initially a diminutive of Dorothy?"

Photos and dolls

It was one of those Saturday mornings when Nancy was in no mood for great shakes in the kitchen. Breakfast would be a packaged affair and everyone could help themselves. She had stacked bowls, cereals and fruit on a tablecloth on one side of the dining table as a gentle hint that no bacon and eggs would be forthcoming today. A collection of dusty photo albums occupied the other side of the table.

She was bent over an album of yellowing colour prints when she heard Harry at the back door. He stomped his feet a few times before opening the door and stepping inside. She watched as he walked over to her with a flower in his hand, leaving a trail of grass and dirt behind him on the tiled floor.

"A flower for the lady," he said, presenting it to her. It was a twig from the neighbour's Poinciana tree, bearing two flowers of an incredible red that she had yet to define. Crimson? Scarlet? Cadmium red?

"Thank you," she smiled. "My flower thief."

"Pfft! One flower. That's not theft, it's neighbourly charity. What are you up to?"

"Just a bit of nostalgia. After seeing those photos yesterday, well, I thought I'd pull out a few albums."

"I forgot that we had those," he said, leaning over to look at the photos before her. He laughed. "Is that you?"

"Yip."

"You were a little beauty, weren't you?"

Nancy contemplated the pony-tailed girl in the picture, smiling at the camera through a missing front tooth. "Mmm. I was?"

"Sure. Pity I hadn't known you then. I might have fallen for you."

"Lucky you, to escape such a fate."

She closed the album and stood up, planting a kiss on his cheek. A photo lay face-down on the table where the open album had concealed it. Harry picked it up.

"What's this?" he frowned, turning it over.

"It's the photo from the book, the one of Cecily's daughter and the other girl. I want to show it to Dorothy."

"What? You just took the photo?"

"Yes. I'll take it back. It's not theft, it's... It's research, investigation."

Harry slapped the photo down on the table. "No, no, no, no. You're the one who wouldn't get off my case about the doll and now you have carried off a photo!"

"It's not..." She hesitated.

"Yes?"

"Okay. Okay. So I'm a thief. Well, shoot me."

"Which would really make me a murderer."

"Daddy is a murderer."

Martha shuffled around the corner, dressed in yellow pyjama bottoms and an off-white spangled T-shirt she was growing too big for but refused to give up. Priscilla hung lopsided from one hand as she squinted up at her parents through sleepy eyes. There was a bruise midway up her thigh where she had bumped into something the previous day. All that the picture lacked was a few tears and a dirty smear across the cheek to make it a poster for parental neglect. Harry had visions of Martha visiting them in prison—he the murderer and Nancy the thief. Happy childhood, no?

He let out a sigh. "No. Morning, Martha. But no, I am *not* a murderer."

"Hello, love," said Nancy, bending down for a hug. "Have a good sleep? Where's your cat?"

Martha shrugged and submitted to a hug from Harry as well. He tickled her. She squealed and hit him with the elephant.

"Help!" he cried. "I'm being murdered by a pink elephant. Help, help, he's going to trample me!"

"Is not, Daddy!" she protested. She held the toy out to him. "See? It's just a doll, Daddy. It's just Priscilla."

"Talking of which," said Nancy. She hesitated. Martha had temporarily diverted them from a loaded topic and she did not wish to stir things up again, but the toy sale was her only link to Dorothy, the Kewpies and Cecily. Besides, her daughter could be a useful ally. "The toy sale is on today."

"And?" Harry asked, on the defensive.

"I thought we could go, Martha and I," she said innocently, not looking at him but glancing at Martha instead.

Martha, sensing the tension in the air, looked from one to the other with big eyes. She hugged the elephant to her chest. Nancy felt a sudden pang of guilt. How could she use her own child as leverage in a silly argument with Harry? She would let the issue pass. There were other ways of getting hold of Dorothy. What was the Internet for, after all? She could contact the Lion's Club and ask for Dorothy's contact number.

"Maybe..." she started.

"Alright," said Harry at the same time, also relenting. He was in an irritable mood. Perhaps a bit of solitude at home was not such a bad idea. He might even take his bike out and cycle off his frustrations. "You go then."

"Are you sure? We could go another time; it's not that important."

"Of course I'm sure. It's important to you. And to Martha as well. Right, possum?"

Martha nodded uncertainly, without smiling.

"But there's one condition." He gestured towards the table with its scattering of photos and albums. "The photo goes back. ASAP."

She nodded and hugged him gratefully. "Oh, thank you, Harry! Thank you. You're a darling."

"Not a murderer?"

"Not even if I were really a thief."

Pie in the sky

"It's like…"

Nancy tried to think of an analogy for what she was feeling. Her mom had a favourite saying—the road to hell is paved with good intentions. But that did not cover half of it. It was the knowledge that you had been given something small and beautiful and promising, like Jack with the beans, and now you had an uncontrollable bean stalk and a hungry giant breathing down your neck.

"It's like trying to pry open the lid of a special can of paint when you don't have the right tools. You keep trying and prying and in the end the lid is so bent out of shape that even with the correct tool you will now never get it open and you either have to jab a hole in the lid or throw away the whole can. I wish Harry had never taken the stupid doll!"

"No, I'll tell you what it's like," said Jenny, leaning forward with her elbows on the table.

It was nearly noon, way past teatime, and the lunch crowd was settling in. They should have been home long ago, but after the fiasco with the photo, Nancy had to gather her wits. A cuppa at the Blue Bower was the only solution she could think of. It would settle Martha as well. She had not expected Jenny to take even five minutes off from a busy Saturday schedule for a tête-à-tête, although she had secretly wished it. As it turned out, Jenny had summarily shrugged off her manager's hat, ordered coffee and cake on the house, and was now giving Nancy her undivided attention.

Nancy stabbed a cake fork angrily at the slice of cheesecake in front of her. Beside her Martha, her eyes still red from crying, was eating an apple and walnut muffin with single-minded concentration. No remedy for shock better than tea and sugary treats, may God forgive her the unhealthiness thereof.

"It's like this," continued Jenny. "Someone gives you—or maybe you buy it on a special—a whole bag of, say, blueberries. It's a treasure. They're so lovely, you just have to do something special with them, cook up a storm, bake a pie, whatever. And then you stumble across a recipe and it's like a story coming together, it's so beautiful. You just have to make it.

"So you've got all the other ingredients, except for one thing, the lime juice. You've got a scraggly lemon somewhere, but it's not going to be enough and you can't go to the shops now, because, well, whatever, you just can't go now. Your car's out of fuel or something."

Nancy smiled and took another bite of the cheesecake, this time with less frustration. Martha had also switched her attention from the muffin to Jenny, if not for the interest of the actual story then for the animated way in which Jenny was holding forth.

"Anyway, the neighbour has a lime tree and you know he wouldn't mind if you just took one, because see, he's away on holiday and you're not going to phone him in Thailand or Paris or wherever just to get permission to pick one lime from his tree. So, you trip over and pick a lime. Or you pick two, just in case. But what you didn't know is that he has a house sitter this time, even though he's never had one before, because see, he now has a goldfish that needs to be looked after, so he can't just up and go anymore and leave the house unattended.

"But you get the limes and you go home. Then you start making this pie and you're so excited because it's going to be exquisite and you're already congratulating yourself, because you're not normally a great cook but this is going to blow the roof off. And everything is going so well and you've got the pastry done to a tune and you pour in the filling and you stuff it in the oven and you wait.

"In the meantime, the house sitter has you clocked for a thief. Sorry, I know, too close to the bone, but there you go. Bear with me. The house sitter thinks you're just a common thief, maybe you're planning a break-in, who knows, and he'll be held responsible, so he's reported your suspicious activities to the police, who are now knocking on your door."

"Please, Jenny," Nancy said, rolling her eye to indicate Martha.

"What? It's just a story. Isn't it, Martha? I'm just telling a story. You don't have a neighbour with a lime tree, do you?"

"Does a Poinciana tree count?"

"No. What? No. Can I please continue my story? Thank you. Where was I?"

"The police are knocking on the door."

"Are they bringing us a goldfish, Aunty Jenny?" Martha chimed in.

"A goldfish? Why? Did I... What?"

"Never mind," pacified Nancy. "No goldfish, Martha. You have a cat, okay? Carry on, Jen."

"Right. The police are taking this with a pinch of salt, anyway, but they have to investigate, so they ask you a few questions, this and that and have you stolen the limes and so on. You explain about the pie and the neighbour and your car and it all gets complicated, so the conversation drifts outdoors as you're trying to make sense of this little thing that has suddenly become so huge you think you might be spending the night in jail or something. And the house sitter comes out and he's actually not a bad guy and you explain the whole thing a second time and you all have a good laugh and the police go on their merry way and everyone is happy."

Jenny paused to take a sip of her coffee. A few feet behind her a waitress was hovering with an empty tray, trying to decide whether to interrupt.

"But what about the pie, Aunty Jenny?" asked Martha.

"Aha! Clever girl! What about the pie? That's the whole point, because while you were having a nice or not so nice neighbourly discussion, you'd forgotten all about the pie. And because you were outside, you didn't hear the oven timer. What you do hear now is the smoke alarm going off, because voila, your pie has burnt to a crisp. Goodbye pie! Goodbye beautiful berries! Better if you'd never gotten them in the first place. *That's* what it's like. Oh, and then—and this is the worst part—then you find that you did after all have a lime, hidden away under a stack of bananas in your fruit bowl!"

"Well, thanks for making me feel better," Nancy said flatly and let her head sink into her hands. "Now I'm a lime thief, as well."

"No, no," Jenny said and reached out a hand to touch her friend's arm. "I was only trying to explain how something really insignificant can just domino into this apparently massive problem. And I say 'apparently' because it's not really important, see. It's not your fault at all. It's just the way the world works sometimes."

"Still, the pie's gone up in smoke, hasn't it?"

Jenny shrugged and smiled ruefully. "Yes. More or less. But you still have the recipe, don't you? Besides, I'll bake you a better one. The cheesecake was good, wasn't it?"

"Will you tell me another story, Aunty Jenny?"

"Sure, darling, but another time, okay." She looked at her watch. "I'd better get back to work. Alright, Nance? You'll be okay? Keep me in the loop and give Harry a kiss from me, but only if he's nice to you, okay?"

"Thanks, Jenny. You're a star. And thanks for the treats."

Playing at playing detective

She could keep one entertained for hours, could Jenny, Nancy thought. Martha had certainly had a good time and recovered from her fright. Nancy hoped that most of the implications of the analogy had passed over her head. Of course, it was not a lime that Nancy had stolen, nor a Poinciana blossom, and she still could not really think of it as theft.

Was there a legal definition of theft? It was such a small, simple word. You couldn't even trace its meaning back through a convoluted history that implicated anything else than its current meaning. Like 'flower' and 'child', the word had always been just exactly what it was, give or take a few pronunciation changes. A thief was a thief was a thief.

The toy sale, now attended with Harry's blessing, had been a disappointment. Even for Martha, who had had no ulterior motives for attending, it was surprisingly lacking in, well, surprises. Perhaps the excitement of the Kewpie dolls was just too hard to match. Perhaps there were just so many previously loved toys that one could appreciate before suffering compassion fatigue. For Nancy, the one thing that had been conspicuously absent was Dorothy.

It was hard to tell whether the sorting of toys they had witnessed the previous week had really paid off. There seemed now to have been just one criterion for categorisation—dolls and non-dolls. The former category was of course the biggest by far and there was no discrimination between large and small, human or animal, fluffy or plastic. Baby dolls or rubber ducks—they were all the same, and they were spread out indiscriminately over all available surfaces. The category for non-dolls included a mishmash of toy vehicles, plastic swords, Lego sets, and balls, restricted to three tables at the back of the hall and watched over by a thin bearded man.

There were at least half a dozen Lions Club volunteers, including Alfred and Emilia, Dorothy's companions from earlier, but of Dorothy herself there was no sign. They wandered among the tables, stopping occasionally when something caught Martha's eye. Despite Dorothy's predictions of a limited clientele, the sale had drawn quite a crowd and not merely elderly sentimental shoppers either. In a town with limited entertainment opportunities, apparently even a second-hand toy sale was worthy of a family outing.

Nancy hung around even after they had done the rounds of the tables twice. But Martha was getting fidgety and any hope of Dorothy appearing was dwindling. In the end she approached Alfred to enquire. He did not recognise her from the last time, although he seemed to vaguely remember a woman and child intruding on their toy sorting. But he didn't know where Dorothy was or whether she would be coming in and neither did he have any contact details for her, although Nancy managed to find out that Dorothy's surname was Sheehan. Emilia was of even less help and looked frankly suspicious when Nancy asked about Dorothy's whereabouts. None of the other volunteers could help and when Nancy voiced the opinion that surely there had to be a list of names and telephone numbers, they looked collectively lost and uncomprehending, so she shrugged her shoulders and left, a grateful Martha in tow.

Martha had a rather pragmatic view of toys, an attitude that sometimes leaked into her appreciation of other things and would later in life set her apart as an extraordinarily creative but no-nonsense architect. To her, toys existed for the sole purpose of being played with. Possession alone brought no joy. Having a dozen dolls stacked up on the shelf or in the cupboard just for the sake of having them made no sense at all. Like marionettes, they only came alive when you included them in your life. Wandering around a room full of toys that you couldn't play with was thus the ultimate frustration. A mild anxiety was brewing in her heart. She longed to get back to her own menagerie—her pink elephant, her cutie doll, her cat—on the dot.

Over the last few weeks a tremor of change had passed through Martha's world. A kitten and a cutie doll had arrived in her life on the same day. Then the doll had been taken off her, because it was an old lady's, but it had still been around, in its little box, in and out of her daddy's car. She had then latched on to the baby doll at the library, which her mother had also taken off her because that too belonged to an old lady. This had, however been immediately and miraculously replaced with another cutie doll. The first cutie doll had then completely disappeared. In the meantime, there had been the trauma of her kitten disappearing into hospital for a day and reappearing all bandaged up. Her pink elephant had thus far been untouched by any disappearances, but you never knew. Who knew what could be happening to all her playmates while she was unhappily trooping around here? They had to get back.

"Mommy," she whined as Nancy buckled her up in the back seat. "I want to play with Snail. Are we going home now?"

It was, however, not to be.

Her failure to find Dorothy at the toy sale was only a temporary setback for Nancy. She was determined to clear up the mystery of the photo. At least the volunteers had been able to give her Dorothy's surname. They came from a generation to whom surnames were still important, something you attached to your first name when introducing yourself.

You weren't merely Alfred or Emilia or Dorothy; you were Alfred Welch or Emilia Miller or Dorothy Sheehan. In that way, connections could be established to shared acquaintances with the same surnames—the Welches from out west or the Millers who used to own the service station in Mount Larcom. You could reminisce about famous inhabitants or keep your mouth shut about infamous ones.

The older people generally also had home phones instead of merely relying on mobiles. It would be easy enough to find Dorothy in the telephone directory.

But Nancy had promised Harry that she would return the photo as soon as possible and she would make good on that promise. There was no time like the present. She took the old photo from her handbag and, balancing it on her lap, took a photo of it with the camera on her smartphone. She suddenly realised that she could have saved herself a lot of trouble by merely photographing the photo in the first place. There would then have been no need to borrow it. It could have stayed safely untouched in Cecily's house. Wasn't that how they did it in the spy movies? Such an elementary mistake, my dear Watson. The lime hidden underneath the bananas. Nancy smiled. She would not make a great detective.

For the first half of the twenty minutes it took them to drive to Cecily's house, Martha was uncharacteristically whiny. She made soft moaning noises and fiddled with the seat belt buckle and kicked her feet up and down, generally getting on Nancy's nerves.

"Stop it, Martha," Nancy said. "I have to drop off this photo, okay? I won't be long."

"But Mommy..." Martha drawled.

"Here," said Nancy, reaching over onto the floor of the passenger seat and handing Martha a bunch of rolled-up sales catalogues she had picked up from their driveway this morning. "How about you are the hostess and you have to buy some food to cook for your guests—see what you can find in there and then you tell me what you're going to make for dinner."

This kept Martha quiet for the rest of the drive. She was still paging back and forth through the leaflets when they arrived at Cecily's house. A taxi was just pulling away from the curb. Nancy waited for it to drive away before parking in the same spot. She left the engine running, opened her door and walked up the driveway to the house.

The key having of course been returned to the cleaner, she could not replace the photo where she had found it, among the pile of books. The next best place she could think of was just inside the house. She was about to slip the photo under the front door when she had second thoughts.

Wouldn't it be odd to leave it there? Who was likely to be the first person through the door next—the cleaner, the police, or perhaps Cecily herself? If it was the police, would they scan it for fingerprints? That would set off a whole string of explanations that would inevitably involve Harry and the excavated doll. She now realised that the doll, lying snuggly in its tin box on the coffee table behind the locked door, was in itself a potential cat amongst the pigeons. Not that either she or Harry was guilty of anything, of course.

She stood up from where she had been crouching, indecisively flipping the photo in her hand. Then she walked back to the street and pushed it into the full mailbox, sliding it in over a thick wad of the same junk mail that Martha was currently perusing, sticking out halfway. As she got back into the car, she thought perhaps the mailbox wasn't really a better option after all. Besides, the photo as it now was would probably get damaged. It needed to be in an envelope at least.

Digging around in the car she found an old bill in the glove compartment. She took the bill out of its windowed envelope, replaced it in the glovebox and walked back with the empty envelope. The overflowing mailbox was locked, but by squashing the roll of junk mail down she could just get a finger onto the photo and with minimal effort pull it out again.

She slid the photo into the envelope and retraced her steps up the driveway to the house. No, mailing it would be better after all, more anonymous, she thought. Back to the mailbox.

She pulled the roll of junk mail out, together with two other old catalogues that had not made it completely into the safe cover of the mailbox and were consequently the worse for wear. Whether Cecily was coming home soon or not, Nancy doubted she would miss two weeks' worth of junk mail. She would just throw it away. The mailbox was now significantly less full, and she could easily fit the enveloped photo through its opening. With the envelope held between two fingers, ready to be dropped, she hesitated again—should I, shouldn't I?

A sudden loud barking from next door frightened her into action and she let go. The photo dropped with a soft papery sound onto the other mail, beyond retrieval.

Nancy slid back into the driver's seat with a small sigh. As she reached for the door to close it, a man appeared from nowhere and held the door open. Nancy gasped.

The man's secure grip prevented her from closing the door. There was a faded tattoo of a shark on his forearm and he scowled at her from beneath bushy grey eyebrows. His other hand had a firm hold on a lead at the end of which a Kelpie was excitedly straining forward, wagging its tail furiously while keeping up a high-pitched barking.

"Um... hello," Nancy managed.

"What the hell do you think you're doing?" the man asked.

"Excuse me? I was just... I was..."

"Yes? Snooping around the property while no-one's looking. I saw you last time, lady. Don't think you can get away with it. Shut it up!" he shouted at the dog, giving its lead a jerk which in no way diminished the noisy barking. "I'll have the police on you."

"Mommy?" Martha, who had been totally occupied in virtual meal planning until then, spoke in a scared voice from the back seat. Nancy reached out a comforting hand to her, without taking her eyes off the man. She pocketed her own panic and drew a deep breath before addressing the man.

"I was just delivering something. Now," she said and pulled at the door again. "If you don't mind, we were just leaving."

The man let go of the door so suddenly that it slammed shut, the inside handle catching Nancy on her knee. She yelped. The dog suddenly stopped barking and looked at Nancy, its head tilted quizzically. As she pulled away, Nancy could see in her side mirror the man still gesticulating and glowering at her. Behind her Martha burst into tears.

Of gardens and graves

Cecily wheeled her suitcase into the bedroom and sank down on the bed, stroking her palm over the aquamarine bedspread. It was good to be back. She was exhausted.

There was a dog barking somewhere outside. It sounded like Gareth's. He would have noticed the taxi dropping them off, she supposed. Goodness, he was a sticky beak! She smiled. How he would have liked to know about the adventures she had had the last couple of weeks!

It was good of Michelle to see her safely back. And at last she had been able to show her the garden, Cecily's Folly. She still wondered how they had missed the doll; she was sure that it had to be this garden bed.

"I remember coming back from the funeral and finding Anne in the bathroom, washing the soil off her hands," she had told Michelle. "She was still feverish. She shouldn't have been up at all; it set her back again, and she nearly ended in the hospital. I couldn't believe that flu could do that to a child. She had always been strong and healthy."

"It was a blow, even for me. I had nightmares afterwards, and it wasn't even *my* father."

"Yes. She seemed to slip away from me from then on." The new grevilleas were in full bloom and she touched one delicate flower spike with her fingers. "I found the spade here, and the soil was dug over. I knew she had buried something, but she would never tell me what it was. I only found out later, just before she left. She threw it in my face like an accusation."

"We have laid her to rest now, Cecily."

"We have."

"And I am so glad I could share it with you. But now I must go, or I'll miss my flight. The taxi is still waiting."

Cecily slipped off her shoes and lay down. An hour later, she drifted back into consciousness. She sat up, coughing. Her body still ached at times; the doctor had told her it would be a while before she was back to normal. But being home was a healing balm in itself. A cup of tea would be even better.

When she had made the tea and toasted a slice of banana bread from the freezer, she took it through into the lounge. She would phone Michelle to say a final goodbye. She had been urging her to buy a new mobile phone, but Cecily wondered whether she would go to the trouble. Perhaps it would be easier just to revert to the way she had lived all her life—not unconnected, just connected in a different way.

It was something that few people seemed to understand these days. People were linked in deeper ways. She thought of it as underground connections. A tree's branches did not need to touch those of another one down the street. They could talk in the swaying breath of the wind and the feathery touch of birds. Under the soil their roots reached out to each other and small creatures carried messages of love and remembrance.

She was lost in thought, a wistful smile on her lips, when she saw the scratched cookie tin on the coffee table. It was like walking into a dream.

Of Dorothys and dolls

With the event of the digital revolution and the concurrent boom in ebooks, Nancy had stubbornly refused to believe in the predicted death of paper books. She loved real books and she would not give them up without a struggle. No electronic screen could ever replace the feel and smell of paper and ink.

She had launched a one-woman war and allocated a monthly budget to buy books. She increased her visits to the library from once every fortnight to once and even twice a week and would take out an armful of books, even if she had to return half of them unread. Someone had to boost the statistics and convince the commercial world that people still wanted the real thing.

By the time it finally became clear that printed books weren't going anywhere, anytime soon and that print book sales were again rising, she had a pile of unread books at home and the library personnel were calling her by her first name. Nevertheless, she was no technophobe and loved the immediate availability of knowledge that the internet provided, even if some of it had to be taken with a pinch of salt.

After her failure to find Dorothy again at the toy sale, she was about to give up her quest to solve the Mystery of the Dolls, as she had started to think of it. But the rude man with the dog had, after the initial shock, stirred up an anger in her that not only rekindled her curiosity but set it aflame like a splash of fuel on a smouldering fire. The next morning after breakfast, while Harry accompanied Martha to the park on a father-daughter bicycle "trip", Nancy sat down at her computer and started a search for Dorothy Sheehan.

It failed miserably. Although Google yielded some seventeen people called by that name, none was the Dorothy of the dolls. There was a brief moment of elation when, scrolling through images, she came across a hazy photo that could have been Dorothy in an earlier incarnation, but on further investigation it turned out that the woman with the glasses and dark curls had been a nurse in Virginia, USA, and had been dead for eleven years.

Changing perspective, Nancy then tried to search for teachers from the local schools, but this net was too wide and the holes too big. There were nearly twenty schools in the area and Nancy had no idea where or when Dorothy had been a teacher. This was searching for a needle in a haystack in the digital age—you could use a strong magnet to scan the haystack, but it only shifted your problem. You now had to search for one specific needle among hundreds, not to mention the screws, wires, coins, and lost penknives all attracted to your magnet. A computer hacker in an action movie or the head of the intelligence service might have been able to find Dorothy, but Nancy could not.

If there was any chance of finding her, it would be through footwork and word of mouth and a good bit of luck. Nancy's only links to Dorothy were Cecily and the Lions Club. Since Cecily's disappearance was the reason she was looking for Dorothy, using Cecily to find Dorothy became a circle argument and thus of no use. The Lions Club had thus far not proved of much use either, but it was a resource that, like a closed-down mine, might yield some discarded gems yet for a persistent investigator.

It was easy enough to find the local Lions Club online. The website had not been updated, with the toy sale still advertised on the home page as an upcoming event. Nancy scrolled through all their pages, scrutinising names and photos for any sign of Dorothy, but she was not to be found. There was no telephone number listed, but there was a contact email address and Nancy posted an inquiry asking how she could contact Dorothy.

It being Sunday, that was as much as she could do for the time being. She would just have to be patient.

Taken for a ride

Unlike Nancy (and women in general, he was given to believing), Harry had never had any inherent yearning for children of his own. He liked children in general, as he generally liked people or dogs. Of course he now loved Martha and had done so since her arrival five odd years ago. This had not influenced his desire or not towards having children. However, there were moments when he felt that a child of the male persuasion would have been nice to have. His outing to the park with Martha was a case in point. Whatever the modern tendency towards gender equality, there were certain basic differences between male and female, boy and girl, which were obvious and undeniable in his opinion.

Martha had an untamed streak, and she was no fairy princess, but she was still a girl. This meant that of the three nearest parks available for them to explore on bicycle, only one was suitable. Had she been a boy, as Harry had once been, he was sure she would have preferred Ibis Park or Curlew Park, where the lay of the land had been unadulterated with playground equipment. While the open spaces and bare patches among the trees might have seemed uninviting to the aesthetic eye, it had plenty of natural topography ideal for the ramps and turns and general dare-devilling on wheels that appealed to a boy's adventurous spirit. Even a bicycle still fitted with training wheels like Martha's would not have been enough to deter him.

As it was, Martha showed no interest in these activities of Harry's daydreams and so they turned the other way and cycled the few hundred metres north to Apex Park. Martha did a few turns with her bike on the lawns under the trees, but the thick grass made for heavy going. After a few near misses, she bumped into a eucalyptus and fell to the ground in melodramatic slow motion. She was up again before Harry could reach her, none the worse for wear, but it was the end of her cycling enthusiasm.

"Push me, Daddy!" she cried, running toward the swings. Harry leaned his bicycle against a tree and dutifully followed.

For a while, they were the only ones in the park. Harry found it strangely soothing, giving Martha a gentle push every time the swing's pendulum brought her within reach. Her back under a striped blue T-shirt was warm and real beneath his hand. She talked in spurts of sentences that he could not follow. But her words did not seem to have any communicative function anyway, so there was no need to respond. In the branches above them, noisy miners kept up their own screeching conversations, while a pair of magpies foraged on the ground.

The arrival of three other children, all boys, brought him out of his reverie. Martha was saying something and the lilt of her voice demanded an answer.

"What was that, Martha?"

She repeated what she had said, but she was moving away from him, talking into the flow of air around her face, so that her words were lost in the wind and the bird noises. Harry watched the smallest of the three boys as he waited for her to swing back. He seemed younger even than Martha, with a mop of dark hair, and was rushing for the netted rope climb.

Now there's another fearless creature, he thought. Boys rush in where angels fear to tread. The other two held back, whether from a lack of enthusiasm or a sense of responsibility, looking around at Harry and Martha and the two bicycles. A woman in slacks was coming through the trees towards them and he wondered whether she was the children's mother.

He withheld his hand from Martha's back, slowing her down, and on her next approach she turned her head around inquiringly. He smiled and grabbed hold of the swing's rope, letting its momentum carry him along with her until they came to a stop.

"I can't hear you, possum. What did you say?"

"It's that nice lady, Daddy."

Harry glanced back at the woman, who had now reached the play area where the older boys were standing. She was older than he had thought at first, with undyed grey hair and black-rimmed glasses, more likely to be a grandmother than a mother, and looked out of breath after her walk. She seemed to be admonishing the boys, but in a friendly manner. He did not recognise her as anyone he had ever seen before.

"Do you know her?" he asked Martha.

She nodded, sliding out of the swing seat without further comment. She walked over to where her bicycle stood and held onto it possessively. The woman turned to glance at her and Martha gave a tiny wave.

"Oh, hello," the woman said, her face brightening.

"Hello," Martha replied.

"Are you well? Where's your Mommy?"

Martha hesitated and then nodded, deciding that would be enough answer for both questions. Harry had collected his own bicycle and came towards Martha, nodding at the woman in greeting. She smiled back at him, her cheeks dimpling in wrinkles. He wondered whether he should say something. But Martha had now turned away and was already pushing her bike across the lawn, so he just shrugged in explanation at the woman and followed. They were back on their bikes and on the pathway, heading for home, when Martha cleared up the mystery.

"It's the doll lady, Daddy. She gave me the cutie doll."

Harry considered turning around, but for the moment he couldn't remember what Nancy had wanted with this woman. It had something to do with the photo and the dolls. Some days he just couldn't keep up with her reasoning. He couldn't keep up with Martha either, who was now enjoying at full speed the last downhill stretch before she would have to push her bike up their street. Her bicycle performed its own variation of a speed wobble despite the extra training wheels.

He abandoned all thought of Dorothy and raced to catch up with his daughter.

If her internet search had been a let-down to Nancy, the news that Dorothy had been within hand's reach was an even greater frustration. She groaned.

"Why didn't you say... why didn't you ask her?! Is she still there? I have to find her."

"What was I supposed to tell her?" he asked to Nancy's disappearing back as she rushed out to the car. "I didn't even speak to her. I think. We only..."

Yes, he wondered, what had we done? It wasn't a conversation, really. Or could a nod and a smile and a shrug be called a conversation? Perhaps not. Was it only a conversation when you actually said something, real words? Communication and conversation weren't necessarily the same thing. So perhaps one could say they had communicated. He would have to ask Nancy where the word conversation came from. Converse – didn't that mean opposite? Was conversing the same as opposing, then? Goodness, did anyone ever really know what they were saying, really, literally?

"So?" he asked, when Nancy came back. But her expression was answer enough, more communication without conversation. "No Dorothy?"

"No Dorothy. Another wild goose chase."

"Not her or not there?"

"Not there," said Nancy, cupping her face in her hands and dragging her fingers through her hair. She smiled ruefully at Harry. "The bird has flown," she said. "Any suggestions?"

"Let it go?"

"Argh."

"Oh, come on, Nance, it's not really important, is it? I mean, we returned the doll and we have one of our own, so that seems like a fair enough deal. No use chasing after flown geese, so to speak."

"Perhaps you're right. I would have liked to know, though, about the doll. But I guess a bit of mystery in life is a good thing. Spices things up."

"Even if it is never solved?" he asked.

"Especially if it is never solved."

Tails and tales, revisited

By Monday afternoon, there had been no response from the Lions Club and Nancy was ready to let go of the whole doll story. She also realised that she had neglected to return Snail for a check-up with the vet over the weekend. Not that either the kitten or Martha seemed to mind. Nancy had never seen anyone—human or animal—take to illness with such alacrity as Snail. Or perhaps it was just the attention she thrived upon.

Nevertheless, Nancy had booked in an appointment for the late afternoon to have the bandage removed. They were a few minutes late, because she first had to pick Martha up from kindergarten. Martha, excited to see her cat, had then opened the cat carrier in the car and Snail had slipped under the passenger seat, cone and all, from where she had to be retrieved once they arrived at the vet clinic. They were ushered in immediately. In the doorway of the other consultation room a grey-haired woman stood talking to another vet with her back to Nancy, a young boy of about four clutching at her dress.

Nancy was halfway through the other door, the carrier with Snail carried before her like a shield and Martha shuffling in behind her, when the woman turned around and Nancy recognised her.

"Oh!" she cried, coming to a sudden stop. She pushed the cat carrier into the arms of the baffled vet. "Excuse me. I won't be a second. Dorothy!"

Dorothy smiled in immediate recognition. It is she, thought Nancy on seeing her again. It has to be Dorothy in the photo. Those dimpled cheeks and the small mole beside her mouth were unmistakable.

"Hello, Nancy. What a nice surprise! I saw your little girl only yesterday," she said. She gestured towards Martha, who, torn between her concern for her kitten and the safety of her mother's side, and now confronted with another complicating issue, hovered midway like a cat on a rickety fence.

"I know, I know. I went to look for you and you were gone. Is this your grandson?"

"Yes, this is Neil. He's the youngest. We just brought in a magpie that's been injured. Found it next to the road. They think it might have a broken wing."

"A bird in hand," Nancy said.

"What was that?"

"Oh, nothing, just my mind running away. Listen, Dorothy..." Behind Nancy the vet cleared her throat. "I have to go. Our cat. But could you give me your phone number; there's something I wanted to ask you."

"I'll just wait for you," Dorothy said. "You go on in."

Snail was checked over and pronounced at a satisfying stage of healing, so that her bandage could now be permanently removed, revealing a strangely bare and blunted tail end, decorated with a row of stitches like short misplaced whiskers. Martha frowned at the sight and did not quite trust the vet's pronunciation that it would all become fluffy and nice again. She longed to touch the exposed skin, on which a soft down was now just starting to grow, but did not yet dare. Snail was bundled back into her carrier, the cone to stay on her head for a few more days, and when Nancy had paid, they walked over to where Dorothy and her grandson were waiting.

The boy was staring in fascination at a young Border collie that had crawled under a chair, twining its lead around the legs of both the chair and its owner. The pup's antics had set of a frantic barking from a terrier on the other side of the room. Neil edged closer to the action, but Dorothy grabbed hold of his shirtsleeve and pulled him away. She stood up.

"Shall we go outside?" she asked Nancy, her eyebrows furrowing at the noise.

With Snail safely stowed in the car and the two children surreptitiously eyeing each other from opposite ends of a garden bench outside the clinic, Nancy took out her mobile phone and searched for the photo she had taken of Cecily's photo. She held it out for Dorothy to see.

"The twins," Dorothy said. There were tears in her voice.

"I was a schoolteacher," Dorothy said, nodding towards the two children as if in explanation.

"Yes, I know," said Nancy.

"You know?"

"You told me, when we met in the library."

"Ah, yes, I did." She smiled. "Best years of my life, you know. Best years of theirs."

"With you?"

"Oh no, any child, anywhere. It should be a great time, don't you think—growing up, exploring, learning, making friends. You can't beat childhood for stacking up experiences. They're like sponges."

On the bench Neil and Martha had moved closer together, although keeping up appearances by apparently ignoring each other. Neil was now on his knees, facing backwards over the back of the bench. Martha followed suit. An elderly man with an equally elderly fox terrier came out of the vet clinic's door. As they came nearer, the dog halted, sniffed the ground and lifted his leg against a shrub growing behind the bench, balancing on arthritic legs to dribble his urine against its trunk. The children squealed with equal parts disgust and delight.

Nancy thought she knew enough about young children stacking up experiences to keep Dorothy talking for hours, but she wanted to get back to the photo and Dorothy's connection to Cecily. She touched the screen on her phone and it lit up again.

"And this is you, right?" she asked, indicating the photo. Dorothy nodded. "And the girls—were they your pupils?"

Again, Dorothy just nodded, as if not trusting her own voice. But then she spoke, tersely.

"Michelle," she said, pointing to the girl on the left. "And Anne."

"Twins?"

Dorothy chuckled. "You'd think so, wouldn't you? Everyone thought they were twins. They just looked *so* alike. They had a right royal time taking people for a ride. But no, not twins, though that's what we used to call them."

"And this one—Anne—she is Cecily's daughter?"

"Yes! Yes, that's Anne. You know Cecily? Did she give you the photo?"

"Um... I wouldn't say I know her, exactly. My husband does her garden. But I got the photo from her, or rather that's where I saw the photo, yes."

"Why?"

"You knew Cecily?" Nancy sidestepped the question.

"Of course I did. I still do."

"You know she's been missing?"

"I heard something, yes. We're not bosom friends; I see her once in a while, maybe two or three times a year. But it's still a small town at heart. The boom is all just fluff, window dressing, outsiders coming and going again. Everyone else still knows everything about everyone."

"Hmm. So, the dolls..." She looked from the photo to Dorothy's face and then quickly away. Tears were now flowing freely down the older woman's cheeks. Nancy felt like an intruder. Borrowing a photo from the empty house of a missing person was one thing but poking your nose into the private griefs of someone you barely knew standing right next to you in a very public space, was an entirely different matter. There was something deep and sad at the bottom of this and as much as she wanted to clear up the mystery, she did not want to create any more misery.

She laid a hand on Dorothy's shoulder in comfort and turned towards the children, who had in the space of a few minutes become firm friends. They had found a beetle and were both squatting next to it on the ground. Neil poked at it with a stick, while Martha watched intently. The thought crossed Nancy's mind that their next cat might be called Beetle.

"Michelle was my favourite," Dorothy said, sniffling into a tissue, and Nancy turned back towards her. "I tried not to show it, of course, but children have a way of knowing. I've always felt guilty about that somehow, felt that I had failed Anne, though it was no-one's fault. It could just as well have been the other way round, really. They both suffered for it."

"What happened? Why... where do the dolls come in?"

"They got the dolls as a birthday present. Birthday presents, I should say. Their birthdays were close, though, Anne's first— in October—and Michelle's about a month later. Funny the things you remember. Some birthdates just stick in my head. I can even remember the birthday of my own English teacher— thirtieth of April. Always remember it, for some reason.

"Anyway. The dolls were Cecily's idea and if I remember correctly the girls both got them on Anne's birthday, so that Michelle wouldn't feel left out, you know.

"They became fixated with the dolls, absolutely entranced. You know how it is with children. One toy or game or doll becomes the centre of their world for months on end."

"I know," said Nancy. "I remember we had marbles when I was in primary school. And yoyos, they were another craze."

"Exactly. The girls took those dolls everywhere. The two were more or less inseparable, at school and out of it. Academically they were moderately good, I'd say among the top ten of their class, not that the classes were very large, mind you. But they were lovely girls – well-behaved, polite, caring. I had them from Year Three onwards.

"They lived only a few blocks apart. Their dads were business partners; they had a successful business—building, property development, something like that. And the parents played tennis together, as did I for a while. I was never any good; I mainly did it to please my husband. He played golf."

Dorothy paused, looking at the photo on Nancy's phone with a wistful smile. "I don't remember this photo, but it looks like our house in the background. That tree there is an old she-oak, a lovely old tree. They must have come over to play there."

"But the doll from the toy sale, the Kewpie doll we bought, that's not...?" asked Nancy.

"Oh, no, I don't think so," said Dorothy. "That could be any old doll, I think; the Kewpies were quite popular at some stage. It's just the... I don't know, the trigger, perhaps? The connection that made me think of the twins again."

"Synchronicity."

"If you like."

"Well, yes. Because we found..." Suddenly Nancy wasn't sure how she would tell Dorothy about the doll from Cecily's garden without revealing that Harry had taken it. Although he had already returned it. "So, what happened to the dolls?"

Dorothy sighed. She took the few steps towards the bench which the children had now vacated for a more interesting environment on the ground among the flowers and shrubs. She patted the seat next to her and Nancy also sat down.

"It was at Cecily's house. The girls must have been ten or eleven at the time. There was a party of some sort. I think it was just a dinner party. It was the two couples—Cecily and Jack Stone, and Michelle's parents Margaret Boucher and her husband Malcolm—and my husband Alex and myself, and then another couple we knew, the Wintertons. And of course, the children. We had three boys at that stage, Anne was an only child, Michelle had a younger brother of six or seven, and the Wintertons had two toddlers and a third one on its way. It was a full house, I can tell you!"

"Eight adults and, uh, eight children?"

"That many? Yes, well, it wasn't unusual, really. We seldom used babysitters; the children just went along. They were well-behaved and when they got tired, we packed them off to bed in a room and collected them when we went home.

"It was a lovely evening. We always had lovely evenings. And Jack and Malcolm together were a scream; they could make you laugh till you cried. Literally. Jack was a big man and not only tall but heavy. He played tennis and all, but perhaps he overindulged on the beer afterward, who knows. Cecily never said anything. He was a very social man, outgoing. He also smoked, but most of us smoked, then, although I never could stand the smell of it; it just made me nauseous. They all knew that. I never allowed Alex to smoke in my house. Or maybe it was stress—don't they blame all diseases on stress nowadays?

"So, anyway, we were having dessert and Jack went into the garden for a smoke or perhaps, you know, men like to take a leak against a tree. Like dogs they are. Looking at the stars, they called it. But then he doesn't come back. His dessert sits there half-eaten and we're about to clear the table, when someone—it must have been Cecily—suddenly wonders where he is. And then the twins come in screaming."

"What happened?"

"They'd found him in the garden. Down and out."

"Dead? Not dead?! Oh dear."

"Yes," said Dorothy, wiping the drying tears from her cheeks. "Dead as a... Dead."

"Heart attack?"

"Yes. We stormed out, well, the men did. We tried to comfort the girls. Cecily was stunned, pale as a sheet. They were in shock, of course; we all were. The men tried to revive Jack, but it was too late. We called the ambulance, but he was already gone. Just turned forty and with a young daughter."

"How terrible! The girls... Oh god!"

"Yes. It somehow melded them together even closer. I've often thought it was like a lightning strike on two rocks lying next to each other. It melted them, melted them into each other, you know? They had shared this horrible experience and the only way to turn that they could think of, that made any sense, was towards each other. It was hard on Cecily, seeing her daughter turn towards someone else for comfort and leaving her out in the cold."

Nancy nodded.

"But the dolls?"

"I'm coming to that," said Dorothy, smoothing her dress over her thighs. "Margaret and Malcom were from England, originally. I think Michelle must have been born over there. They'd been in the country for some years, say seven of eight, perhaps more. But after Jack's death, the business floundered. Malcolm just couldn't cope, couldn't get it on track again without Jack. They had all their family in England still, Margaret's parents and sisters and Malcolm's mom and so on. So, they left, went back there within the year."

"And the children? The 'twins'?"

"Poor girls, they were heartbroken. I don't know who had it worse, Michelle going back to a birth country about which she wouldn't remember anything or Anne staying behind without her dad, in the very house where the tragedy had happened. Of course, I don't know what happened to Michelle, but Anne didn't cope very well.

"She turned inwards, no-one could get through to her. We discussed her, Cecily and I, many a time. I tried to help, but she rejected everybody. She turned into a sulky teenager, left school as soon as she could. Cecily offered to send her over to England to visit Michelle, but I think by then they weren't even in contact anymore."

"What happened to her, to Anne?" asked Nancy. "Does she still visit Cecily?"

Dorothy sighed and wiped at her eyes again before looking up. She held Nancy's gaze for a long moment before looking down into her lap, where her hands were knitted into an anxious tangle.

"She just left, went north somewhere. Had Cecily frantic with worry. Then she phoned one night from a friend's house in Bowen, before... She... There was a beach party; she must have had too much to drink. No-one really knew what happened, whether it was an accident or... Anyway, she drowned."

Nancy could not speak. It felt as if someone had ripped out her throat. She blinked her eyes, dazed.

"Now the dolls," Dorothy continued. "Michelle presumably took hers with her. Anne—she was very sick with flu on the day of her father's funeral and had to stay at home. So, she buried her doll in the garden." She gave a sad chuckle. "It must still be there, somewhere in Cecily's beautiful garden."

Gluing things together

When they arrived home, Nancy was surprised to see Harry's ute already parked in the carport. It was only four. She still felt raw with the news about Anne's death and the buried Kewpie doll and was looking forward to unburdening by sharing her grief with Harry. She had been prepared to hold out, like coping with a painful wound while you sat in the doctor's waiting room. But now there would be an early reprieve.

She smiled eagerly, pushing Martha in front of her down the pathway to the door. Martha had spent the morning making hand puppets out of old socks at kindy and had insisted on putting them on in the car. The blue shaggy-haired, button-eyed puppet on her right hand was having an intense conversation with the too small whiskered red sock on her left hand, which by some inexplicable rule of quantum physics slowed down her feet, so she stumbled under her mother's impatient shove. Nancy was obliged to carry her daughter's bag and hat, as well as the cat carrier, with her own handbag slung over her shoulder.

They reached the front door in a jumble of elbows and knees and captive fingers, just as Harry opened it from inside. He put out a hand to keep Martha from falling, pulling off two inexpertly glued-on sock whiskers in the process. Martha looked at him in distress.

"Daddy! My whiskers!" she cried.

"I'm sorry, darling," he said. "I'll fix it."

"You're a murderer!"

"Yes," he said. "So they say. Hello, Nancy."

"You're home early," she said and, having regained her balance, planted a kiss on his lips. "I've got news."

"Yes?"

"Can we go inside? Or were you going out again?"

"No, um, it can wait. Come in."

"I found out about the doll, from Dorothy," she said, pushing past him into the house, a wailing Martha in tow.

They released Snail from her carrier. Then while they hunted for a tube of glue and tried to glue the puppet whiskers back on and found that project glue does not easily stick to cotton socks and finally resorted to needle and thread to restore the puppet to its former glory, Nancy told Harry all about the twins and the Kewpie dolls and why one had been buried in Cecily's garden.

"She must have known about it, then," said Harry.

"Who? Cecily?"

"Yes. And she must have known that it was buried in that garden bed. I wonder..."

"Yes, I see. I see! Why didn't she tell you before you started digging? Do you think it has anything to do with her disappearance? Maybe we should tell the police. It could mean something."

"The police," said Harry, sighing, "would be only too happy to know."

"Why do you say that?" Nancy asked.

"I'm actually on my way to see them. Come, sit down and I'll tell you before I go."

But Nancy was too restless to sit down, so they stood talking at the kitchen counter. She listened with increasing agitation, her fingers nervously playing with the glue and thread and tufts of old sock spread on newspaper among the fruit bowl and a dirty coffee cup left over from lunch. From her room they could hear Martha's resumed sock dialogue.

"I haven't told you about the spade," Harry confessed.

"Your missing spade? What has that got to do with anything?"

"Remember the neighbour found it in his shed?"

"Yes. And you went to fetch it."

"Except it wasn't there when I got there. The police had confiscated it."

"Why? When?"

"A random coincidence."

Nancy was going to protest this tautology—a dead corpse, she winced, a round circle!—stopping to correct it, but she ignored the impulse and left Harry to continue.

"Before I got there, one of the officers went back for something and saw the spade. It had some marks on the back. Turns out it's blood. They think it's Herbert's blood, male, same blood group and so on. They're going to do a DNA analysis as well, to confirm it."

"What?! But... I thought he had drowned. And how... I mean, I know it's your spade, but..."

"It doesn't prove anything, I know. I don't know how the spade got there, I don't know why it's got his blood on it, but it has. Which is why they have been digging up the new garden bed."

"What?! Fred's? That you planted? Why, do they think... Do they..."

"I'm the suspect again. The gardener, remember?" Harry grinned unconvincingly. "Always the first suspect."

"So Herbert didn't drown? But didn't he go fishing in the storm? You said they found his boat."

"They found the boat, but no body. And then the spade."

"For god's sake, Harry, when? Why didn't you tell me?"

"I didn't want to upset you. Besides, I didn't do it, didn't kill anyone. And now..."

"Of course you didn't!"

"But the spade made me a suspect. And now..."

"You probably forgot it there and Herbert used it and... Maybe he hurt himself and got some blood on it. *Before* he went fishing. How could he go fishing after someone had killed him? How could he be dead and *then* drown?"

"I don't know. But," Harry paused, drawing his fingers through his hair, "but now, they *have* found him. Herbert. That's why I have to go in again. God knows why I would want to kill poor Herbert. I can think of some people I might want to kill, but Herbert is not one of them."

"I'll get straight to the point, Harry," said DI Brian Parker. "As you now know, we have found Herbert Ainsley's body."

"Yes," said Harry. And it wasn't in my garden beds, he thought, still silently fuming at the upheaval—literally, Nancy, literally—that the diggers had caused to the newly planted garden.

"I apologise for messing up your garden. But," the detective patted the neat stack of documents in front of him into an even neater pile, "you understand the seriousness of the situation."

"I understand, Detective."

"You're not going to ask me where we found him?"

"I suspect you're going to tell me, anyway."

"He was buried."

"What? I thought he drowned."

"Do you now? Well, maybe he did. But the cyclone did us a favour—swirled him around and then buried him under a layer of sand at Canoe Point. Someone saw his foot sticking out."

Harry's spine tingled. He imagined Nancy and Martha coming across a body while walking on the beach. He stared at Brian Parker.

"Okay. Now, if you could just remind me, Harry—for how long have you known the deceased?"

"If you mean Herbert, I don't really know him."

"Yes, but you do his garden. You did his garden."

"I do the garden of the property, under the instruction of Fred Holmes, the owner. I seldom had any contact with Herbert."

"Alright, let's accept that for the time being. You don't know him. But for how long have you been doing his garden? And let's just assume it's his garden, please, and not get tied up in semantics."

"I think it's been just over a year now," Harry said. "The old people moved out and then the house was empty for a couple of months before he moved in."

"And you," the detective said, leaning forward with a frown, "didn't get to know him at all? In a year's time?"

"He comes and goes, Inspector," said Harry. "He's either working or sleeping or fishing when I'm there. So, no. I've met him, of course. We have a quick chat now and then, but mostly he keeps to himself. He seems a nice enough bloke. Seemed."

Parker nodded, tapping a finger on his documents. He opened the top file and extracted a few pages, stapled at the top corner, then closed the file again and put them on top, tapping the stack into alignment before continuing. There was a photo of someone attached to the papers. From his upside-down vantage point Harry couldn't see who it was, but it wasn't Herbert. It looked like a woman with dark hair.

"Now, Harry, for how long have you known Tanika Watson?"

"What?" This was such an unexpected turn that for a second Harry could not remember who Tanika was. Her name was like a Russian phrase in the middle of an English sentence and his brain stumbled before recognising it. He guessed that it was her on the photo.

"Watson, Tanika Watson. You do know *her*?"

"Of course I do. She's my estate agent."

"*Your* estate agent?"

Who is the one getting tied up in semantics now? thought Harry. He shrugged. "I have some properties I rent out. Gardening is not the most lucrative business."

"Some properties. Three to be exact, yes? And you have known Miss Watson for about..." Parker made a show of consulting his notes, "... ten months?"

"I guess so."

"Not to mention that she recently moved into your street. Quite handy, that."

"It's not my street!" Harry protested.

Parker held up a hand. "Now, now. What would you say is the nature of your relationship with Miss Watson?"

Harry felt himself blushing under Parker's direct gaze. He remembered the smell of sweet spices and Tanika's appearance at his open car window.

"As I said, she's my estate agent, at Real Property. She took over from Helen as property manager."

"An improvement, would you say?" Parker asked with a slyly insinuating smile. He tapped on the photo of Tanika on the page in front of him.

"She's still fairly new. But she's capable. We get on well enough."

"Capable." He paused just long enough to make the word expand with all kinds of possibilities. "She is also, of course, the agent for Fred Holmes and for the deceased Mr. Ainsley." The detective looked at Harry, waiting for a response, as if this latest statement should be of some considerable significance. Harry could not think what he was getting at and shrugged without answering.

"You don't find that strange, Harry?"

"Um... no?"

"No? Such a *capable* woman, able to handle the affairs of all these men."

"I am sorry, Inspector," said Harry, his hackles rising. "But what exactly are you driving at?"

"I'll ask you again – what was your relationship with Tanika Watson?"

"Listen, Inspector, if you're trying to insinuate that I had some kind of, some... that I had an... some personal relationship with her, you're dead wrong!"

"An affair would be the word you're looking for, Harry. Dead wrong, am I? As dead as Herbert Ainsley? No, just sit back down, please. Thank you." He tapped the files again. "We have reason to suspect a little affair between you and miss Watson. 'Your house or mine'—does that ring a bell?"

"That's... just..." Harry said.

"The walls have ears, Harry. We'll need to look at your mobile and your emails, of course."

"That can't be evidence enough. We were joking!" Harry said, shaking his head.

"Ha!" DI Brian Parker leaned back in his chair, his arms stretched out straight, palms down on the table. "I'm still digging, Harry Green, digging in the good old dirt like a gardener. And who knows what we'll come up with? We now have Herbert and he is still going to tell us a few things, even after a fortnight. Sand does a better job at preserving bodies than water does, Harry. Looks like someone gave Herbert a mighty smack on the head.

"So, let me warn you. We have your spade. We can prove beyond a reasonable doubt that the blood on it is Herbert's. Someone—and I'm not naming any names—whacked him one with your spade and then someone dumped him in the river.

"You had means. You had opportunity. All we lack is motive. Something like, let me see, passion? Jealousy? That's as good a motive as you can get."

"I still don't get it. Even if I had an affair with Tanika—which I didn't—why would I kill Herbert? What has he got to do with anything? I told you, I didn't even know him!"

"Oh, but your dear agent did," smirked the detective. "No use denying it."

"No, but..."

"She wasn't just his agent, either. Lovely miss Tanika Watson knew our Herbert very well, didn't she? She knew him in the Biblical way, you might say. Now that's what I call real property. Enough to make any other man *green* with envy, not so, Harry?"

Parker smiled at his own pun. He pushed back his chair and got up. "Thank you, Harry, you can go. For now. Oh, and better get those plants back into the ground, hey?"

Someone else's property

Harry was already halfway through his flat white before Tanika arrived. The coffee scalded his throat as he quaffed the rest in big nervous gulps.

"Hi," he said, pushing back his chair. "I need a refill. What are you having?"

"Sorry I'm late, Harry. I'll have a green tea, thanks."

It was the kind of thing Nancy used to drink way back when they were still dating—green tea or camomile or some herbal infusion—and it made Harry even more uncomfortable ordering it for another woman.

"What's up, Harry?" Jenny asked, coming up to the counter as he was paying for the new order. She nodded at Tanika in her red Real Property work shirt. "Property issues?"

"I guess you could call it that," he said. "How're you doing?"

When he had called Tanika after his visit to the police station, she was about to head out to an acreage property on her way home and had suggested a quick meeting away from the sticky-beakers at her office. A meeting between owner and agent would not have been anything out of the ordinary and Harry would have preferred the anonymity of the familiar, so in an immediate countermove he had suggested the Blue Bower, where the presence of Jenny, his wife's best friend, would at least prove that the meeting was no lover's tête-à-tête.

They exchanged a few pleasantries and then Harry returned to his table. The café closed at five-thirty and they were the last customers. Tanika had a work folder open in front of her but closed it when Harry sat down.

"Busy?" he asked.

She started to say something, then shrugged and sighed.

"Look, Harry," she said, looking down at her hands on the folder. Her nails were painted a dark red, but the pedicure was spoiled by signs of nail biting. The sparkling silver bracelet was gone from her wrist. "I'm sorry that you got involved in this. It's about Herbert, isn't it?"

"Um... yes," he said.

"It wasn't an affair, you know." She looked up and her eyes were shiny with tears.

Harry swallowed at the offending word rolling so easily off Tanika's red lips. "Um... no?"

"It was a relationship. I mean, what's wrong with that? Neither of us were married," she said, her voice taut. She swallowed.

"I'm sorry. I really didn't know. About you and Herbert. I'm sorry that he's dead, but..." He broke off as the waitress brought their drinks. "Thank you."

Tanika nodded, her eyes bright with tears. "I wasn't sure, you see. It was so precious and wonderful, and I just wanted to hold onto it for a bit, for myself, before telling anyone. I was afraid it would disappear once other people knew. That's why we kept it secret."

"I understand." He wished he could comfort her but under the circumstances he did not dare.

"And now he's dead." She stifled a sob. "I'm so sorry about your garden; I couldn't believe they would do something like that. And now they've found him, did you know?"

"Yes. Yes, I know. Look, Tanika," he said, biting his lip and looking away from her lovely face where the tears were ruining her make-up. "I don't know what happened between you and Herbert, and it's your private business as far as I'm concerned. But why does the police think we... you and I... that we had something going on?"

She gave him a blank look. Her eyes darted to the sides.

"Because that's what the police are saying," he continued. "Apparently, I was having an... an affair with you, as was Herbert. So I got jealous and bumped him off with the spade. A crime of passion, it's called. A lover's triangle."

"I should have told you earlier," she said, pursing her lips and looking away again. Then she suddenly looked back at him, eyes wide. "My God! Of course!"

"Yes? Well, it's none of my business. But could you tell the police? About us. Not about us, about not-us. Whatever, you know. There are two sides to a story. And three sides to a triangle, of which I am not one, okay? I mean, just tell them we aren't... involved. I don't care about you and Herbert. Sorry, I don't mean that in a bad way. It's just..."

"It's not Herbert. I wasn't talking about Herbert."

"Not?" Harry said, frowning.

"No, I meant..." Tanika stopped. Her face suddenly stiffened as she stared over Harry's shoulder.

Harry turned around in his chair. His heart sank as he recognised the man walking towards them with a grin on his face.

"Look what we have here," said Detective Inspector Parker. "A lover's tryst, a twosome! Well, the triangle is about to get squared. Don't get up, Harry. Miss Watson, we'd like another word, please. Somewhere private?"

Tanika got up, leaving her tea unfinished. She gave Harry a glance and a shrug that could have meant anything. Harry watched her guided out of the café by the detective, who followed the undiminished sway of her hips with a cynical look. Neither looked back.

He slowly sipped at his coffee, pondering the ways of attraction. You could not hide sexual allure, just as you could not hide a body in a flower bed. Should you even try? As he left the restaurant, waving a goodbye to Jenny, he found himself wishing for the uncomplicated days pre-Tanika. How did he ever get pulled into this maelstrom?

Cecily returned

The phone rang on Tuesday morning while Harry was brushing his teeth. He grunted something indecipherable hoping Nancy, scrabbling around half-naked in the walk-in wardrobe looking for clothes, would be able to answer it. He flushed and spit and turned around to see her holding out his ringing mobile as if it were an Eastern brown snake just woken from its winter hibernation.

The phone was lighting up, undeniably, with the name 'Cecily'. Harry thought, in no particular order, or perhaps all at the same time, such is the workings of the human brain under stress—police, missing and murdered, Herbert, spade, doll, police. Then he pressed an index finger to the green answer icon, while Nancy, still in her pyjama knickers, watched him, a pink T-shirt clutched against her naked breast. She looks like Martha with her elephant, Harry thought inconsequentially, it's the same colour pink.

"Harry speaking," he said cautiously.

"Good morning, Harry. How are you?"

"Cecily? Is that you?"

"Yes, of course, Harry. Are you well?"

"But, aren't you…" He couldn't think of a word that would make sense. Gone? Missing? Dead? "We thought…"

"Yes, I'm sorry about last week, Harry. I stayed away a bit longer than planned." She gave what sounded like a happy chuckle. "I would have let you know, but I'd lost my phone. We were going to look up the number, but then I was in hospital and, anyway, it's looking good, isn't it?"

"It is," Harry said slowly, thinking *We? Hospital? Good?*

"The garden, I mean. It's looking really good, thank you, Harry."

"You're welcome," he said. And repeated for the benefit of Nancy, who was staring at him in disbelief, "You're welcome, Cecily. I'm glad that you're back."

"You had some good rain here."

"We had."

"Not as much as we had. Up north, I mean." She chuckled again, like a schoolgirl with a happy secret she could now share. "I've never seen so much water, Harry. Not in my life and I've been alive a long time."

"I know. And we saw it on the news, the flooding. Were you okay?"

"Oh, we had an adventure! We got a bit wet. Look, I'll tell you next time. Tomorrow? No, it's next week, isn't it, when I'll see you again?"

"Yes. But... your phone..."

"I lost it at the Coffee Club and then someone handed it in to the police. I only got it back yesterday. So, Harry, the garden bed—did *you* find the box? With the doll? Only, it was in my lounge, you see, when I got back."

"Um, yes, well... I'm glad you're safe, Cecily."

"Thank you so much, Harry. We'll talk next week, then. Bye now."

Fred's affairs

As much as he wanted to rush to Cecily to see her in person, to confirm that he wasn't dreaming, and to hear her explanation, there were more pressing matters on Harry's agenda. Now that the police had found Herbert's body, he had been given permission to restore Fred's garden to its previous undisturbed state. Well, thank you very much, but shouldn't they have restored it themselves?

Somehow, he had been expecting and yes, dreading, that the police would still be all over the place. But there was no sign of them. Instead, it was Fred's white car that was parked in the driveway. There was, however, no sign of Fred.

Harry knocked on the front door, though he wasn't sure what he expected. Cecily may have come back from the dead, but surely Herbert was in no position to do so and Fred wasn't going to be inside either. There was no answer, so he pushed open the side gate, now without police tape, and walked around to the back.

He groaned at the site of the garden. More than half of the plants had been removed and the garden bed dug up like a tilled land. The plants were stacked on the lawn against the shed. Although the policemen had taken care to put each root ball in a plastic bag, without the support of a pot the soil was falling away, and the plants leaned sideways like a group of drunken blokes against a bar.

The door to the shed stood open and not having spotted Fred anywhere else, Harry looked inside. Fred was sitting on an upside-down wheelbarrow that Herbert kept in the shed alongside a collection of crates, toolboxes and camping gear. It smelled of mould and rust and stale fertiliser.

As Harry's silhouette darkened the doorway, Fred looked up. His movements were slow and listless. He seemed to Harry bowed down in despair.

What did he really know about his client? Only that he was some kind of engineer, either semi-retired or only employed part-time. That he presumably had a wife in Bundaberg who never accompanied him on his visits up here. That he did not share his tenant's love of fishing. That he preferred foxtail palms to golden cane palms. In fact, he knew even less about Fred than he did about Cecily. It was the realisation of how unconnected he was to any of his clients, even those he had "known" for years, that now made Harry's shoulders slump, rather than the sight of Fred's sad demeanour.

"Harry." Fred got up to shake his hand.

"Morning, Fred. I didn't expect you here. You saw the garden?"

"I did, yeah. Bastards! It was looking so good."

"Yes. Looking for Herbert. What a waste! I suppose you know they've found him."

Fred blanched. He looked around the shed as though searching for something. Then he went back to his seat on the wheelbarrow.

"They've found Herbert," he pondered. He waved a hand vaguely around the shed. "Take a seat somewhere, if you want."

Harry surveyed the layer of dust on the shelves and the crates and tools and on a stack of old newspapers. There were some fold-up camping chairs in their carry bags leaning against what looked like an old boat engine and he contemplated pulling one out. He could not see any other way that he could practically or comfortably sit down. Besides, he wanted to get back to the garden and get the plants back into the ground. He was in no great mood for conversation.

"I'm good, thank you. I'll stand."

"As you wish." Fred stopped speaking and chewed on his lip, considering. His eyes clouded over and he stared at his feet on the dirty shed floor without seeing. Then he shrugged and heaved a heavy sigh.

"My wife just called," he said. "They're looking for me, the police."

"Looking for you? Are you also, um, missing?" Harry asked, knowing it sounded daft, but at this stage anything was possible. He wouldn't have been surprised if Fred had declared him, Harry, to be missing as well. Although lost was perhaps a better word.

"What? I don't know. Am I?"

"Why would they otherwise be looking for you?"

"I'm married," Fred said, as if that explained everything.

Harry was getting more and more confused. If Fred's wife had just called, it went without saying that he would be married, he thought. But why on earth would the police be looking for him? Had he done something to his wife? He could not think of any reasonable reply, so he just nodded gravely. Go with the flow.

"Happily married," Fred went on. "Heading for twenty years now, can you believe it? Me and Francis. You haven't met Francis, have you? No, you haven't. She never comes along. She doesn't like this place, never did. And I get it, you know. Six years. I get it."

Harry didn't get it, but he nodded in understanding and waited for Fred to continue.

"Anyway, we go back a long way. We've been through some stuff together, had our share of arguments and mishaps, I suppose, like everybody else. She's threatened to leave me before. Hell, she did leave me once! For a week, then she was back.

"She's just... She's an angel, you know. Six years she put up with this place. And me on FIFO for most of that time – fly-in fly-out, fly-in fly-out. It's hard on a relationship."

No relationship was always plain sailing, Harry thought. Yet people persisted in loading extra stress onto the fragile threads that knit relationships together. Many people in this town had FIFO jobs. He himself had once considered applying. You flew in to a work site—mainly in the mining industry—did your shift of seven or ten or twelve days and then flew back home for a similar period of rest. It was all about the money. The pay was good, and the mining company did not have to invest in permanent housing, infrastructure, and the general social niceties that made up a village or town. No schools or churches or cinemas or parks, no malls or professional services or garden centres. But it could wreak havoc on a marriage. Why this was something Fred suddenly felt impelled to discuss with his gardener, Harry couldn't guess.

"So, a man gets lonely, you know. And we weren't only blokes doing FIFO and... Anyways, I had a bit of something with this girl at the site. Long story short, Francis finds out, leaves, comes back, I get a job in Bundaberg and we're out of here. All good. Even the property market colluded. We had tenants in two ticks. And a great gardener." He flashed a quick smile at Harry.

"Sit down, Harry. You're making me nervous."

"I'm good, thanks," Harry repeated, but relented enough to move over to the grimy work counter and lean against it. Fred waited until he was settled before continuing.

"So, we got our first tenants. That was a bit before your time." For a moment Fred mused in silence and Harry wondered whether there had been another "bit of something" with a tenant. He had an uneasy feeling about where the conversation was heading.

Fred wasn't a handsome man. Not that he was unpleasant to look at, but his face lacked a certain unity of design. His nose was a bit too long and his eyes a bit too small. His cheekbones were undefined and his chin too prominent. But he had a full head of dark hair just touched by grey and when he smiled something shifted in his face, as if for those brief moments everything was indeed in perfect place and designed by a master.

He smiled now, but grimly, and his eyes were those of a caged animal.

"We used Real Property from the start. Always had good service. Oh, maybe not always. We once had an issue with a plumber that they'd called in for a blocked drain, that I didn't like. Wouldn't use him again. But for the rest, they've been good." He looked up at Harry. "But you also use them, of course. Not the plumbers. The estate agents."

"I do," Harry said. "And they're good, yes. I don't have any complaints."

"Helen – did you know her?"

"I did." Surely not Helen, thought Harry. Fred and Helen? His mind did not want to go there. "Dark hair, shortish and... She was Irish, I'm sure."

"That's her. Solid."

Harry grinned cautiously. Helen had indeed had her feet firmly on the ground in more ways than one.

"Now Tanika," Fred continued, shaking his head and blowing a sigh through his lips. "Oh, man."

The light went on for Harry. Fred and Tanika! Did Fred fall into that delicious trap? And did she find his smile a fatal attraction? Or could he have some other hidden charms? Harry had never pretended to understand the minds of women, especially not when it came to their attraction to men.

Then he had another thought—wasn't Tanika supposed to be having an affair not-affair with Herbert?

Fred was looking at him with eyebrows raised and head tilted. "You know?" he said.

Harry shrugged, looking away.

"I mean," Fred continued. "I just... God knows, I love my wife. I love Francis. But sometimes..." He waved a hand as if shooing away flies. "Sometimes, I don't know, I just need to breathe. Damn, Harry, I..."

Harry waited. There were many things he could have said, about fidelity and trust and triangles and consequences, but it all seemed too complicated, like a parcel wrapped with multiple layers of criss-crossing tape. He didn't know where to start, so he just stared at Fred, waiting.

"Okay. I'm just going to tell you. So." Still Fred wavered, blinked. "Okay. So, we hit it off, Tanika and I. Big time. Lots of empty houses, you know. I came up every couple of months or so. You know that. Just for a few days at a time, a weekend. And she's okay with that."

"She is?"

"Oh come, it's not serious, really. It's not even an affair; it's just a ..."

"A bit of something."

"Yeah," Fred smiled, relieved. "Exactly, and I mean..."

They both startled as Harry's mobile rang in his pocket. He peered at the screen, raised his eyebrows, and looked at Fred before walking out of the shed to answer it. When he came back after a few minutes, there was a look of baffled surrender on his face.

"It was my wife," he said. "The police are, um, looking for me." And yes, he thought, I am missing, completely lost.

Triangles and other calculations

They waited in the shed, Fred on his wheelbarrow and Harry against the workbench. After some minutes of uneasy silence, Harry picked up one of the camping chairs, shook it out of its bag and carried it outside, where he sat on the lawn, looking at the sad garden, until the police arrived soon afterwards.

DI Brian Parker strolled into the garden with Berkley in tow. He smiled tightly at Harry, who stood up from his chair to face the detective.

"Good day, Harry. Gardening, are you?"

"Detective. I'm trying my best. But I keep getting interrupted."

"So sorry, Harry. Think of me as your ad break. But," Parker relented, "we might be able to stop interrupting you. So, here's what's happening. As you know, we have some evidence pointing to you assaulting Herbert Ainsley. Really, I should just arrest you on suspicion of murder. Prime suspect." He shrugged. "Fortunately for you, there's some inconclusive evidence."

"Inconclusive?"

"Berkley?"

Berkley nodded at his superior and cleared his throat. "We have recovered Ainsley's body. From the beach. He drowned. Oh, did you know that? Sorry. So, we have matched the blood on your spade with his. That creates enough evidence to arrest you, as the inspector has pointed out. What you also probably know..."

"Oh, get on with it!" Parker interrupted. "You're like a bloody lawyer. Point is, Harry—the spade with which you bashed in Herbert's head matches the wound on that head, which we have now found."

"You've found his head?" Harry asked incredulously.

"No, no. You know we found his body, which happens to have his head attached, which forensics tells us happens to have been bashed in by *your* spade."

"But you just said he drowned."

"He did, he did," said Berkley. "But only after..."

"He died from drowning after being bashed on the head," said Parker impatiently. His eyes flicked to the open shed door and Harry thought he saw a flicker of amusement in his face.

"But he went fishing. He could have hit his head on a rock."

"Not so. The injury to his skull matches a blow from a spade. So, all you have to tell us now, Harry, is how you got him into the river."

"What? You're not serious! How? Why? Why would I even do something like that?"

"There's no shortage of motive, Harry," said Parker.

"Surely you don't still believe... Didn't...?" Harry now also looked at the shed. Was Fred hearing all this? Telling Parker about Fred's affair with Tanika could exonerate him by shifting the blame squarely onto Fred's shoulders. As much as he deserved it, Harry couldn't make up his mind whether he should expose Fred.

"As I told you before. Passion is always an excellent motive. What with the lovely miss Tanika sharing her properties and all. You..."

They all looked up as there came a loud clanking from the shed, followed by the appearance of Fred. He had a splintered piece of timber in his hands and he looked murderous.

"You!" he shouted at Harry. "You too!"

Harry shrunk away, keeping the camping chair between him and Fred. Parker and Berkley, however, stood their ground. Now there was a definite glint of amusement in Parker's eye. He stroked a hand over his thin hair as if patting a cat.

"As I predicted, the triangle squared. Mr. Holmes, what a totally expected pleasure."

A walk in the park

Chris was at the barbeque with his back to them, gently blowing into the fire to encourage it into flowering. Jenny spotted them and waved them over. She stood up to hug Nancy.

"No Martha?"

It was a glowing Saturday afternoon after yet another rain shower the previous evening. Every man and his dog were out and about in the parks or on the beach. At the adjacent picnic hut a family of eight or more were sprawling onto the lawn with food carriers, eskies, chairs and strollers. A small black poodle tied to a chair leg kept darting in and out under the chair, in which a large woman sat as if she had been poured in.

"She's with a friend," said Nancy.

"Oh?"

"Yes, can you believe it? His name is Neil, and he has, according to Martha, two dogs and a rabbit and a cage full of budgies."

"A boy?" asked Chris, waving wood-smoke out of his eyes.

"A boy," said Harry. "Already."

"You'd better watch out, Harry," laughed Jenny. "Your father-daughter relationship is about to get complicated."

"Don't talk to me about relationships," groaned Harry.

Jenny glanced at Nancy, who smiled and shook her head. She poured herself a glass of white wine and clinked it against Jenny's. "Cheers!"

There was a responding chorus of clinks all round. Harry joined Chris at the fire. The warm afternoon air around them warbled with the sounds of summer.

"So, it turns out you're not a murderer after all," said Chris.

"I'm not. I'm not a murderer and I'm not an adulterer, either."

"Well, thank God for that."

"Indeed," said Nancy.

"Nancy tells me it was the neighbour, what's his name?" asked Jenny.

"Not the neighbour, the owner, Fred. I still can't quite believe it. I mean, I know the man. I thought I did. Anyway, he's not really a murderer."

"But he *is* an adulterer." Nancy banged a fist on the concrete table to emphasise her statement.

"So he is," Harry agreed.

"But there was a neighbour."

"There always is. Ask Nancy, she reads all those murder mysteries and apparently, except for the cleaner and the gardener, they always suspect the neighbour."

"Oh shoot, Harry, that's not what I said!"

"You did, you did. You said..."

"Okay, but tell Chris about the neighbour," said Jenny.

Harry looked at Nancy, lifting his eyebrows. She looked back, her eyes narrowed. Then she grinned. He lifted his beer in salute.

"There you go. Nancy will tell you. Ready for the meat, Chris?"

"Right," Nancy began. "There are two neighbours. Not neighbours of each other or even near each other. That's what neighbour originally meant, you know—a nearby farmer. Anyway... but I wish *you* could tell it, Jenny, you're just a much better storyteller than me."

Jenny waved her off with a laugh, but then relented, embroidering it with the gift of a natural raconteur.

"Two people went missing in different parts of town and two neighbours watched. They did not see their neighbours disappear, but they saw enough.

"Fred was a womaniser, which in my opinion makes it sound way too romantic, like a Don Juan opera, and it's just the way with men and it's all okay. He has a fling here and a fling there and meanwhile he's actually married. His poor wife just has to put up with his shenanigans. Until she's had enough.

"She gives him an ultimatum and they move down to Bundaberg, where she has been wanting to go forever and where he is closer to home and she can keep an eye on him. Except of course they still have the property up here and he keeps a close eye on *that*, especially when the estate agent changes to the delectable, what was her name again? Yes, Tanika. In which Fred meets his match. Because Tanika is really something for the eye and she doesn't mind advertising it either *and* she doesn't mind keeping a few balls in the air at the same time, excusing the pun.

"So, Fred and Tanika has this thing going. Until Tanika meets Herbert. Then she starts shedding Fred like an old skin. Now Herbert is a bit of a hermit, a lone crab who just pops his head out to work and then goes fishing. So, when he goes missing, at first everyone thinks he's just gone fishing. Everyone except Tanika, who had a liaison planned for which he never shows up. And of course Fred, his landlord.

"You see, Fred did have a bit of flu going into that weekend, as he told Harry and the police, the storm weekend. Well, a bit of flu, which actually means the man flu, doesn't it?" Chris looked away from the barbeque to grin at her but didn't comment. She took a sip of wine before continuing.

"Now Fred is moaning and groaning and feeling sorry for himself and possibly, just possibly, hinting that another woman would have been more sympathetic. His poor wife has to run around keeping him happy, until he presumably takes it too far and she's had enough. He says, she says, and on Friday night somewhere after midnight—which would make it

Saturday morning—she says enough is enough and she kicks him out. She literally throws his car keys at him and locks him out of the house.

"Old Fred mopes around a bit and then he gets in his car and drives. He drives around town for a while, chewing the cud, getting his anger up, swearing at his wife. He'll show the stupid cow, he thinks, so eventually he heads north, because he's got a house there, hasn't he? Never mind that he has a tenant in the house. He also has Tanika.

"He comes to Tanika's apartment around five in the morning, but she's not there. And then for whatever reason, like a homing pigeon, he decides to go to his own house, the one that Herbert is renting. Maybe he thinks Herbert will be at work or out fishing or God knows what. He's not allowed on the property without his tenant's approval, but he goes anyway, he is in such a mood.

"Of course, Tanika is secretly visiting Herbert. It's not an affair, she says, because neither of them is married, they just want to keep it a secret for now, a delicious secret. She parks her car just a little way down the street to make it less obvious and she slips out of the house before the neighbours wake up. What she doesn't know is that Fred has just drawn up near the house and he sees her kissing Herbert goodbye at the door. She doesn't see him when she leaves.

"Fred wants to kill her. But he doesn't *really*, he is too smitten. What he wants to do at that moment is to kill his usurper, the hermit crab Herbert. He wants to smash in his empty snail shell of a skull. So, Fred goes into the back garden and spies on Herbert, planning revenge. He is still planning when he sees Herbert coming to the back door. Because Herbert *was* going fishing that morning, and he wanted to get out and back before the storm hit. He didn't bet on getting hit by Fred.

"Herbert is coming out and Fred is looking around for something to bash his head in and there is nothing at hand except a broom and a flowerpot that's way too heavy and then, voila, there is a spade! It is Harry's spade, which he forgot there two days earlier when he was moving the paving stones or something. So, wham! Herbert gets knocked out cold by Fred with Harry's spade.

"Now Fred is a philanderer, but he's not really your murdering type, so he gets the fright of his life when he sees Herbert lying there. He doesn't even check whether Herbert is dead, which he isn't, not yet. Fred flings the spade across the fence into the neighbour's yard and takes to his heels. And no-one sees him leaving, except—ha!—the neighbour's five-year-old son, who is also up early, because his dad is taking them to a go-cart rally (which by the way gets cancelled because of the cyclone) and he is way too excited to stay in bed. Mind you, he doesn't see Fred flinging the spade, he just sees him leaving the property, so when he later finds the spade in the garden, he doesn't make the connection. The police sniff that one out later.

"Oh, what's this?!" she suddenly cried.

A Labrador puppy chasing a ball had bounded over and nearly landed in Jenny's seat. Harry stepped in to grab him by the collar.

"Sniffing you out," said Chris.

The dog's owner arrived out of breath and apologetic. Harry recognised him as the son of one of his clients. They had a brief conversation, before the young man clipped a lead to his dog's collar and walked away. It gave Harry a buzz of contentment, meeting like this, outside his work environment. He watched as the man walked away. Studying music, he thought. That's interesting. Something else he didn't know about a client.

"And I didn't know they had a new puppy," he said aloud. "I was wondering where the other dog had gone. Bitten by a snake, apparently. Sorry, Jenny, carry on."

"Thank you. Now, the young boy. You might doubt the evidence of a five-year-old. His word against Fred's, saying he was too sick to drive this far. But Fred also ran out of fuel on the way up. He nearly made it. The CCTV camera caught him filling up at the servo on the Bruce Highway just before the turnoff into town, early that morning. So that's compounding evidence.

"The rest is really assumption based on lack of evidence. Herbert woke up, probably more than a bit concussed and confused, and he did go fishing. No-one actually saw him leaving home. Goodness knows everyone was focusing on the storm, weren't they? It's like those magicians—the more you watch their hands, the more they're able to deceive you, right before your eyes. A bloke walking his dog saw him in his ute with the tinnie near the esplanade at eight, said Herbert nearly ran him over and didn't even notice."

By the time Jenny had finished her story, with many interruptions and exclamations from all parties, the meat was cooked, and they could sit down to a meal. A barbeque for Jenny was, of course, not about the meat, and there was a more than ample supply of salads and grilled vegetables and sauces.

"So Fred didn't murder Herbert either?" asked Chris.

"No," said Harry. "No-one murdered Herbert. He drowned. Fred got charged with assault, though."

"And Harry got his spade back."

"But what about the other neighbour? You said there were two neighbours."

"Cecily's," said Nancy with a shiver. "You tell it, Harry. That man gives me the creeps."

"Cecily is my other client that went missing, remember, the old lady?"

"Yeah, the one Nancy bumped off," drawled Chris. She made a face at him and winked at Harry.

"She also turned up, but alive. Long story, but she'd gone off with an old friend to Bowen, got caught in the storm, got pneumonia or cold-exposure and was in hospital up in Proserpine for two weeks."

"You have to tell it like a story, Harry!" Nancy protested.

"You tell it then. No? Well, anyway, Cecily's neighbour is an old fellow they call Grumpy Gareth. On everybody's case, it seems, a real sticky beak and a meddler. Cecily knocked on his door to get help with her car, because it wouldn't start. That was the Thursday morning. So the police had it wrong; I wasn't the last one to see her."

"The gardener," mused Chris.

"I'm telling you."

"Why didn't he tell them? Or did he?"

"Nope. Not till much later. Seems he didn't like the police interfering in *his* street. He's been warned about his dog a couple of times, so he doesn't like them. He's a real old bastard. If something had happened to Cecily, he could have been had for perverting the course of justice."

"He's the one who shouted at Nancy, isn't he?" asked Jenny. "And had Martha in tears, poor girl."

"She's a tough girl, though, our Martha."

"Oh, isn't she just. Here's a cheers to her."

"Cheers!"

"Cheers!"

They ate and drank and talked, while the afternoon stretched its languid limbs like honey through the town. Only a few blocks away Martha was curled into a ball on the lawn of her new friend's house, being enthusiastically licked by two dachshunds. Neil shouted in glee and joined the fun.

On the wall in her lounge Cecily was hanging a newly framed photo of herself and Michelle—a selfie—against a background of golden grevilleas, while Gareth sat on his veranda, patting his dog and staring at nothing in particular. A car door slammed next door and his dog gave a tentative questioning bark, but Gareth closed his eyes and didn't get up.

On the other side of town Tanika was showing a house to a potential buyer, a middle-aged man with deep dark brown eyes. Despite a lot of interest, it had been empty for months, but she had a good feeling about this one. She smiled at the man and walked ahead of him into the main bedroom with the view onto the river, her hips swaying.

As the four friends finished their barbeque lunch and started packing up, the black dog that had been curled under the ominously heavy chair of his owner, pricked his ears. He sniffed the air and gave a quick high-pitched bark before darting out from under the chair. His leash reigned him in, but he stood barking at the end of its reach, staring into the park's leafy gardens. He could smell it, oh, he could smell it, however much his stupid humans denied it.

Under the drooping leaves of an elephant ear a tiny black and white creature flattened its ears and gave a frightened meow. Not long now, and it would dart out in front of someone, to be picked up and cuddled and given a new home. Yes, here they came now, this was it, this was its destiny and its story.